"What is it you're hiding?"

She knows! Jess's unending questions had made him say too much. He should have known he could never get involved with her. God, how he hated the questions, the lying. What he'd become.

"I don't hide," he responded. "It's more like I try not to make waves, to stay invisible."

"Why?" she asked.

What could he say to her? He'd already told her too much. What was it about this woman that made him break his self-imposed rules over and over again?

Jess moved closer to him, so close all he had to do was lean forward and kiss her. She touched his arm, letting her hand slide down to his, and the sensation was shockingly intimate. Jess was powerless.... He reached out and pulled her up against him, his lips crashing down on hers.

"See," she said softly. "If you're so busy being invisible, your perfect match—your soul mate— can't see you. What if she walks right past?"

Rob could barely breathe. He thought of his deception, of the lies. How could he have a soul mate? At times like this he felt he didn't even have a soul.

Dear Reader,

What is it about mysterious men that makes our pulses race? Whether it's the feeling of risk or the excitement of the unknown, dangerous men have always been a part of our fantasies, and now they're a part of Harlequin Intrigue. For the first six months of 1996 we'll kick off each month with a Dangerous Man. You see, you made the twelve DANGEROUS MEN from 1995 such a hit that we're bringing you a sextet of the sexy but secretive men in 1996. This month, meet Rob Carpenter in *No Ordinary Man* by Suzanne Brockmann.

For Suzanne Brockmann, writing is as necessary as breathing. Although she lives west of Boston, she vacations at least twice a year on Siesta Key in Sarasota, Florida, where this book is set. This is Suzanne's first Intrigue novel, though she is the author of seven books.

With our DANGEROUS MEN, Harlequin Intrigue will keep you on the edge of your seat...and on the edge of desire.

Regards,

Debra Matteucci
Senior Editor & Editorial Coordinator
Harlequin Books
300 East 42nd Street
New York, New York 10017

No Ordinary Man
Suzanne Brockmann

Harlequin Books

TORONTO • NEW YORK • LONDON
AMSTERDAM • PARIS • SYDNEY • HAMBURG
STOCKHOLM • ATHENS • TOKYO • MILAN
MADRID • WARSAW • BUDAPEST • AUCKLAND

For Melanie and Jason, extraordinary kids

"Country Waltz" by ©1992 Eric Ruben and Suz Brockmann. Lyrics used with permission.

ISBN 0-373-22365-X

NO ORDINARY MAN

Copyright © 1996 by Suzanne Brockmann

This edition published by arrangement with Harlequin Books S.A.

® and TM are trademarks of the publisher. Trademarks indicated with ® are registered in the United States Patent and Trademark Office, the Canadian Trade Marks Office and in other countries.

Printed in U.S.A.

CAST OF CHARACTERS

Jess Baxter—She has a secret admirer...one she could do without.

Rob Carpenter—Underneath his short brown hair and businesslike wingtips, he is no ordinary man.

Kelsey Baxter—Jess's six-year-old daughter believes that like Beauty and the Beast, her mom and Rob will marry and live happily ever after.

Stanford—Jess's neighbor who's pushing forty...and never been kissed.

Ian—Her ex-husband refuses to believe their relationship is over.

Pete—The new bartender at the club, his eyes follow her every move.

Frank—He's very helpful, but what does he want in return?

Stan—The unassuming next-door neighbor who sees all.

Dr. Selma Haverstein—Her psychological profile of the killer fits Rob like a glove.

Prologue

Her apartment building was not very hard to get into. He just rang all the doorbells in the lobby and waited for someone to buzz the inner door open. Once inside, he quickly took the stairs up to the third floor.

He opened the door a crack, just enough to be able to see down the hall to her apartment door.

He had followed her as she did her chores today, as she did every Saturday. He had left her at the video store, knowing that she'd stop to pick up her dry cleaning and then come home. She had no idea he'd be waiting for her.

None of them ever had any idea.

As she emerged from the elevator and approached her apartment, he tensed. The timing had to be perfect. He had to wait until she unlocked the door, and was heading through . . .

He sprang.

She didn't even have time to yell. His hand was over her mouth, the knife at her throat. She knew who was in control, who was in charge. She knew not to struggle. They were alone in her apartment, and finally, the game would come to an end.

He could barely wait.

Chapter One

"It was a dark and stormy night," Doris drawled across the telephone line, "when suddenly a mysterious stranger appeared from the shadows of the mist."

Jess Baxter laughed and peered out the screen door into the small circle of light thrown onto her back deck by the porch lamp. "First of all," she said to the older woman who was her day care provider and longtime friend, "It may be night, but I've got all the lights on, so it's not dark. Secondly, it's certainly not stormy, and there's no mist in sight. *And*, Rob's hardly a stranger."

"He's hardly Elmer Schiller, either," Doris countered, referring to the shy, elderly little man who had been the previous tenant in the small apartment attached to Jess's house.

"No, he's not," Jess had to agree. She heard an odd, slow, shuffling, thumping sound that had to be Rob Carpenter, her new tenant, carrying *some*thing heavy up the stairs to the deck and to the door of the apartment.

"I mean, when it comes down to it," Doris said, "what do you *really* know about this guy?"

"Oh, come on, Doris," Jess replied, moving back into the kitchen and pouring herself a glass of iced tea. "He's lived down the street for months." For the past six months, Rob had rented a neighbor's house while the family was away in Europe.

"Where'd he come from?" Doris asked. "Where'd he live before he moved into the Hendersons' house? What's his family like? Where did he grow up? Any deeply rooted psychological problems? Any tendencies towards violence? Does he prefer to use a knife or a gun when committing murder...?"

"You've been watching too many bad TV movies of the week," Jess scoffed, trying not to glance out the screen door as the subject in question went past, carrying another box.

"Might I remind you that there's a serial killer on the loose?" Doris persisted. "The fact is, you *don't* know anything about this guy."

"Next time I'll be sure to put 'Choice of murder weapon' on the rental application," Jess said dryly.

"I worry about you and Kelsey," Doris stated firmly. "Living all alone. Maybe you should get a big dog."

"Maybe *you* should take stress reduction classes."

"This is the guy who comes to your shows all the time," Doris said. "Right? The guy you've told me about?"

"Well, yes," Jess said, drawing designs in the condensation on the outside of her iced tea glass. "I've mentioned him once or twice."

"A few more times than that, hon. I've heard quite a bit about Mr. Rob Solid-And-Dependable-Businessman. Mr. Rob Polite. Mr. Rob Ordinary-Guy-With-Real-Nice-Eyes. I think you've got a bigger role than tenant in mind for this one."

Jess rolled her eyes. "Doris!"

"*I* think you think this Rob might be good father material."

"Really, don't start."

"Honey, I'm not accusing you of anything *wrong*," Doris said. "It's been two years since you kicked Ian out. It makes sense that you're a little itchy for some male company. And heaven knows you could use some help both paying the bills and raising Kelsey. But don't hitch yourself to some guy you don't really know just to—"

"Doris," Jess singsonged warningly.

"I mean, if it's all hot and heavy between you two, if he makes your heart beat harder, then God bless him, but still, make sure you know what you're getting yourself into," Doris said, rushing her words in her haste to get them out. "Ian Davis was no prize, but he never got violent—at least not with you or Kelsey. But you always hear about these polite, quiet types who end up taking a machine gun and—"

"Gee, I'm going to sleep really well tonight," Jess said.

"For all you know, this Rob could be the guy everyone's looking for—the serial killer," Doris persisted.

"He could also be Elvis Presley," Jess said, "alive and in disguise, hiding from his adoring public."

"Jess, I'm serious."

"Rob needed a place to live," Jess interrupted her friend. "There's nothing going on, *and* I have no plans for there to *be* something going on. I needed a tenant. Fast. Both for the money, and for the fact that if Rob didn't move in, Stanford Greene was going to."

That silenced Doris. "God," she finally said.

"Yes," Jess agreed, pushing open the screen door and carrying the cordless phone out with her onto the deck. "God."

"That creepy guy who lives next door with his creepy parents?" Doris asked.

"Yes," Jess said, glancing over at her neighbor's house. It was in dire need of a paint job and some serious repairs. Creepy indeed—both the house and the people who lived inside. Stanford Greene's mother had decided that since her baby boy was pushing forty years old, it was high time he got married. She'd also decided that Jess would make the perfect little bride for her baby. When Mrs. Greene had heard that Elmer Schiller was moving out of Jess's apartment to live with his daughter in Fort Myers, she'd thought that Stanford's moving *in* would be a perfect way for her darling son to get to know Jess better. But perfect wasn't quite the word Jess had in mind. She could just picture pudgy Stanford with his ear pressed to the paper thin walls, listening to every phone conversation Jess had. She could just see him staring at her all day from the deck, rather than from the other side of the wooden fence that separated their two yards.

"I take it all back," Doris conceded with a shudder. "Well, some of it anyway."

Jess leaned on the rail of the deck, looking down at the driveway below. The trunk of Rob's car was open, lit by the dim garage light, but her new tenant was nowhere in sight.

"I'm sorry, am I making too much noise?" a soft voice said, and she spun around, heart pounding. "Maybe I should move the rest of the stuff up in the morning," Rob added. "I know it's late, and I don't want to wake up your daughter."

Rob must've been inside the apartment. But Jess hadn't heard the door open, or the sound of his footsteps on the deck. It was as if he'd suddenly appeared, instantly standing next to her, conjured up by her vivid imagination.

He was taller than she remembered. And even though he was a good five feet away from her, it seemed as if he were standing much too close.

"You startled me," she said breathlessly.

"I'm sorry," he apologized again.

His eyes were brown. They were average brown—neither deep chocolate nor tawny amber. Just…brown. They were level and steady and mostly hidden behind circular wire-rimmed glasses. But every time Jess met his gaze, something very hot and very dangerous sparked. This time was no exception.

His hair and face were slightly damp with perspiration. But he hadn't bothered to roll up his shirtsleeves, and his tie wasn't even loosened.

Despite the protestations she'd made to Doris, Jess found Rob Carpenter incredibly attractive. She wouldn't admit it to her friend, but she couldn't deny it to herself.

On the surface, he seemed so…average. He had conservatively cut brown hair, brown eyes, a medium build. He always dressed the same way—like a computer programmer. Tonight he was still wearing his work clothes—khaki slacks and a long-sleeved button-down shirt with a bland tie. In an elevator full of businessmen, he would blend into the crowd—nondescript, nothing special.

Unless you looked more closely.

His shoulders were broad beneath his crisp white shirt. His body was slender, and his pants hugged his backside almost sinfully. Undeniably, the man had a *great* butt. *And* a great smile. His teeth were straight and white, and his cheeks crinkled charmingly at the edges of his mouth. He was much better than average-looking. In fact, behind those glasses and that unremarkable haircut, he was remarkably handsome. His face was lean, with a strong jaw and a straight, nearly perfect nose. His lips were beautifully shaped, and his smile made his brown eyes sparkle with amusement. Yet there was always a tinge of sadness behind that smile, a hint of tragedy in his eyes.

Maybe that was what Jess found so attractive. Maybe it was the mystery that seemed to linger around him.

Or maybe it was simply the fact that outwardly Rob was a polar opposite to Ian Davis, Jess's ex-husband. The truth was, from his short brown hair to the tips of his well-polished businesslike shoes, Rob appeared to be everything that manic and out-of-control Ian, with his Hawaiian shirts, his long, curly blond hair and his ice blue eyes had never been.

"Jess, are you still there?" Doris asked.

She was staring at Rob. Jess *knew* she was staring, and she forced herself to pull her eyes away. "Doris, I've got to go," she said into the telephone.

"Just remember what I said, hon."

"Goodbye," Jess returned firmly and punched the off button on the phone. She turned back to Rob. "Sorry about that."

"It's okay," he said in his quiet, accentless voice.

"You're hardly making any noise at all," she told him. "I heard you pull into the driveway while I was on the phone and I meant to come out and ask if you needed any help. Can I give you a hand with the rest of your things?"

"No, that's all right." Rob looked over the railing at his car in the driveway below. "I don't have that much stuff, and I'm almost done. There're just another couple of boxes."

"I can help you with them."

Rob shook his head. "No, really. They're both too heavy. They're my free weights. I didn't pack 'em real well—I just threw all the plates into a couple of crates."

Free weights. Rob lifted weights. Funny, she would have never known. If he had a weight lifter's physique, it was hidden underneath his loose-fitting shirt. At first glance he looked so much like a computer nerd, barely capable of lifting a too heavy briefcase, yet here he was, bringing weight-lifting equipment into her apartment.

Her apartment? *His* apartment now. He'd signed a six-month lease just this afternoon. For the next six months, Rob Carpenter was going to be her closest neighbor.

As she gazed up into his eyes, Jess felt again that spark of awareness, that whisper of heat.

But he turned away. "Well . . . I'll, um, get the rest of my, uh . . ."

"I'll get some iced tea," Jess offered, heading for the door to her kitchen. "You look like you could use something cool to drink."

"That would be nice," Rob said, stopping at the top of the stairs and looking back at her, smiling very slightly. "Thanks."

He moved silently down the stairs as Jess pulled open her screen door.

Doris was right about at least one thing. Rob *did* make Jess's heart beat harder. Just one little smile, and her pulse was pounding.

She got another glass from the cabinet and pulled the ice cube tray from the freezer. She added several fresh cubes to her own glass, still sitting out on the counter, as Rob moved quietly past the door, carrying a large, heavy-looking box filled with free weights. The box looked awkward and unwieldy, yet he carried it easily, as if it weighed almost nothing.

He moved silently past the door again, heading back toward the stairs as Jess took the iced tea pitcher from the refrigerator and filled both glasses.

What *did* she know about this man?

Jess knew that Rob worked as a software consultant for some local computer company—she couldn't remember the name—and that he traveled rather extensively throughout Florida and the southeast, sometimes taking as many as eight or nine business trips in a single month.

She knew that he had moved to Sarasota from up north—which city or state, Jess couldn't say. She didn't think he'd ever mentioned it.

She knew he had nice eyes, that he was polite and quiet, maybe even shy.

And that he drove a staid, dark gray Taurus sedan.

He liked to listen to folk music, and he'd attended nearly all of her gigs. He'd come when she played her guitar and sang at local clubs, often bringing along one of the guys from his office—a friendly man named Frank—but never showing up with a date.

She knew Rob liked the food at the China Boat, the small restaurant three blocks south. She'd seen him carrying bags of takeout as she'd driven past, after picking up her daughter from Doris's after school day care. Of course, that didn't necessarily mean he liked the China Boat's food. Maybe it simply meant that he *didn't* like to cook.

They'd really only spoken a few times. Unlike his friend Frank who was very chatty, Rob never stuck around her gigs long enough to talk, as if he were somehow afraid to impose.

That wasn't a lot to go on, but it didn't take much imagination to picture Rob Carpenter fitting easily into Jess's life. Her life and Kelsey's. Her six-year-old daughter actually knew Rob better than Jess did. Kelsey's best friend lived next door to the house Rob had been renting. Kelsey had told Jess that Rob had often come into her friend's yard to play baseball with the two children and her friend's dad. Rob apparently had a natural way with kids. Kelsey—who was usually so reserved around men, thanks to Ian—adored Rob. He'd given both children nicknames—her friend was Beetle and Kelsey was Bug.

Sure, Doris was right. Jess didn't know much about Rob's past. But Kelsey liked him, and that was worth quite a bit in Jess's book.

As Jess put the iced tea pitcher back in the refrigerator, Rob moved past the door again, carrying his last box. Moments later, he tapped softly at the screen.

"Come on in," she said.

He opened the screen door quickly and came into the kitchen without bringing in any of the bugs that were circling the light—not an easy feat. He carried in her evening newspaper. With a quick smile, he handed it to her.

"I was wondering which side of the driveway you wanted me to leave my car on," he said. "Or if you'd prefer that I parked on the street."

"The driveway's fine," Jess said, putting the paper down on the kitchen counter and handing him one of the glasses of iced tea. "Just don't block the garage in case I have to get out before you leave in the morning. And if you ever have anyone stay overnight, any..." She was about to say girlfriends, but she paused, suddenly uncertain. What if he was gay? He couldn't be, could he? No, from the way he always looked at her, she had to believe that he wasn't. Still... "Any *friends*," she continued, "Just have...them...park on the street."

Rob noticed her carefully genderless sentence, and he fought hard to keep his reaction from showing. Jess actually thought that he might be gay. He wasn't sure whether to laugh or feel insulted. Or feel relieved.

Because here he was, standing in Jess Baxter's kitchen. She was not more than six feet away from him, dressed in a short-cropped T-shirt that didn't quite meet the waistband of her cutoff jeans. Although she wasn't very tall, her legs were long and slender, and standing there like that in her bare feet, with a narrow strip of smooth, tanned stomach showing between her shorts and her shirt, she looked like something out of a beach boy's fantasy.

Her short dark hair curled softly around her heart-shaped face, and her eyes had to be the darkest shade of brown he'd ever seen in his entire life.

The first time Rob had seen her, when he'd first moved to Sarasota, to this neighborhood, he'd known that she was someone he should stay far, far away from. When he'd first spotted her with Kelsey, he'd fervently hoped that she was happily married. He prayed that she had someone that she loved, someone who adored her, someone who would protect her.

Naturally, she was divorced, a single mom. She wasn't seeing anyone, wasn't even dating. His bad luck just never seemed to quit.

Still, he'd kept his distance. But he couldn't keep from watching her. He noticed her when she played in her yard with Kelsey. He watched her when she worked in her garden. He spied her when she grocery shopped, early every Thursday morning, like clockwork. He'd even watched her cooking dinner through her uncurtained kitchen window. He also went to her shows, and listened to her play her guitar and sing.

She had a smile as sweet and welcoming as a warm spring morning, and eyes as mysterious as the darkest night sky. Her voice, with its gentle southern accent was velvet—husky and soft and unbearably, achingly, painfully sensual.

When the Hendersons had written him of their impending return, he should have moved clear across to the other side of town. This woman didn't need the kind of trouble he brought with him. But she had seemed as desperate to find a tenant as he'd been to find a place to live.

"You want sugar in that?" Jess asked him, gesturing toward the tall glass of iced tea she'd handed him as she crossed to the cabinet and took down a sugar bowl. Her jeans shorts fit her perfect derriere snugly and she swayed slightly, naturally, as she walked. Sweet God, if she only knew what he was thinking, she'd be convinced beyond a shadow of a doubt of his heterosexuality. "Or would you like some lemon?" she added.

"Sugar," Rob heard himself say. "Thanks."

He should be getting out of there. He should go into his new apartment and organize his things, set up his weight-lifting gear, watch some mindless television sitcom. He should be leaving Jess Baxter alone, not standing in her kitchen, looking at her legs, thinking dangerous thoughts. Instead, he sat down across from her at her kitchen table.

"You know, I realized I don't know that much about you," Jess said, taking a sip of her iced tea and gazing at him with her bottomless dark eyes. She pushed the bowl of sugar and a spoon in his direction.

She was going to ask him some questions. Some personal questions. Rob stirred sugar into his glass, carefully keeping his face passive, fighting the hot surge of anger that pulsed through him. God, he hated questions. He hated lying, he hated all of it. He hated his entire life, loathed what he'd become. *Boring,* he reminded himself. *Make yourself sound unbearably boring. She'll change the subject soon enough.* "There's not that much to know," he said blandly. "I work for Epco, Inc., downtown. I work with computers, you know, software consulting. It's pretty mundane."

God, he hated small talk. But that's all he ever did—all he ever could do. It was too risky to have any kind of real conversation, too nerve-racking to say anything that would make someone take a closer look at him. So he always stuck to small talk. Always. For the past eight years, he'd had his real conversations in his head, with himself. Sometimes he felt well on his way to being certifiably nuts. But he had to keep his interactions with other people to a minimum. He had to be boring. He had to remain invisible.

"I travel a lot," he added, "but I only see the insides of office buildings."

Jess nodded, still watching him. "That's too bad." Her eyelashes were amazingly dark and incredibly long. And she didn't look the slightest bit bored. In fact, she looked interested. More than interested. Attracted. Beautiful, vibrant, sexy Jess Baxter was actually attracted to dull, mild-mannered, boring Rob Carpenter.

Her cheeks flushed very slightly as Rob met her eyes and held her gaze, wondering if she could see past his disguise, wondering if somehow he'd slipped and given himself away. She looked away, embarrassed or nervous. Damn straight she should be nervous around him.

"With my schedule, I don't have time for anything besides work," he added, hoping she'd pick up his double meaning. He didn't have time for anything else, *especially* romance. He couldn't risk the sweet intimacy of a lover's quiet questions or the expectations of shared secrets and whispered confessions.

Jess took another sip of her drink, removing a stray drop of tea from her lips with the tip of her tongue. It was sweetly, unconsciously sexy on her part, and Rob felt his body respond. Man, it had been too long...

"No hobbies?" she asked, one elegant eyebrow arching upward. "No clog dancing classes?"

Rob had to laugh at that. "No," he said. "Sad to say, I had to give it up."

"Music, then," Jess prompted. "You must have an interest in music—I've seen you at some of the folk festivals, and at some of my gigs. You even brought along that friend of yours—Frank. I appreciated your helping pad the audience."

Rob nodded. "I like music," he said. That was true, but he'd really gone to those festivals and concerts expressly to see Jess sing. "But I never brought Frank. We're not friends—more like acquaintances. We both happened to show up at one of the folk festivals and we got to talking—we both work at Epco."

Jess nodded, taking a sip of her iced tea. "How about movies?" she asked. "Kelsey and I saw you a couple of times at the Gulf Gate Mall theater."

Now *this* was something he could talk about. Rob smiled and let himself relax a little. But only slightly.

"We love going to movies," she continued, pushing a stray curl back behind one ear. "We go to everything a six-year-old can see, that is. I've become a Disney expert."

"I'm more into *Pulp Fiction* than *Pocahontas* myself," Rob admitted. "I'm a Spielberg fan. And I like James Cameron too. He did the *Terminator* movies, remember those?"

"Aha." Jess smiled at him as she took another sip of her iced tea. "You *do* have a hobby, if you watch movies enough to be a fan of a specific director."

"I don't know, it's slightly more passive than clog dancing," Rob said, smiling back into her warm brown eyes. God, she was pretty.

"So is stamp collecting."

"You win," he conceded. "I guess I have a hobby."

"We also saw you in Books-A-Million," she said. "Buying a stack of books about two feet high."

"I also like to read. Fiction, mostly."

"But I didn't see you move in boxes and boxes of books," Jess said, resting her chin on the upturned palm of her hand as she continued to gaze across the table at him.

Rob shrugged. "I don't usually live in a place big enough to keep bookshelves. I read 'em, then donate 'em to a local nursing home."

Her big dark eyes softened. "That's sweet."

God, he could lose himself in those eyes. He could just fall in and disappear forever, drowning, suffocating, pulling her down with him. They'd both simply vanish, never to resurface.

"You moved down here from up north," Jess said, wondering if he could hear the breathlessness of her voice, wondering if he knew it was caused by the way he was looking at her. "Didn't you?"

Across the table, Rob nodded, pulling his gaze away from her and giving his iced tea another spoonful of sugar and another stir. She'd been wrong about him, Jess realized. She'd thought he was shy, but there was nothing in those brown eyes that suggested shyness. In fact, his gaze was confident and steady. Rob Carpenter wasn't shy at all. Just…polite. Reserved. Quiet. And as attracted to her as she was to him.

"Where are you from?" she asked.

"All over the place," he answered, glancing up at her and giving her a ghost of his earlier smile.

Could he be any more vague? Jess took another sip of her tea. "I grew up here in Florida," she said. "Out on Siesta Key. My parents still have a beach house there. I use it sometimes when I've got a gig at the Pelican Club."

He didn't comment or offer any information on the location of his own childhood. He just watched her.

"My folks are up in Montana right now," Jess continued, more to fill the silence than because she thought he'd be interested in the whereabouts of her parents. "They're retired and doing the RV thing. You know, the enormous silver cylinder on wheels? Camping without the nasty outdoors part?"

That got another genuine smile out of him. And a response. "They're in Montana, huh? It's pretty out there—different from Florida."

"I've never been to Montana," she admitted. "Have you?"

He nodded, yes, but didn't elaborate. She'd asked another faintly personal question that he wasn't going to answer at any length. Apparently, he was willing to converse about superficial things but he didn't like to talk about himself. But then, to her surprise, he actually volunteered some personal information. "I lived out west for about a year and a half."

"So you really are from all over the place," Jess said. "Where did you grow up?"

His smile faded quickly, but he still gazed at her. There was something else in his eyes now. It wasn't amusement. It had a harder edge. Maybe it was alertness. Or was it wariness? Why should a question about his childhood make him wary?

"Jersey," he finally replied. And as if he somehow knew that he was being too vague again, he added, "Near New York City."

"Really?" she said. "Where exactly?"

"Just across the Hudson River."

So much for "exactly." "Does your family still live up there?"

"I don't have a family." He was still watching her.

"I'm sorry," she murmured, instantly backing down.

"I'm not." He said it so matter-of-factly, it took her a moment for his words to make sense. How could he not be sorry that he didn't have a family?

The first thought that occurred to Jess was that Rob Carpenter didn't want her to know the name of the town he'd grown up in because he'd done in his entire family and was now living under an alias, on the lam. It was a thought that would have made Doris proud. It was also ridiculous. Wasn't it...?

The man was clearly hiding something. Wasn't he? Or was he simply a private person, unwilling to talk about personal things to a near stranger?

Rob gazed across the table at Jess. She was watching him steadily, warily. He knew he made her nervous, he could see it in her eyes. But he could also see her attraction to him, too. It simmered between them like something living, ready to devour them both.

He knew without a doubt that if he reached across the table and put his hand over hers, she wouldn't pull her own hand away. And he could only imagine where that one touch would lead. But that was part of the problem. He *could* imagine. He could see it quite clearly.

Rob pushed his chair back from the table and stood up. "I should get going. Thanks for the drink."

Jess stood up, too. "Feel free to drop by anytime," she said. "Kelsey and I are home most evenings." She shoved her hands into the front pockets of her jeans shorts, a sweetly nervous gesture that exposed another half inch of her flat, tanned stomach. "We're neighbors now. I hope we're going to be friends."

Friends. Rob put his hand on the screen door's handle. He and beautiful Jess Baxter were going to be friends. He couldn't help but wonder just how friendly she intended to be.

Damn, he shouldn't have moved in here like this. For Jess's sake, he should have gone far, far away. Because he knew damn well he wasn't going to be able to resist her. If he was reading her right, and she *was* attracted to him, he didn't stand a chance at keeping his distance. If she made even the smallest attempt to seduce him, he'd surrender. He was strong, but he wasn't *that* strong. And where would that leave him? Where would it leave Jess?

Rob stepped out onto the porch, shutting the door behind him. "Thanks again."

He didn't wait for her to respond. He turned and headed for his apartment door, down at the other end of the deck.

He liked Jess more than he'd ever imagined. It had nothing to do with the physical attraction that drew his eyes in her direction all the time. It had to do with her warm smile and her friendly conversation, and her funny, easygoing outlook on life.

Yeah, he liked her, and he'd seen an answering attraction in her eyes tonight—for her sake he should clear out right now. He should just get in his car and leave.

JESS RINSED THE ICED TEA glasses and put them in the dishwasher, feeling oddly unsettled. She'd set out to find some facts about her mysterious tenant, but all she had now were more mysteries.

He had no family and yet he was glad about that.

He grew up somewhere near New York City, but when she'd asked him where exactly, he'd continued to be vague.

Jess picked up the newspaper that Rob had brought inside, and went to check on Kelsey. It was supposed to be Kelsey's job to bring the afternoon paper in each evening, but occasionally her daughter forgot. It was all part of being six years old.

Kelsey was fast asleep, the bedsheets twisted around her like some kind of Roman toga. Jess smiled, pushing Kelsey's damp brown hair back from her warm, round, freckled face. She hadn't expected that her quiet conversation in the kitchen with Rob would disturb her daughter. Kelsey would remain sound asleep throughout the noisiest thunderstorm. The kid could sleep through anything.

It probably came as a form of self-protection, from the days when Kelsey's father was still living with them. Ian Davis, with his shaggy blond curls and mocking blue eyes was the first violinist and concert master of the Sarasota Symphony Orchestra. He was flashy, arrogant and selfish. And interminably loud and often rudely, nastily abusive. Jess's ex-husband was jealous as hell, and would start a fight with her over something as innocent as a friendly smile she gave to the attendant at the gas station.

Yet fidelity wasn't in Ian's vocabulary when it pertained to himself.

Jess could still feel the giddy sense of freedom she'd felt on that day two years ago, when she'd packed up Ian's things and sent them to the SSO office with a letter from her lawyer.

She carried the newspaper into the living room. Doris had been wrong. As tough as things were financially, Jess didn't need—or want—a man around. She and Kelsey were getting along just fine on their own.

Of course, Ian still didn't agree. According to him, their relationship was in no way over. He came around constantly and left the key to his condo in her mailbox, on her porch, in her car. Did he really expect her to come crawling back to him? Jess would send the key back, but she'd just find it again several days later. Finally, she tossed it into her junk drawer. Game over. Let Ian think he won.

As Jess set the paper down on the coffee table, the headline caught her eye. As usual, it was about the Sarasota serial killer. It was amazing. Sarasota wasn't that big a city. Sure, there was crime, but nothing ever like this. It was disconcerting to think that a madman was out there, prowling the streets, hunting down and killing young women.

The latest victim was twenty-two years old. She had come home from graduate school for spring break, to visit her parents. Her body had been found, raped and murdered, in her own bedroom. Jess shivered as she read the interview with the police.

The killings had been going on for six months now, although the media and the public had only known about it for half that time. The FBI were closemouthed about whether or not they had any suspects. They warned all area residents—women in particular—to keep their doors and windows locked, and to avoid going out alone, particularly at night.

Jess stood and locked the front door.

Of course, with Rob Carpenter living in the attached apartment, she should feel safe. The walls were so thin, she wouldn't have to scream very loud for him to hear. Unless of course, she thought with a wry smile, remembering Doris's words of warning, Rob himself was the Sarasota serial killer.

But that wasn't really such a funny joke. True, Doris was probably just being melodramatic as usual, but the fact remained that Jess didn't know very much about Rob at all. He was a stranger. On top of that, it seemed oddly coincidental that he should have moved to Sarasota six months ago—right before the murders started.

Jess mentally gave herself a shake. Oddly coincidental? She was getting as bad as Doris. Sure, he had moved to Sarasota six months ago. But so had lots of other people. It wasn't odd, it was just plain coincidental.

Rob was just a nice, quiet guy who didn't like to talk about his past. No big deal. Jess didn't like to talk about her marriage to Ian. That didn't make her an axe murderer. Maybe Rob had been married to some stinker. Maybe he'd had a lousy childhood. Maybe he just wasn't comfortable talking about his personal life. He'd opened up quickly enough when she'd asked

him about movies and books. Of course, that was just glorified small talk.

Rob was just a nice, quiet guy.

Still, Jess stood up and locked the back door anyway.

THIS PART WAS THE BEST. He had brought the rope, of course,
and the knife. He loved the look on her face when he tied one
end of the rope around his own ankle. And he loved it even
more when he told her to tie the other end around her leg.

But first, he ordered her to get herself ready—to put on her
makeup while he got undressed.

She was crying by then, but that was okay. They always cried
around this time.

She would stop soon.

Chapter Two

"Hey, Bug, what's happening?"

"Rob!" Kelsey's voice carried clearly inside from the back-yard. "You're home!"

Jess moved to the kitchen window and watched as her daughter leapt from her swing set and ran to greet Rob.

She glanced at the clock. It was almost five—earlier than he usually came home.

It had only been two weeks, but it seemed as if Rob had been living in the spare apartment forever.

It hadn't taken long to settle into a routine of sorts. He would come home from work and play in the yard with Kelsey. Jess would come out after a while, and invite him to join them for dinner. He would refuse, except for the times she hadn't bothered to cook. If she was planning to send out for pizza or Chinese food, he'd agree to eat with them—but only if he could pay. Since last Monday, Jess had been insisting they split the bill.

Why? Because they'd been eating an awful lot of pizza and Chinese food lately.

The evenings had quickly settled into a routine, too. Jess and Kelsey would plan to play a game or rent a video, and they'd invite Rob to join them. Sometimes he'd stay. Sometimes he'd take his car and go out—where, he never said, and Jess never dared to ask.

Rob always kept their conversations light, never getting personal. He talked about the weather, baseball, Kelsey's school. Small talk. Although last week, the subject of Ian had come up, after Jess's ex paid her a particularly unpleasant visit.

Jess had felt Rob watching her after Ian finally left. She'd glanced up at him and tried to smile. "Sorry about that," she'd apologized.

Rob shook his head. "I wasn't sure whether to leave and give you privacy, or..."

"I appreciated it that you stayed," Jess said, meeting his eyes. "Ian was drunk again and he's something of a wild card even when he's sober." She laughed, but there wasn't much humor in her voice. "He drinks, and then he thinks that he wants me back. I don't know why. He didn't want me when we were married."

Rob leaned back against the rail of the deck, still watching her.

"I'm sorry," she said again, trying to shake herself out of the depression that always followed one of Ian's visits. "I don't mean to sound so bitter."

"He's pretty screwed up," Rob commented. He hesitated, looking down at the stained boards of the deck before he continued. "Jess, may I ask you a personal question?"

Silently, she nodded. This entire conversation was pretty personal. She'd half expected Rob to run away after Ian had left—to distance himself from her sordid personal life. But he was planted rather firmly against the deck railing, clearly not going anywhere.

Rob was quiet for another moment, choosing his words carefully. "Has Ian ever... hit you or Kelsey?"

"No," she answered honestly. "He never did that. He had temper tantrums and tore up the living room a couple of times. He smashed a full set of dishes once."

"But he never hurt you?" Rob persisted.

"Not intentionally," Jess told him. "One time he broke a window, and I got cut by a piece of flying glass, but that was an accident."

"It starts that way," Rob said. "An accidental burn. An accidental cut." His voice got harder, rougher with emotion. "An accidental fist in your face."

Jess stared at him.

"I think you should get a restraining order," Rob continued. His eyes were almost steely behind his glasses. "What if he comes around here when I'm not home? What if next time he 'accidentally' hurts Kelsey?"

Jess was shocked. "Even though Ian doesn't pay much attention to Kelsey, he'd *never* hurt her," she protested. "He's her *father*."

Rob laughed, his voice harsh. "Oh, Jess," he said. "You have no idea what a father can do to a child."

"But you do know," she ventured, realizing what he was saying. "Don't you?"

Something changed in Rob's face, as if he suddenly became aware of the fact that he'd said too much, that he'd given himself away. As Jess looked at him, she saw an array of emotions parade across his face. His eyes flicked toward his apartment door, and she knew he wanted to run away from this conversation.

But he didn't leave. He met her eyes squarely, and he answered her. "Yes."

Watching him, Jess realized that she and Kelsey were important to him—important enough for him to risk revealing some of the past that he kept so carefully concealed.

His father had abused him. There was no doubt of that in Jess's mind.

"It started with accidents, too," Rob said quietly. "You were lucky you got out of your relationship when you did. I didn't have that option."

Jess felt her eyes fill with tears as he straightened up. "Think about getting a restraining order," he said again, ending the conversation by going into his apartment.

He hadn't brought the topic up again, but Jess couldn't forget that tiny piece of himself that he'd allowed her to see. She was positive that the only reason he'd told her as much as he had was because he so very much didn't want the same thing to happen to her or to Kelsey.

But despite that one incident, Rob continued to keep his distance. He never, ever stayed after Kelsey had gone to bed.

Funny, Kelsey's bedtime seemed to be getting later and later these days.

Jess wasn't sure whether to be grateful or insulted that he hadn't yet asked her out. She could see his attraction each time she glanced into his eyes. Still, part of her liked the fact that he was moving at a snail's pace. It was gentlemanly. It was romantic. At the very least it was different.

But another part of her was frustrated beyond belief. This was the part of her that filled her dreams with steamy, erotic visions of her new neighbor, the likes of which she'd only imagined. And boy, had she imagined. She dreamed of Rob kissing her relentlessly. She dreamed of his arms around her, his hands caressing her, their naked bodies pressed together, straining to become one . . .

The sad reality was, if she was *really* lucky, he'd stay for dinner and afterward they'd play Candy Land.

Jess went out onto the deck.

She could see Rob and Kelsey, crouched in the dirt, heads close together as they examined something at the edge of the garden.

As Jess started down the stairs, he glanced up.

For the briefest instant, she saw hunger in his eyes and raw desire on every angle and plane of his lean face. But it was gone so quickly, Jess was left wondering if she had imagined it. Still, her mouth was dry and she had to moisten her lips before she spoke.

"Hi." A brilliant opener. No doubt he'd be too dazzled by her conversational skills to even hazard a reply.

But he smiled, apparently undaunted, standing up and brushing off his hands. "Hey."

"We found a worm," Kelsey informed her. "But it's all dried up and yucky."

"Kelsey, please don't—" Jess sighed as her daughter wiped her muddy hands across her clean T-shirt "—get your shirt dirty." She sent Rob a look of amused dismay. "Too late."

"Sorry," Kelsey said, frowning down at herself, her forehead wrinkled with her distress.

"It'll wash out. But go up and change, please," Jess said. "We've got to get going."

Kelsey headed for the stairs up to the deck with her normal explosion of speed. She was like a miniature rocketship—either standing still or moving at the speed of sound.

Jess turned back to Rob. "You're home early," she said. "I was sure we'd be gone before you got here."

He didn't ask where she and Kelsey were going. Come to think of it, except for that one time he never asked anything that was even remotely personal. "They were having a party back at the office," Rob explained. "The music got too loud. I wasn't getting any work done, so I thought I might as well come home."

Where are you going? He didn't ask the question, but Jess could see it in his eyes. He wanted to know. So why didn't he simply ask?

"I was going to leave a note on your door," Jess said, answering the question anyway. "I got a call from the Pelican Club out on Siesta Key. Tonight's entertainment canceled and they asked me to fill in. I've got to be there in an hour."

"The Pelican Club." Rob poked at the garden with the toe of his shoe, burying the mummified worm under a clod of dirt. "Nice place. I've gone to see you play there before."

"I know," Jess said quietly, watching him.

Rob glanced up at her, and the power generated as his eyes met hers seemed to sizzle the very air around them. He quickly looked away and the sun's reflection on his glasses hid his eyes.

"Will you come with us?" The words were out of her mouth before she'd taken the time to think. But as soon as she said them, she realized that she was, essentially, asking Rob Carpenter out. She immediately backpedaled, adding, "Doris can't baby-sit tonight, and all of the local kids are going to a dance at the high school, so I'm stuck and Kelsey's going to be there, too. I'm sure she'd love to have someone to eat dinner with while I'm playing." Lord, now it sounded as if she wanted Rob to come along as a baby-sitter. And that wasn't true at all. "I'm doing this badly," she continued almost desperately, "but it's been a while since I've asked a man out and . . . you're probably busy. Sorry, I'm . . . sorry."

"I'm not busy." If he was looking at her, she couldn't tell. The sun's reflection still kept her from seeing his eyes. But he didn't say anything else.

"Would you . . . Do you . . . want to come?"

Rob didn't respond at first, as if it were a question that required deep thought to find the answer. But he lifted his head and met her eyes again when he did speak, and his gaze was steady and very certain. "Yeah," he said. "I'd like that."

Jess smiled at him, her entire face lighting with her delight, and Rob felt more of the defenses he'd erected against this woman eroding, just totally melting away.

He couldn't help but think about that evening last week when, after Jess's ex-husband had put in an appearance, Rob had found himself telling her about his *father,* for God's sake. He just stood there, watching and listening to himself tell her things he hadn't told anyone. Ever. He'd had to force himself to stop talking, to walk away before he told her more. And now he'd gone and told her he'd like to go on a date with her. What was he thinking? Where was his mind?

Dear God, he was in trouble here. It was all he could do not to reach out and touch her smooth, sun-kissed cheek with his hand. She'd just asked him out and like a fool, he'd accepted, pushing them both one step closer toward the hell and heart-ache that was inevitable. God help them both.

"Great," she said. "Give me fifteen minutes to get changed and then we can go. Mind if we take your car? My clutch is acting up again and—" She looked around the driveway, and then out toward the street. "Where *is* your car?"

"I lent it to...someone," Rob replied, unwilling to tell her that he'd intercepted Ian again, just moments ago, out on the street in front of her house. Ian had come with the excuse that he needed to borrow Jess's car. Rob had lent Ian his own car, simply to keep him from hassling Jess. Ian was supposed to return it later tonight. "I didn't think I'd need it. I could call a cab and—"

"No," Jess interrupted. "That's not necessary. My car will get us there." She smiled, another burst of sunshine. "I'll drive along the bus route just in case."

"If you want, I can take a look at your car," Rob said. "I'm pretty good with foreign engines."

He could see surprise in Jess's eyes. What kind of computer geek knew the first little thing about cars? But she didn't say a word, didn't ask one single question. She simply accepted whatever minuscule tidbits of personal information he threw in her direction. She respected his privacy. Yet he could tell that she hoped he'd open up and really talk to her. Too bad, be-cause that was one thing that wasn't going to happen. He was going to leave her with all of her questions still unanswered.

"Pull your car out of the garage," Rob said evenly. "I have to make a couple of phone calls first, but then I'll check it out."

"All right," she responded. "Thanks."

She used her key to trigger the automatic garage opener and the door that was built right into the side of the house rolled up. She disappeared into the dark, cool gloom and after a mo-ment the car started with a muffled roar.

Unable to shake the feeling that he was being watched, Rob glanced up at the neighbor's rundown old house. Sure enough, there was Mr. Greene, sitting in his wheelchair on his porch, staring down at him with cold, baleful eyes. Rob had seen the old man out there when he'd come home even late at night—past 2:00 a.m. Mr. Greene was always watching. He looked as if he were judging, condemning, like an aging Roman ruler, ready to give the signal of thumbs-up or down.

Thumbs-down. That seemed to fit this situation perfectly.

God, he had to stop this before it got out of hand. He had to tell Jess he couldn't go to the Pelican Club with her. He had to tell her that he needed to move out.

Jess backed out of the garage, then cut the engine and climbed out of the car. As she walked toward Rob, a breeze blew, ruffling her dark hair, leaving one silky lock out of place. He couldn't stop himself. He reached up to smooth it back down, and as he touched her, their eyes met and she smiled. And all of the words he needed to say dried up in the heat of his desire. Everything that he knew he should say and do instantly became as hard and as unrecognizable as the worm Kelsey had found.

Rob wanted Jess more than he'd ever wanted a woman before. It was more than pure physical need, although there was plenty of that. But there was also emotional need—a vast, empty longing for a normal life, for a chance to feel at peace.

"I better go get dressed." Jess's voice was slightly breathless as she pulled away from him. "I don't want to be late."

Rob watched her walk up the stairs, wondering how, after this was over, he was going to live with himself.

JESS LOOKED AT HERSELF in the bedroom mirror. The dress she was wearing dated from her college days at Berkeley School of Music. It was black, with a cuffed, low V-neckline that plunged down between her breasts. Her arms were bare, and the full skirt ended midthigh. The skirt used to be a lot longer, but Jess had taken her scissors to it, in an attempt to update her wardrobe without spending any money. The end result was still elegant, with the added bonus of a lot of leg. And that's show biz, she thought wryly, slipping into her black pumps.

Rummaging through her purse, she found her makeup. She ran a brush quickly through her shiny, dark hair, dug her dangling onyx earrings out of her jewelry case and put them on.

"I'm ready," she sang out as she carried her guitar onto the deck and locked the door behind her.

Both Kelsey and Rob looked up as she came down the stairs. But while Kelsey merely glanced at her mother from her perch on the swing set, Rob's eyes were riveted to Jess.

He wiped his hands on a rag and lowered the hood of her car, latching it firmly. "You look beautiful," he said. Then he frowned. "I thought the Pelican Club was casual."

"*You* can be casual." Jess smiled. "I, as your evening's entertainment, want to be noticed."

Rob nodded. "You'll be noticed."

"Thank you," Jess said. Lord, he looked so serious, standing there like that, trying so hard to hide his attraction to her. But he couldn't hide it entirely—which was a good thing, especially since he was the one she wanted to notice her.

As his eyes lingered on her legs, Jess felt a momentary flash of apprehension. She was finally going on a date with this man—because *she* had asked *him*. He'd been living next door for two weeks, but she still didn't really know him. Who was he? Where had he come from? She knew his father had abused him as a child. Rob had a background as different from Jess's own happy childhood as she could imagine.

Jess put her guitar into the trunk and her bag into the back seat, trying to dispel her uneasiness. "How does the car look?"

"You were right," Rob said, tossing the rag onto the floor of the garage and lowering the door. "The clutch needs to be replaced. It should be okay for the next day or two. It could even last as long as a month. But sooner or later it's going to go."

"Probably when I'm already late for an important audition," Jess said, rolling her eyes.

Rob moved toward her, but stopped a good six feet away, careful as always not to get too close. "I'd offer to replace it for you, but I don't have the tools for it. I could see if I could borrow some, though."

"Thanks, but no." Jess shook her head. "I can't take advantage of you that way."

"Yes, you can," Rob said quietly. "I'd love to do it for you. I'm just not sure if I'll have a free weekend before the clutch goes out."

Jess had to turn away, afraid that he would see the sudden longing in her eyes. Despite all of his secrets, she liked Rob too much. She liked his direct approach with Kelsey, the way he talked to the little girl as if she were a grown-up. She liked his gentle smile and his warm laughter and the way his eyes crinkled at the edges when he was amused. She liked the way his hand had felt in her hair.

But at the same time, he was a mystery. He was intriguing, with a dark past, possessing more than a hint of danger.

And she was intrigued.

Jess turned back to face him. "Thank you," she said simply. If he'd been standing any closer, she would have leaned forward and kissed him. But he was too far away. She took a step toward him—

"Yoo hoo!"

Jess looked up to see Mrs. Greene standing on her porch, next to her husband's wheelchair. The bright pink-and-orange flowered muumuu she was wearing over her large girth rippled slightly in the evening breeze.

"Where are you going?" Mrs. Greene called out. She wore a pair of binoculars around her neck and she lifted them to her face, turning a dial to bring Rob into better focus.

"I'm singing tonight out on Siesta Key," Jess said patiently, hiding her exasperation. It was *good* her neighbors were always watching her house, she told herself. She didn't have to worry about burglars or vandals. The nosy Greenes were better than a guard dog.

"Oh, really?" Mrs. Greene called. "Where?"

"The Pelican Club," Jess replied.

"And the new tenant's going along?"

"His name is Rob Carpenter, Mrs. Greene," Jess said patiently. "You've met him before." She turned to Rob. "Rob, you remember Mrs. Greene. And Mr. Greene," she added. It was easy to forget the silent, angular man in the wheelchair. He faded to almost nothing alongside his enormous, talkative wife.

"Of course," Rob acknowledged.

"Too bad Stanford's not back from the store," Mrs. Greene said, referring to her only son. "I'm sure he'd love to go along with you. I don't suppose you could wait twenty minutes...?"

"No, I'm sorry." Jess tried her best to sound regretful. "We're already running a little late. Maybe next time." She turned toward the backyard, praying that Stanford wouldn't come home early. "Okay, Kel," she called, trying not to sound as if she were suddenly rushing. "Wagon train, ho!"

Kelsey came running, stopping to pick the newspaper up off the lawn. She carried it with her into the back seat.

"Bye, Mrs. Greene," Jess called out as she and Rob and Kelsey all climbed into the car. But Mrs. Greene had already gone back into her house.

Jess glanced at Rob as she started the car. He didn't say anything—he didn't even smile. But she could see amusement in his eyes.

As Jess pulled out of the driveway, old Mr. Greene watched them from his wheelchair on his porch, craning his neck as they moved out of sight. "Seat belts fastened?" she asked her daughter.

"Check," Kelsey said. "What does s-e-r-i-a-l spell?"

Jess exchanged a quick look with Rob. He leaned toward the back seat. "Let me see that, Bug."

Kelsey handed him the newspaper.

Jess pulled up to the stop sign at the end of the street and looked down at the paper Rob now held. "It spells *serial,* Kel," she said distractedly as she silently read the headline, "Sarasota Serial Killer—Victim Eleven." She quickly skimmed the article. Another murder had occurred, this latest not more than a few miles from her neighborhood. The victim had been another young woman. She had been raped, and her throat had been cut. And like all the other victims, she had been found naked, in her own bedroom, with her face heavily made up, and with a ten-foot length of rope tied tightly around her left ankle. What kind of man could do such a thing? A person who had grown up with constant pain and violence, perhaps? Jess's eyes slid toward Rob and she found herself wondering . . . No, that was ludicrous. Wasn't it?

"Who are all those ladies?" Kelsey asked, leaning forward to look over Rob's shoulder.

The newspaper had run studio photographs of all of the victims to date. There were ten of them—eleven after last night.

"Mommy, they look kind of like you," Kelsey said. "So pretty. Is it some kind of beauty contest?"

Jess looked closely at the pictures. Kelsey was right. All the women *did* resemble her. They all had dark hair, and most of them wore it short. They all had faintly heart-shaped faces, with large dark eyes . . .

She swallowed, fighting the wave of fear that gripped her. How unpleasant to realize that she fit the description of the type of woman the killer liked to murder most. . . .

She turned back to Kelsey, trying hard to make her voice sound natural. "Someone killed those women," she replied. "The police are trying to catch him."

"Until he's caught, you're going to have to be careful, okay, Bug?" Rob said.

Jess put the car into gear, but she saw Kelsey nod very seriously in the rearview mirror.

"You have to remember to stay close to the house. Don't go anywhere alone. Especially at night," Rob instructed. "Jess has to remember that, too."

Jess looked over at him.

"You've got to keep the doors and windows locked," he said in a low voice. "Promise me you will, okay?"

He cares about me, Jess thought, suddenly deliriously happy despite the frightening newspaper story, despite the fact that Rob remained such a mystery. "I promise," she agreed. She glanced at Kelsey as she pulled out onto the main road, heading west toward Siesta Key and the Pelican Club. "Okay, Kel," she added, "You got your drawing pad and pencils?"

Kelsey rummaged through her backpack. "Check."

"You got your Star Trek dolls?"

"Check."

"How about the sticker book, coloring book and crayons, giant monster mazes book?"

"Check, check and . . . check."

"Look in my bag for me. Did *I* forget anything?"

Kelsey opened Jess's bag and peeked inside. "Extra guitar strings, capo, tuner, two cords," the girl said. "Pitch pipe, Swiss army knife and your little box of picks."

"Thanks. Okay. Now tell me again. What are the rules?"

"No talking to you during the set," Kelsey recited. "And stay close, where you can see me. I won't go out of your sight, and I won't talk to strangers."

"Good," Jess said. "Course, this time it'll be different, because Rob's here." She glanced up and found him watching her, and felt a flash of warmth. *Rob's here.*

"Rob and I are going to eat dinner while you sing," Kelsey said. "I'm going to have the broiled scrod."

"Oh, Bug, what a thrill." Rob grinned as he turned sideways in his seat to look back at Kelsey. "I can't tell you how often I've longed for a dinner date with a beautiful woman who actually knows what she wants to order before we even walk into the restaurant."

"We Baxter women are known for our decisiveness," Jess said, then laughed. "Of course, I realized as soon as I said that, that I can't decide which song to open my first set with."

"'Country Waltz' or 'Jamaica Farewell,'" Kelsey suggested.

"I can't start a set with a song that has *farewell* in the title," Jess protested.

"Then 'Country Waltz,'" Kelsey said. "There. You decided. No sweat."

Jess looked at Rob and grinned. "Life should always be so simple, shouldn't it?"

THIS TIME HE FELT IT begin as he was in the car. He had gotten depressed again after last night, and even thought about turning himself in. But as he slipped out of his depression and into the warm feeling of expectation, he basked in the rush of knowing that he would, that he must, strike again.

For a moment, he wondered what made him know that it was time again to start the game. The thought had barely formed before it was pushed aside by an almost giddy confidence. The urge was upon him, and he would fulfill it. He was totally in control, completely unstoppable. His senses were so keen he had to turn the radio down to barely a whisper to keep the sound from hurting his ears. He put his sunglasses on to protect his eyes from the brightness of the blue sky.

When the car stopped at a red light, he tried to identify the taste in his mouth. Then, as the light turned green, he smiled and surged forward.

Of course.

The taste in his mouth was blood.

Chapter Three

The Pelican Club's outside bar was already crowded, and Jess quickly set up the house sound system. She was still fifteen minutes early, but this job paid particularly well. If she left a good impression, it could become a weekly gig. She tried not to think of all the things in her life that needed to be repaired or replaced. Instead she concentrated on adjusting the small mixing board and hooking up the microphone and the cord from her guitar.

She tuned up quickly, put her gleaming guitar into a stand, and crossed to the bar.

The bartender was a man she'd never seen at the Pelican Club before. He was different from the usual beefcake-types she'd met there in the past. He was older, shorter, slighter. He was average height and build, with short dark hair that curled slightly in the humidity and looked as if it hadn't been combed after he'd taken a shower. He wore the tight red T-shirt with khaki shorts that were the standard uniform for all of the staff at the Pelican Club. He had a typical beach bum's two-day growth of beard, but something about him seemed oddly out of place, as if he didn't belong here.

"Hi, I'm singing here tonight," she said, when he looked up from replacing glasses in the overhead rack. "Lenny said someone named Pete would be on duty...?"

"I'm Pete." He had silver-gray eyes and a smile that came and went far too quickly, leaving his rather angular face looking almost stern. "You're Jess Baxter. You look just like your picture."

"My picture...?"

"The manager pinned it to an easel in the lobby," Pete explained. "Where it says, 'Tonight's Entertainment.'"

He leaned his elbows against the bar, his body relaxed and loose. But his eyes were watchful and sharp, and he seemed to study her face, her dress and her body beneath it.

"I'm going to start in a few minutes," Jess said, backing away from him. Glancing around, she spotted Rob and Kelsey sitting at a table at the side of the crowded deck. Rob had his back to the railing that looked out over the water. As their eyes met, she felt a familiar surge of energy and excitement. She had to force herself to look back at Pete. "I'll need you to turn off the tape that's playing."

Pete nodded. He gestured with his head toward Rob and Kelsey. "Is that your family?"

"My daughter," Jess said. "And...a friend."

The bartender nodded, glancing again at Rob. It was a seemingly casual move, but Jess couldn't shake the feeling that those odd, silvery eyes missed nothing. "Just let me know when you want the music turned off," Pete said, moving away to serve a customer.

Jess crossed the room, toward Rob and Kelsey. What *was* it about the bartender that seemed so odd? Sure, his eyes were an unusual color, and he didn't smile very much, but that wasn't it. There was something else that seemed wrong.

"Problem?" Rob asked, rising to his feet as she approached their table.

Jess shook her head. "No, just stage fright, I guess." She took a deep breath in and let it out in a rush, forcing herself to smile. "Believe it or not, after all these years of performing, I still sometimes get it."

"You know, I read a book once," Rob told her, "that said what you call something, what you *label* it, helps determine whether or not you feel positively or negatively about it. Like, some people get what they call 'stage fright' and become terrified or sick from it, but other people call that same feeling 'excitement' and they get pumped up and really jazzed about a performance. It's the same feeling of anticipation—that kind of butterflies in the stomach feeling—but what these different people label it determines how they're going to react to it."

Jess was looking at him peculiarly, her eyebrows slightly raised. "You're not following me, are you?" he added.

But she shook her head. "Yeah, actually I am," she said. "And I agree with everything you just said. You're right. Usually I don't call this feeling stage fright." She looked out over the rail at the calm water of the harbor. "But tonight, for some reason, I'm particularly nervous." She turned to look at him again. "I think I'm more nervous about being here with you than I am about singing," she admitted frankly.

But before he could respond, she changed the subject. "You do read a lot, don't you," she said.

Rob nodded, relieved to be on safer ground. "Yeah," he replied. "That's usually what I do when I'm not working." But not by choice. He didn't say those words aloud, but as he met Jess's eyes, he knew that she could read his face as clearly as one of his books.

"I like books," he said almost defensively. He just wouldn't spend *all* of his time reading—living a fantasy life—if he had any kind of choice.

But he hadn't had a choice in so long . . .

Jess was watching him. Her dark eyes were so perceptive. They were bottomless and warm and incredibly gentle.

"Why do you hide?" she asked quietly.

His first thought was, God, she knew. But how could she possibly know? She was speaking figuratively, not literally. "I think of it more as trying not to make waves," he said. "Or trying to be invisible."

"Why?" she asked.

Why? What could he say to her? He'd already told her too much. Again. What was it about this woman that made him break his self-imposed rules over and over again?

Jess searched Rob's face. For a few moments, he'd let his guard down, and she'd been able to see an array of emotions cross his face. But now again, his eyes were guarded, his expression closed.

Invisible. That was a good word for the way he held himself, for the way he made himself blend in. Except right from the start, Jess had been able to see past that. But, clearly, she was the exception. Not everyone would take the time to search for the real man.

"What if," she said softly, "you're busy being invisible, and your perfect match—your soul mate, so to speak—can't see you? What if she walks right past?"

This conversation had long since gotten out of hand. Rob forced himself to smile. "I'm not too worried about that," he said, trying to make his voice sound light. "Look, I'm going to the bar. Can I get you something to drink?"

Jess shook her head, no, and Rob just barely made it over to the bar. What if he was invisible and his soul mate *could* see him? He glanced back at Jess as she sat next to Kelsey and she gave the little girl a hug. She looked across the room at him and smiled, and he could barely breathe. How could he have a soul mate? At times he felt he didn't even have a soul.

By the time the bartender served him a glass of soda, and he walked back to Jess and Kelsey, he was able to smile again.

"I'm going to start singing. Give me a kiss," Jess said to Kelsey, leaning over to smooch her daughter's smooth cheek.

"Break a leg." Kelsey didn't even look up from her coloring book.

"Don't drink more than one glass of root beer for each set."

Kelsey carefully selected a turquoise-colored crayon from her box. "What if I'm thirsty?"

"Water has been known to quench thirst."

Jess stood up, tilting her head to look up at Rob. Their gazes locked, and she felt a dizzying warmth that started deep in the pit of her stomach and spiraled upward.

For once he was close enough so that all she would have to do would be to lean forward, and his arms would go around her. And then if she lifted her face to his...

He wanted to kiss her. Jess knew just from looking, from the way he gazed at her mouth, from the heat and longing in his eyes.

But it was crazy. They were standing in a room filled with people—including her six-year-old daughter.

She wanted to kiss him, too, but instead she touched his arm, letting her hand slide down to his hand. The sensation was shockingly intimate as he intertwined their fingers. Jess felt herself sway toward him.

This was crazy. Still gazing into her eyes, he reached out, cupping her face with his other hand. She stood on her toes, lifting her mouth to his.

Their lips met, featherlight and gentle. His mouth was warm and sweet, and she wanted more.

But she pulled away, shaken by the intensity of her desire. His breathing, too, was unsteady as he stared at her.

"Wow," Jess finally said. She managed a shaky smile. "Can you hold that thought for about—" she glanced at her watch "—four hours?"

But it was as if Rob didn't even hear her. "I'm lost," he murmured, shaking his head slowly. "Dear God, I'm totally lost."

Jess glanced down at Kelsey, who was taking great pains to appear absorbed by her coloring book. Which meant she hadn't missed that kiss.

That kiss... He had *kissed* her. She felt a sudden burst of intensely perfect happiness. With a flash, she could see herself with Rob and Kelsey, laughing together in the kitchen, cooking dinner. Cooking *breakfast*. She could picture them taking trips to the beach, gazing up at the stars on a clear night. She could imagine a future filled with laughter and song.

"I'm lost," Rob whispered again.

Not me, thought Jess. I'm found.

HE WAS CONFUSED.

It was an odd feeling.

For so long, he'd known exactly what he'd needed, and exactly what he had to do to *get* what he needed.

He still knew. But never before had the temptation to do otherwise been so powerful, so sweet.

Rob looked down at Kelsey, still coloring away in her book. She was part of the temptation. With very little effort, he could slip into the role of father. Father, husband, lover, friend. Soul mate. He could be normal, have a healthy family, make brothers and sisters for this little girl, make babies with her vivacious, beautiful, heart-stoppingly sexy mother.

Jess.

She stepped gracefully onto the small stage. Picking up her guitar, she sat on the stool, crossing her long, slender legs as she adjusted the microphone.

She met his eyes from all the way across the room and smiled.

She was temptation incarnate. She was unlike any woman he'd ever known—except maybe his own mother. But his mother was just a shadow. An elusive, ghostly memory from his early childhood, hovering just out of range of his peripheral vision.

Jess was real.

She was flesh and blood.

Blood.

His stomach hurt and he tried to stop thinking, stop feeling.

He watched Jess nod to the bartender, and the man faded out the taped music that had been playing. Softly, she began to play, taking the introduction around twice as her fingers warmed up.

As she started to sing, her voice was soft and light. Even through the sound system, it barely cut above the noises of the bar. She kept her eyes down, singing the first verse of the song almost as if to herself, and slowly the crowd quieted down. They had to quiet down if they wanted to hear her smooth, rich, alto voice at all. By the time she was ready to sing the refrain, Rob could've heard a pin drop. She looked up at the audience then, smiling as if they were all friends who just happened to drop by while she was singing in her living room. She looked around, meeting the eyes of individual people in the crowd.

"It's just a simple country waltz," she sang. "The kind you hear all the time. So darlin', let this dance be mine."

Jess let her eyes rest on Rob as she sang the second verse. "The music pulled us out across the floor. You held me oh so tight." Her voice caressed the notes as she looked into his eyes.

God, how he wanted her. He wanted to kiss her, to devour her, to fall back on his bed with her, her body underneath his. He wanted to lose himself in her, to hear her cry out his name.

His hands were clasped tightly in front of him on the table, and he looked down, away from her for a moment, closing his eyes briefly. When he looked up, she was still watching him, and he knew she couldn't help but see the heat in his eyes.

"Your smile, it set my heart on fire," she sang, her own desire thickening her voice. "I hoped that you'd be mine, and stay and dance with me all night."

Her eyes were telling him that she was singing this song for him. She was giving him an invitation to become part of her life tonight. But not just tonight. Every night. Jess was not a one-night woman. Her invitation would last from now till death do us part.

Death.

God, if she only knew . . .

Jess stepped off the stage and nearly ran right into Stanford Greene.

"Evenin' Miss Jess," he said, in his thick southern accent. He was standing much too close—they were nearly nose to nose. His eyes watched her unblinkingly. She was reminded of the baleful stare of his father, sitting in his wheelchair, out on the porch.

"Stan!" she said in surprise. She took a step backward, trying to achieve a more normal distance between them. He never seemed aware of anyone's personal space. "What are *you* doing out here?"

He shuffled toward her, his hat in his fat fingers. She moved back another step, bumping against the hard wood of the bar. All this time, and the man *still* hadn't blinked.

"Ah came to hear you sing. Mama sent me over. She thought it might be a good thing for me to get to know you a little better. Us both being unwed, you with a small child to raise . . ."

Jess carefully kept her face neutral. "Oh," she managed to say.

He leaned closer to her and spoke conspiratorially. "I think she wants a grandkid of her own." A thin strand of the greasy hair that he kept combed across his bald head was dislodged, and it hung down in front of his left ear, almost to his shoulder.

Jess wasn't sure what to say. "Well," she hedged. "That's nice . . ."

"Yes, ma'am." He didn't move. His watery eyes moved down to her low neckline.

Jess tried hard to keep her voice pleasant. "Um, Stan, have you got a table, a place to sit?"

"No, ma'am. Ah have just arrived."

Jess grabbed the empty bar stool next to her gratefully, patting the smooth seat. "Well, here you go. Why don't you sit right here, order yourself something to drink? I'm going to start singing again really soon, and right now I have to go check on . . . on Kelsey," she said, clutching at her daughter as an excuse, "so I'll see you later, okay?"

"Yes, ma'am."

Stanford Greene, Jess thought, shaking her head as she made her escape, easing her way through the crowd. Did Mrs. Greene honestly think that Jess and Stan . . . No, it was too awful to consider. What was that saying—not if he was the last man on earth?

Just as Jess approached Rob and Kelsey's table, a strong hand seized her above the elbow.

"Jess! Darling! Taking your union break, I see."

She froze. The slightly bored, cultured voice was unmistakable. She slowly turned around.

Ian. Wearing a Hawaiian shirt unbuttoned nearly all the way, and a scruffy pair of safari shorts. His shoulder-length blond curls looked as if they had exploded around his face, and his pale blue eyes were rimmed with red. Her ex-husband had been drinking.

"Oh, damn." She quickly glanced at Kelsey. The little girl's smile had faded, and she was coloring again, giving her book her total, undivided attention.

"A gracious greeting as usual," Ian said, slipping his arms around her waist. Jess turned her head away before he could kiss her on the mouth. Instead he kissed her just underneath her ear, letting his lips trail down toward her throat.

She tried to break free, but he held her too tightly. "Ian, stop it," she whispered. If she struggled too hard, there'd be a scene. Lord, if there was one thing she *didn't* want tonight, it was one of Ian's scenes.

"Delicious," he murmured, still nuzzling her neck. "Absolutely delicious. Don't you think, Robert?"

Rob. He was coming to her rescue.

"That's enough, Ian," Rob said evenly, pulling Jess gently away from the other man.

"Yes, sir," another man added. "Don't be obnoxious, Ian."

It was Frank Madsen—Rob's friend from his office. No, not his friend—an acquaintance, Rob had called him. Jess hadn't noticed Frank at first, standing quietly behind Ian.

"You don't mind if we join you?" Ian asked mockingly, pulling another chair up to the table and sitting down. "You all know Frank Madsen, right? Of course you do. I first met him at one of your gigs, Jess. And he works over at that computer place with Robert, isn't that correct?"

Jess smiled tightly at Frank as he shook hands briefly with Rob. She had to get Ian and his abusive mouth away from Kelsey. "Actually, Ian, I *do* mind—"

He tossed a ring with two keys onto the table. "Here are your car keys, Robert," he said. "Thank you so very much."

Jess looked up at Rob in surprise. "You lent *Ian* your car?" she said.

I'm sorry, his eyes said. His arm was still protectively around her, and she felt her pulse quicken from the warmth and solidness of his body next to hers. "He had some kind of emergency," Rob told her quietly, "and I didn't need it.... He was going to drop it off tonight, so I called and left a message on his machine that I wouldn't be home—that I'd be here, with you."

He clearly hadn't expected Ian to come all the way out here to return his car—and to hassle Jess. But despite the words of warning he'd given her recently, he obviously didn't know Ian very well. Certainly not well enough to lend him his car. But Rob was always loaning people his car. Jess remembered a few months ago she'd heard that he'd even let Stanford Greene borrow it.

"I told you just to leave it in the driveway," Rob said to Ian. "With the key under the mat."

Ian shrugged expansively. "I thought I'd do you a favor and bring it out here."

"I have to get ready for my next set," Jess said abruptly. "And no doubt Ian has someplace else to be ... ?"

"Actually, no," he replied, sitting back in his chair and stretching his legs out underneath the table. "Frank and I were just talking, weren't we, Frank?"

"Ian—" Frank said in a warning voice, shaking his head. He met Jess's eyes apologetically. He was older than the rest of them, in his midforties at least, with straight golden brown hair and rather nondescript hazel eyes. He was tall, quite a bit over six feet, with a paunch starting out front. He looked like a former football player gone to seed, still quite handsome, but fading around the edges.

"I was wondering just how many men in this place want to make it with my ex-wife," Ian mused. "I'd guess there are three right here, sitting at this table."

Kelsey put down her crayons and stared at her father, hostility on her small face.

Rob squeezed Jess's shoulder, then crossed around to Kelsey, digging several quarters from his pocket. "C'mon, Bug, why don't you go play a video game?"

"With you?" Kelsey asked hopefully.

Rob glanced across the table. Jess nodded once. Yes. She wanted Kelsey away from there. She could handle Ian, particularly with Frank nearby.

As Rob led Kelsey away, Ian laughed. "Look at that guy, auditioning for the part of 'Daddy,'" he mocked. "Isn't that sweet? It makes me want to puke."

"Ian, please leave," Jess said quietly. She could feel the bartender watching them, his sharp eyes picking up the undercurrents of trouble.

Frank stood uncertainly near the table, unsure whether to sit or stand or leave Jess and her ex-husband alone.

Ian leaned forward. "Can you believe I saw Stanford Greene sitting at the bar?" he said, his voice lowered to a loud stage whisper. "How on *earth* did you persuade him to leave his mommy's basement? Really, Jess, he's not quite your type. I just can't imagine the two of you together. Well, actually, I can, and it's really rather hideous—"

Frank made his decision. "Ian, leave Jess alone. Let's go. I'll drive you home."

"Without seeing Jess's last set? We couldn't!"

"Yes, sir, we certainly could," Frank said firmly.

"You go then," Ian said with a shrug. "I'm staying."

"Excuse me. My break's almost over." Jess smiled one last time at Frank, then escaped into the crowd. When Ian became so absolutely pigheaded, there was no use arguing with him. She could only hope that he wasn't loaded enough to start heckling her during her set.

She headed toward the bar, hoping to get a cool glass of soda to ease the headache that had started with Ian's arrival. But she caught sight of Stanford Greene's unblinking stare directly in her path, and made a quick detour to the stage. There were only a few more minutes before she had to go on, and she might as well spend the time tuning her guitar....

A hand touched her lightly on the back of her neck, and she jumped, spinning around. "Oh! Frank, you startled me!"

"Sorry." The older man smiled apologetically. "I just wanted to say that I'll try to keep Ian away from you."

She looked up into Frank's kind eyes. "Ian's not your responsibility."

Frank shrugged. "It's not a problem. I'm happy to run interference." He paused. "You know, Rob gave me a call, to let me know you were playing out here tonight. I guess you got this job sort of last minute, huh?"

"The manager called me just this afternoon."

Frank nodded slowly. "Good for you," he said.

Jess gazed across the club, to where she could see Rob's brown hair near the pair of video games in the corner. "I can't believe Rob lent *Ian* his car."

"Good old Rob." Frank smiled. "I've borrowed his car several times myself in a pinch."

"He's very generous," Jess said.

"Yes, sir, he is, indeed." Frank hesitated. "I didn't know you two were . . . dating."

Jess smiled. "Tonight's our first date," she said. "If you can even call it a date. I mean, Kelsey's with us, and I'm performing...."

Frank nodded. "Oh. Well, I guess I'll see you around."

He turned to go. Jess put her hand on his arm, and it was Frank's turn to jump.

"Sorry." She smiled gently at his tense expression. "I just wanted to say, if I don't see you after the set, thanks for coming. I'll talk to you soon, okay?"

He nodded. "Okay."

Jess strapped on her guitar, and sat back up on the stool. From over at the bar, she caught a glimpse of the bartender, Pete, watching her.

All evening long she'd been aware of his pale gray eyes following her around the room.

She met his eyes almost defiantly, and he smiled. Or at least he moved his lips upward in an approximate facsimile of a smile. This was not a man to whom a broad, heartfelt smile was a natural expression. It was strange that Lenny should hire him as a bartender. He normally liked retired bouncers—big, tall men with biceps the size of her thigh. Either that, or Lenny hired out-of-work stand-up comics. This Pete was obviously neither.

He wasn't skinny, but he was no Arnold Schwarzenegger. As for his sense of humor... well, he was no barrel of laughs, either. There was something strange about him, and it was more than just the way he always seemed to watch her—after all, she was a performer. People were *supposed* to watch her.

Adjusting her microphone, Jess began to play a soft, soothing instrumental. She closed her eyes and before too long, she lost herself in the music.

HIS BODY WAS HUMMING. Every nerve was stretched tight, taut, ready to snap.

He couldn't have her.

She was singing. Her beautiful, rich voice washed over him. It should have been calming, peaceful—instead it tore like barbs into his already sensitized skin. And the sound of the applause cut through him like a knife to his brain.

But he couldn't leave.

Not with the stage lights making her silky dark hair gleam. Not when she looked out over the quiet audience and sang directly to him. For him. She *had* to be singing for him. He knew that she was.

He couldn't leave, and he couldn't stay. He just sat, feeling the rage building, boiling in his veins.

Chapter Four

It was after one o'clock before Jess put her guitar in the trunk of her car.

The parking lot was nearly empty, and inside the Pelican Club the lights were going off, one by one.

Rob was carrying Kelsey, and he gently put the sleeping child into the back seat and fastened the seat belt around her. He backed out of the car, careful not to hit his head, and quietly shut the door.

This wasn't the way Jess had imagined their evening out would end. They had separate cars—and hers had a sleeping child in the back seat. Odder yet was the fact that if they said good-night here and both went home, they'd end up back at the same house.

Rob was watching her, his face hidden in the shadows.

"Well," Jess said, to fill the silence. "That was a real circus, wasn't it?"

He looked away. "I'm sorry about Ian showing up."

"You didn't know."

"I should have."

"Well, now you do."

"I felt bad for Kelsey," Rob said.

Jess glanced toward the car, where Kelsey was still sleeping, and shook her head. "Ian ignores her," she said. "It's unbelievable. He doesn't even say 'hi.' And it hurts her so much. I try to keep him away from her." She sighed. "That's not necessarily the answer, but for now, it's easier for Kelsey."

"It could be worse."

They lapsed into silence. Jess could hear the sound of the waves lapping at the dock alongside the restaurant. In the grass and trees, insects buzzed and chirped. Somewhere down the street, a dog barked.

"Well," she said again. "I'd better get Kelsey home."

Rob looked up. "Jess, I have to tell you," he said in a rush of words, "that I can't..."

But before he could finish, the last of the bright club lights went out, plunging them into sudden darkness.

"...that I can't do this," Rob concluded softly.

It was velvet, the darkness—soft and warm and enveloping them totally, cutting them off from the rest of the world and from each other.

"Whoa," Jess said, reaching out for him, suddenly uncertain which way was up. "It's dark. Where are you?"

"Here," he answered. His hand gripped her arm, just above her elbow. "I'm here."

"Can't do what?" she asked. "I don't understand." His grasp turned into a caress as he ran his fingers up her arm to her shoulder. There were other people on the other side of the parking lot, but the darkness was complete, giving Jess and Rob privacy for the first time all evening.

She stepped forward even as he pulled her into his arms.

"Oh, God," he breathed, holding her so tightly. "Oh, Jess."

She could feel the warm solidness of his arms, the hard muscles of his chest, the athletic strength of his thighs. She fit against him perfectly, as if he'd been created with her in mind.

He groaned, and she could feel his arousal growing, pressing unmistakably against her. "I can't do this," he said again, his voice hoarse. "I can't kiss you—"

But then he did. He lowered his head and took her mouth fiercely, with an intensity that left her breathless. It was a kiss nothing like the gentle brushing of lips they'd shared inside the club. It was a kiss that claimed her, filled her, possessed her.

Jess kissed him back passionately, hungrily, exploring his mouth eagerly as he seemed to inhale her. She'd been wanting to kiss him like this all evening long. She'd been anticipating this incredible rush, this roller-coaster pleasure ride of emotional and physical sensations that she knew kissing Rob would bring.

His hands were in her hair, on her neck, sliding down the bare V-back of her dress, moving down even lower to press her hips closer to him.

And still he kissed her. He kissed her as if there were no tomorrow, as if he, too, had been waiting much too long for this moment.

It was nothing like she'd imagined, and better than her wildest dreams.

Rob was so quiet, so calm, so careful. She'd imagined sweet, gentle kisses, softly whispered questions, asking her permission to touch her, to move each small step beyond a simple kiss.

But he kissed her wildly, relentlessly, his hands sweeping urgently across her body, cupping the curve of her derriere, weighing the swell of her breasts, his thumbs caressing the sensitive, erect points of her nipples. He knew exactly how to touch her to make the heat of desire flood through her, to make her gasp with need and tremble with longing. His thigh pressed insistently between her legs, and she opened herself, pressing the heat of her most intimate place against him.

The rocket of desire that soared through her was so intense, she gripped him harder and kissed him even more deliriously, urging him on.

Urging him on...?

Was it possible that mild-mannered Rob Carpenter was going to make love to her right here, in the darkened parking lot of the Pelican Club?

There was no denying that she wanted him. But not here. Not like this. Not with Kelsey asleep in her car....

Jess pulled away. It was only the slightest movement, but Rob instantly released her. He stepped back, still supporting her, but now from an arm's length away.

She could hear his breathing, ragged and quick as he struggled to regain his control.

"Oh, my God," he whispered. "I'm sorry—"

"No," Jess said quickly. "Don't apologize. Come home with me. That's where we should be. I want to stop—but only until we get home."

Across the parking lot, a car engine started with a roar. As it pulled out, its headlights swept across them. Rob released her and took another step back, pushing his disheveled hair out of his face.

"I can't," he said tightly. God, she would never know how much he wanted her. She'd never know how close those kisses had come to pushing him over the edge. She'd tasted so sweet, she'd felt so right in his arms. She'd so clearly wanted more...

"Jess, I'm sorry—"

Another car started up. Rob looked down at Jess. Her lips were parted and moist, and her cheeks were flushed with desire. She wanted him to come home with her, to come with her into her bed. Her dark eyes were molten, wanting him...

In a sudden flash, he saw another woman, only this one looked up at him with pain and fear in her eyes. There was blood everywhere, so much blood... He was covered with the blood, with *her* blood. And as he watched, the pain and fear drained from those eyes, leaving them lifeless, glazed, dead...

Rob backed away. "I'm sorry...." he said again.

"It's okay—"

"No, it's not," he said savagely, and turning, he bolted for the other side of the parking lot, for his car.

"Rob, wait—"

Jess started after him, but the light disappeared with the car that left the parking lot, leaving them again in darkness. Dammit, what was wrong with him? She couldn't chase him—she couldn't leave Kelsey.

She saw the sudden flash of headlights and heard the squeal of tires as his car pulled away.

He was gone. Just like that.

HE HADN'T PLANNED IT, but suddenly the need was so great, he had to do it.

This area was unfamiliar to him. That was bad. But the drive back to his own neighborhood would take at least half an hour. And once he was there, he wouldn't be guaranteed satisfaction.

More importantly, he couldn't wait that long. Already, he was burning.

Suddenly he knew the solution, and he pulled into the parking lot of one of the fancy condominium high rises that sat directly on Crescent Beach. It was risky, the car could get towed, but it must be done.

The beach was dark, and a thick fog was rolling in off the gulf. Several of the high rises had flood lamps that lit part of the beach, but most of them didn't.

The darkness, the fog and the late hour didn't keep a few hardy couples from strolling along the edge of the water, hand in hand. Occasionally, a crowd of partying teenagers would pass by, but mostly the beach was empty.

Empty and very, very dark.

The powdery sand shifted into one of his shoes. As he sat down on a wooden beach chair to wait, he emptied it out.

It didn't take long until he found her.

She was walking alone, dressed in a windbreaker, her hair tied back with a scarf.

She wasn't as young as she should be, and he didn't even know the color of her hair. It wouldn't be as good, as complete.

But it would be done.

He flicked his knife open.

WHEN JESS PULLED INTO the driveway, Rob's car wasn't there.

She hadn't really expected him to be there, waiting for her, but at the same time, she couldn't help feeling disappointed.

And hurt. Not to mention confused as hell.

What had just happened between her and Rob? Had she missed some vital and important moment? Had she misunderstood something he'd said?

One moment he'd been kissing her as if his single goal in life were to make love to her, and the next he was running away from her as if she carried the plague, shouting his apologies over his shoulder.

The entire episode had been too strange.

I can't kiss you, he'd said—right before he'd kissed her.

And what a kiss. She'd never been kissed that way before. She'd never been kissed so hungrily, so passionately—as if she were the only woman in the world that he wanted.

Except he didn't want her.

She'd invited him to come home with her, to make love to her. True, she hadn't used quite those words, but her meaning had been clear. She'd been ready to give herself to him, totally.

And he'd run away.

He'd rejected her.

Don't cry, she ordered herself sternly, trying to force back the tears that were flooding her eyes. It wasn't the end of the world. It only felt like it right now.

A tear escaped, and she closed her eyes, letting her head fall back against the headrest.

What was wrong with her? Why was she always attracted to men who ended up hurting her?

In the back seat, Kelsey stirred and sat up groggily. "Are we home?"

Jess quickly wiped her face. "Yeah," she said. "We're home."

"Where's Rob?" Kelsey asked, more awake. "Didn't we need to drive him home? Where did he go?"

Jess pushed the remote and the garage door slid up. She glanced at her daughter in the rearview mirror as she pulled into the garage. Even in the dimness, she could see that Kelsey's eyes were dark with worry.

"Rob lent his car to Ian," she explained. "Ian returned it to him, so Rob's driving it home."

But Kelsey didn't seem to hear, or understand. "Was it Ian's fault?" she asked suddenly, her small face tight. "Did he make Rob go away?"

"What?" Jess turned on the car's interior light and looked at her daughter.

Kelsey looked down at her hands. They were clasped tightly in her lap.

"Kel, I don't understand what you asked about Ian," Jess said. "I need you to explain. Please?"

Kelsey looked up at Jess, tears in her big eyes. "When we were at the Pelican Club, you seemed so happy. I saw you and Rob kissing. While you were on stage, I asked Rob if he was in love with you, you know, like Ariel and Prince Eric in *The Little Mermaid.*"

Jess's heart caught in her throat. "Oh, Kel." What did he say, she wanted to ask. Lord, she thought, look at me, about to pump my daughter for information, like a lovesick seventh grader.

"He said that it was more like *Beauty and the Beast,* and then he looked really sad." Kelsey took a deep breath. "But I was happy, because in the movie, the Beast comes back to life and he marries Belle in the end, and I thought that meant you and Rob were gonna get married, and we could all live happily ever after."

There was a moment of silence while Jess took all of that in.

Kelsey added darkly, "Then Ian showed up, and he was so rude to you, saying those mean things, and I was so mad at him, and when me and Rob played video games, I was really just pretending to play, really, I was so mad at Ian...."

"I'm sorry, Kel," Jess murmured, reaching back to pull her daughter up to the front seat and into her lap.

"Then Rob told me that it wasn't Ian's fault that he acted so rude. He told me that Ian was upset 'cause he still loved you, and *I* told Rob that if Ian still loved you, then he wouldn't be so mean to you, and I told him how Ian used to yell so loudly and break things and make you cry, and I was glad he didn't live here anymore. I told him that I *hated* Ian."

"What did he say?" Jess asked, looking down into her daughter's fierce face.

Kelsey blinked, her angry expression changing. "Rob told me that it was okay for me to be mad at Ian. He said he was pretty mad at him, too. But he said that I should probably give Ian a break, because he's my father, even though he doesn't want me to call him Daddy. And Rob said that he thought maybe someday, when I'm older, I'd be able to get to know Ian, and maybe then I might even like him a little bit. He said that maybe by that time, *Ian* might be a little older, too, and that that would help."

Jess didn't know whether to laugh or cry.

"Rob's a pretty smart guy," she said. She took a deep breath. "Kel, Ian didn't chase Rob away." Jess had done that all by herself. "Okay?"

"Okay." Kelsey's face was still skeptical. "So, are you going to marry Rob?"

Jess hugged her daughter close to her. "We've gone on one date," she told her. One date, and there wasn't likely to be another. "People don't get married after just one date."

"Prince Eric and Ariel did," Kelsey countered. "And so did Belle and the Beast."

Jess gave Kelsey a kiss. "If only," she said, "life could be as simple as a Disney animated movie."

"MURDER ON SIESTA KEY—Victim Twelve?"

The sensational newspaper headline caught Jess's eye at the gas station, inside the little attached convenience store.

A woman had been murdered on the beach on Siesta Key. Last night. Not more than a mile from the Pelican Club.

Jess quickly skimmed the article. The coroner's report estimated the victim's time of death at about 1:30 a.m.—just shortly after she had left the club. Minutes after that disastrous kiss.

Where had Rob gone after that? What had he done? He certainly hadn't gone onto Crescent Beach and slit a woman's throat. Had he?

The unpleasant truth was that Jess couldn't say that for sure. She didn't know Rob well enough. She knew he had a dark side and a violent past. But just how dark and violent?

According to the article, the police were hesitant to link this death to the Sarasota Serial Killer. All of the previous murders had been committed in the victims' own bedrooms—this killing was done right out in the open, on the beach, not far from where Jess's parents owned a house. And the woman didn't fit the killer's usual type. She was older, with light brown hair.

Not that it really mattered. Either way, the poor woman was dead.

And Jess couldn't seem to shake the feeling that the dead woman could well have been *her*.

Chapter Five

"Robert Carpenter. Nickname Rob. Born September 13, 1962, in Jersey City, New Jersey," Rob said aloud as he rinsed his razor in the bathroom sink. It always helped to recite exactly who he was and where he had come from every morning. He gazed at himself in the mirror as he finished shaving. "NYU, class of '85, computer science. Took time off between sophomore and junior year to travel out west. Got a job at Digital directly out of college, moved to a small software design company before the layoffs—a company that has since conveniently gone out of business. Moved to Sarasota less than a year ago."

He rinsed his face, splashing cold water on his cheeks as he gazed up again into his ordinary brown eyes. "Outside interests include books, folk music, movies . . . and being boring as hell."

Rob leaned closer, trying to see what Jess saw when she looked into his eyes. He couldn't figure it out.

He knew what he saw in her. She was a vivacious, happy, friendly lady with a cheerful disposition and the ability to smile in the face of disaster. In fact, Rob knew her better than he knew himself these days. She'd caught his eye the day he'd moved to Sarasota, and he'd watched her for months. He'd watched her playing with her daughter in the yard, saw the love they shared. He'd even sometimes followed them on a Saturday when they went to the beach or out shopping. He'd envied them their casual happiness. More recently, as they welcomed him into their lives as a friend as well as a tenant, Jess had talked without reservation about her warm, wonderful parents and her happy childhood. He'd fantasized at great length about being a permanent part of their perfect little world.

He'd fantasized about more than that, too.

Jess. Yeah, he'd fantasized about her also at great length.

But now he was avoiding her.

The past few days had been hell. Each day, he had left for work early in the morning and hadn't returned each night until long after midnight.

He wanted so badly to see Jess, to talk to her, to touch her. Yes, this project he was working on required some overtime, but not so much that he was forced to stay until midnight. He stayed late because he couldn't risk running into her. He knew he wouldn't be able to stand the temptation. He could still taste that kiss. . . .

Rob also knew that whatever time he came home from work, he'd do no more than lie awake in his bed for most of the night. And when he *did* finally fall asleep, he'd dream about being a part of Jess's life. He'd dream about being normal, about being a husband and father.

But then reality always intervened in the form of the dawn. He would stagger out of bed and into the bathroom. And there, in the bathroom mirror, he would be faced with his bleary-eyed reflection—and the fact that he was not, had never been, and would never be normal.

What right did he have to dream about being Kelsey's father? His own father had been one hell of a lousy role model. The only thing Rob's father had taught him was how to beat the crap out of a kid like Kelsey—how to degrade her and crush her self-esteem into oblivion. Oh, yeah, and he had also learned from his dear old dad how to intimidate and hurt without leaving bruises behind. He knew how to be feared and hated.

What goes around comes around.

Rob got dressed, carried his suitcase to his car, and then climbed back up the stairs and onto the deck to knock on Jess's kitchen door.

He took a deep breath, forcing his speeding heart to slow. Yes, he was going to see her, but only for the briefest moment.

He knocked then waited as he heard her movement in the kitchen, as the door swung open. Jess stared out at him through the screen. She was wearing shorts and a T-shirt, and her feet were bare. Her hair was slightly messed, as if she hadn't gotten around to brushing it yet this morning. Her eyes were guarded.

"Hi," Rob said, wishing that she would smile at him, but knowing that she wouldn't. He looked away from her, down at the deck. "I, uh, just wanted to let you know that I'm going out of town tonight."

Jess pushed the screen door open, a gesture that invited him inside. She had just finished pushing and prodding Kelsey onto the kindergarten bus, and had been getting ready to leave on her regular Thursday morning grocery run when Rob had knocked on the door. But the groceries could wait. She wanted—no, *needed*—to talk to him. But he shook his head, still not quite meeting her eyes.

"I've got to get to the office—I'm already running late," he said. "We've got a project going and we're working around the clock."

Jess stepped out on the deck, joining him in the hot morning sunshine. "Gee, and I thought you were just hiding from me."

He was tired. She could see it in his eyes, on his face, in the way he was standing. But he smiled at her words. It was a sweet smile that touched his eyes with sadness and made her heart turn over.

"I was doing that, too," he admitted. His smile faded, leaving only the sadness in his brown eyes. "I'm sorry about…what happened." He rubbed his forehead as if he had a bad headache. "The bottom line," he continued, "is that I really had no right to go out with you in the first place. I thought I could handle it—you know, being with you—but I couldn't, and I'm really sorry, Jess. The last thing I wanted to do was to hurt you."

"I don't understand," she finally said when he didn't speak again. "Are you telling me that you're married?"

He shook his head. "No."

"Engaged?"

Another head shake.

"Seeing someone else?"

"No, Jess, it's not that at all . . ." But he didn't explain.

"Then what?" She willed him to look up, to meet her eyes, and finally he did. "Are you some kind of priest?"

That got a rueful smile. "Not even close." He paused, looking away again. "I just . . . I need some space, some distance. I got too close, Jess, and I needed some time to back away. I still need time."

She crossed her arms, wondering if he could read the unhappiness in her face as clearly as she read his. Why wouldn't he be more specific? Why did he need space? There was clearly an explosive spark of attraction between them that in her mind was well worth the time and effort it would take to explore it. She liked him and he liked her. Why not see where that might go?

And unless Rob had some dark secret that was keeping him from starting a relationship with her . . .

"I'm sorry," he said. "I really am."

"That's too bad," she told him quietly. "Kelsey misses you."

He met her eyes then. Kelsey missed him. Did Jess miss him, too? He didn't say the words aloud, but she saw the question in his eyes.

She looked so sad, so fragile. Rob forced himself to take a step back, away from her. God help him if he gave in to this damned urge to put his arms around her.

He took another step back, and cleared his throat. "I'll be gone for two weeks," he told her. "With any luck, it'll be a few days less."

Jess nodded, her beautiful dark eyes watching him soberly. "Where are you going—if you don't mind my asking?"

"Orlando."

"Kelsey's going to be so jealous." She was trying so hard to be casual, to pretend that he hadn't created this big, awkward chasm between them. "I'm not going to be able to convince her that you're hard at work instead of running around Disney World."

Rob had to laugh. "I'm not going to have time to get within twenty miles of Disney World," he said.

"*That* she'll find scandalous," Jess told him with an answering smile. "Going to Orlando without paying homage to the Great Mouse is sacrilege."

"Tell her I'm sorry," he said. But the apology in his eyes was for more than Kelsey. It was for Jess, too.

She nodded again, looking away from him. "I guess we'll see you when you get back."

Rob couldn't help but think that if he'd made love to Jess, if he'd followed the urgings of his body and become her lover, then it was very likely that he would be kissing her goodbye right now. She would be in his arms, her beautiful body fitting so perfectly against his. Kissing her goodbye? Hell, with Kelsey at school, he'd swing her up into his arms, carry her into her bedroom and make love to her all morning long.

He was a fool.

Rob watched as she went back into her house.

Time, space, distance.

Two weeks in Orlando didn't seem long enough or far enough away to cool this fire he felt every time he so much as thought of Jess.

He knew of only one way to douse it, and douse it permanently.

"MOM-MY!" Kelsey came rocketing out of the kitchen door, bellowing at the top of her powerful little lungs.

"I'm right here, Kel," Jess said mildly, "not down the block."

"It's really hot inside," Kelsey said, following her inside, "and I couldn't get the air conditioner to turn on."

Jess cursed silently, setting her guitar down on the kitchen floor. It *was* hot in here. Carefully, she kept her face expressionless. Kelsey followed her down the hall to the thermostat for the central air system.

Jess tried every trick in the book, but couldn't get the system to switch on. It made not a sound, not a wheeze, not a cough or a hiss. Sometime during her afternoon round of piano and guitar lessons, the ancient air-conditioning had finally gone belly up.

Kelsey's face was worried. She knew more about their financial status than a six-year-old should. She knew Jess didn't have the money for a repair of this magnitude.

Somehow Jess managed to smile at her daughter. "Help me open all the windows," she said.

The outside air wasn't any cooler, but with the help of the ceiling fan, it at least gave Jess the sensation of circulation.

"Are you going to call the repair guy?" Kelsey asked, catching her lower lip between her teeth.

It would cost sixty-five dollars just to get the repairman to come out. Before Jess called, she was going to make damned sure she couldn't fix the thing herself.

"Maybe later," she said. "Kel, why don't you run down to Carlos's house, see if he can play for a few minutes before dinner?" If she didn't get Kelsey out of there, the little girl was going to follow her around, getting more and more worried.

As much as she liked playing with her friend, Kelsey hesitated. "Are you going to try to fix it?" she asked. "Maybe I can help."

Jess hugged the little girl. "I'll take care of it," she said. "Don't worry, all right?"

Unconvinced, Kelsey went outside. Jess watched from the deck until her daughter reached Carlos's yard, then pulled a clean filter from the garage. Armed with the filter and the Swiss army knife she kept in her gigantic purse, she found the key to Rob's apartment, where the filter duct was located.

Like a good landlady, she knocked loudly, even though she knew he was in Orlando. There was no answer and she unlocked the door.

The apartment was dark and quiet. And impeccably neat.

This was the first time she'd been over here since Rob had moved in, she realized. With the exception of the weight-lifting equipment stacked in the corner, the modestly furnished living room looked no different than it had after the last tenant moved out.

It was odd. He had put no knickknacks out, no pictures on the walls, no magazines or books on the coffee table. There was no dust anywhere, and the wall-to-wall carpeting looked as if it had been recently vacuumed.

The kitchen area was just as sterile. The counters were wiped clean and the stove was spotless. The sink had been recently scoured and a small, white dish towel hung neatly on the rack near the refrigerator. There was nothing personal here, either. There were no quirky magnets on the refrigerator, no calendar hanging on the wall, no food out on the counters.

Jess opened the cabinets. There was no food in there, either. The refrigerator held a six-pack of soda and a jar of peanut butter, some mustard and mayonnaise and salad dressing. But that was it.

The only thing in the freezer was a large plastic container. Curious, Jess pulled it out and opened one corner—and nearly dropped it on the linoleum floor. It was filled—*filled*—with money. Dollar bills. *Big* bills. God, there must have been more than twenty thousand dollars right there in that container. Maybe more.

What kind of man kept twenty thousand dollars in his *freezer?* Rob always paid his rent in cash, Jess realized. Maybe he didn't use the bank. Maybe he *couldn't* use the bank. Maybe he had something to hide. She put the money back, careful to leave it exactly as she found it.

The filter duct was in the bedroom closet, and Jess went into that room with somewhat shaken curiosity. If he kept twenty thousand dollars in his freezer, what was she going to find in his bedroom?

Again, there was nothing personal out on top of the dresser. A small bowl held some coins, but that was it. The bed was neatly made, covered by a bland, tan bedspread. Jess was disappointed. She'd been half hoping his bed would be covered by a zebra-striped comforter, or something with a big, bold tropical pattern.

She slid open the closet door.

She hadn't *really* expected to find any skeletons or gruesome body parts in Rob's closet, but what she *did* find was awfully mundane.

A dozen dress shirts hung there, still covered in plastic from the dry cleaners. Five or six pairs of pants hung next to the shirts, along with several business suits. Way in the back of the closet, in the corner, was a pair of worn-out hiking boots. One had fallen over onto its side—chaos and anarchy among all the neatness and order.

Unable to stop wondering about all that money, Jess pushed the clothes aside to access the air conditioner filter, and as she did, she caught a whiff of the fresh, tangy soap Rob used. Turning abruptly away, she crossed the room and opened both of the windows.

There was no breeze blowing. The outside air hung motionless and hot in the blazing afternoon sun. But with the windows open, at least she could pretend that she didn't have to breathe in Rob's unmistakable and very masculine scent.

Damn him for not wanting her, and damn her for wishing he did—for wishing he would hang some of these sweet-smelling clothes in her own crowded, messy closet.

It was probably just as well that Rob *didn't* want to become involved with her, Jess told herself firmly. She didn't need a secretive man with a violent past who kept more money than she made in a year in a box in his freezer.

She opened the screwdriver blade of her Swiss army knife and quickly unfastened the screws that held the metal air vent in place. The old filter slipped easily out. It wasn't very dirty—certainly not enough to clog the system.

Still, she replaced it with a clean filter and reattached the metal grill.

Snapping the Swiss army knife shut, she gathered up the old filter and let herself out of Rob's quiet apartment, careful to lock the door behind her. The cooling system's compressor housing was on the side of the house, near Kelsey's flower garden and the Greene's porch. Leaning the dirty filter against the garbage shed, Jess stepped carefully over her daughter's sunbaked marigolds and began opening the compressor housing.

"Is it broken, Miss Jess?"

"Hi, Stan," she said, glancing up at her neighbor, who was leaning on the fence that separated their two yards. She'd been expecting him. He appeared nearly every time she worked out in the yard. "Well, it's not working, that's for sure."

From what little she knew about engines and compressors, this one sure didn't look good. It was black with grease and age and crud.

"Hot day."

"Yes, it is." Thank goodness for that fence. It was the only thing preventing Stanford Greene from coming into her yard and peering over her shoulder.

"I understand congratulations are in order," he said.

Jess glanced up at him, wiping her sweaty forehead with the back of her hand in a vain attempt not to get engine grease on her face. "Congratulations for what?"

"Kelsey informed me that you are going to remarry."

Jess straightened up. "You're kidding."

"She said you and your new tenant were making wedding plans."

Jess swore softly under her breath. "I'm sorry. That's not true," she told him.

Stanford watched her expressionlessly. "Mama always punished me severely when I lied."

"Kel's not lying," Jess said. She crouched down and tried to wipe the grease from her fingers on the grass. "Not really. She just got too caught up in a fantasy world. When you're six years old and you want something really badly, reality starts to blur."

Stanford was watching her unblinkingly. Lord, what was she doing, attempting to explain her daughter's forays into fantasy worlds with a man who was quite clearly and firmly anchored in a far-off world of his own?

"A lie is a lie," Stanford said self-righteously.

"Not always," Jess said, standing up and closing the compressor housing with a bang.

"Did you fix it?" Stanford asked.

Jess shook her head. "Nope. It's dead, Jim."

"My name is Stanford," he said.

"I know. I was making a feeble joke," Jess said. "Don't you watch 'Star Trek'?"

"Yes," he said. Then he smiled. His teeth were crooked and yellow. "Oh. That's what the doctor always says. I get it."

"See you later, Stan," Jess said, going inside the house to call the repairman—and watch the remainder of her checking account get flushed down the tubes.

THERE WAS GOING TO BE one hell of a thunderstorm tonight.

Jess had awakened at the first rumblings of thunder, and she stood now at her opened front door, watching the row of palm trees that lined the road shiver in the rising wind. A flash of lightning lit the sky to the west, and the sound of thunder grew more ominous. The first large drops of rain hit the ground as a car pulled slowly onto the street, its headlights streaks of bright in the darkness.

The rain fell, faster and faster, and the wind carried a wave of wet toward the screen. Jess pushed the window shut, then scrambled to check the other open windows in the house.

Lightning flashed again, and the thunder that followed was nearly instantaneous and deafening. She went into Kelsey's room, but her daughter was fast asleep. It was true. Kelsey *could* sleep through anything.

Jess moved quietly back into the hallway. Another bolt of lightning lit the dark night, clearly illuminating her reflection in the mirror for a brief instant. Her eyes looked worried, her face somber.

The repairman had made it out to the house early in the evening. He didn't have the part to fix the air-conditioning system right away, and the bad news didn't stop there. It was going to take another two days, at least, to order the part. *And* the part and labor were going to cost around five hundred dollars.

Five *hundred* dollars.

A gust of wind shook the house, and the lights in the living room flickered, came back up, then went out, plunging Jess into total darkness. It covered her completely, smothering her.

Fighting a flare of panic, she groped her way into the kitchen and found the flashlights. Turning them both on, she carried them into Kelsey's room.

The rain made a roaring sound as it fell hard on the shingles of the roof. But it wasn't loud enough to mask a muffled thud from Rob's apartment.

Jess frowned. Rob wasn't home—he was in Orlando. Had she left a window open in his apartment this afternoon? She groaned, imagining the flood of water on the living room floor, or worse—on the bed.

She left one flashlight on in Kelsey's room, checking to make sure the little girl was still sleeping soundly, then hurried to the kitchen door.

As she stepped out onto the deck, Jess was instantly soaked by the warm rain that was blowing in sheets. Lightning flashed and she jumped, spooked, and rushed for the door to Rob's apartment. Her key stuck in the lock, and she jiggled it until it finally opened.

She closed the door, shutting out the rain and the wind, and flashed her light around the living room. The beam from the flashlight made the shadows of the furniture jump about grotesquely on the walls.

The living room window was tightly shut—she hadn't opened that one this afternoon—so she went into the bedroom, heading for the window beyond Rob's big bed.

But something made her turn her head back toward the other side of the room, and she froze, imagining a dark shape, a man, standing there. It's a chair, she thought, or the closet door is open. Isn't it?

Before she could aim her flashlight in that direction, lightning lit the room.

It *was* a man. The bursts of unearthly light reflected off the broad expanse of a muscular chest, and gleamed off a long, deadly-looking knife.

Jess swallowed a scream and dove across the bed, trying to reach the bedroom door first. She felt a strong hand grab her ankle, and she kicked out in panic as she realized he wasn't going to let go. She swung the flashlight up toward where she imagined his face was, using it as a weapon. She connected with something solid, and the flashlight fell out of her hand, the light bouncing wildly as it hit the floor.

The hand still held her, and she shrieked as she felt herself pulled down off the bed and onto the hard bedroom floor. Her head hit the floorboards with a nasty crunch, but still she fought back.

Then the man's heavy body was pressing down on top of her, and she could feel the coldness of his knife at her throat.

Rob, help, she thought, unaware that she spoke the words out loud.

"Oh, God," the man said, his voice hoarse. The pressure from both the knife blade and his weight lifted, and Jess felt herself being gently picked up. "Jess . . . I'm sorry—"

She opened her eyes slowly as he placed her on the bed. Lightning flashed again, and she could see him leaning over her, dark hair falling over his forehead.

"Rob?" she breathed. Her head was spinning. That knife! The way he'd leapt at her—as if he were defending his very life. And what was he doing here? He was supposed to be away, in Orlando on business.

His eyes were slightly wild, and he was still breathing hard, but it was definitely Rob. His face was filled with concern. "God, I thought you were—" He broke off, shaking his head. "Someone else," he finished inadequately. "Breaking in."

He'd thought she was someone breaking in—maybe to take all that money he had in the freezer. Jess sat up, and the pounding in her head made her reel. Rob's strong arms were there, holding her, pushing her back down against the pillows, but she resisted. She couldn't deal with any of this right now. "Kelsey," she said. "I can't leave her alone for long. If she wakes up—"

She felt Rob's fingers exploring her head, and tried to bite back a cry of pain as he found the bump.

"Oh, Jess," he said again, "I'm so sorry."

Lightning flashed, and despite her throbbing headache, she suddenly became aware of how tightly he was holding her. Their faces were only inches apart, and his eyes looked almost blue in the dim light. That was odd. Jess knew his eyes were brown. And where were his glasses?

Her gaze traveled down to his chest. Yes, just as she had speculated, he had the body of an athlete. He was solid, powerful-looking, his muscles well-defined.

And, oh, my Lord, he had a tattoo! Mild-mannered, bespectacled Rob Carpenter actually had a tattoo! *Two* tattoos! One was a snake, coiled, ready to spring, up high on his left arm, near his shoulder. The other was a sword. It, too, was on his left arm, but on the inside of his forearm, several inches above his wrist.

"You scared me to death," Jess said softly. "Holding that knife like that . . ." Her mouth was dry, and she wet her lips nervously. She didn't dare move. She could feel his heart beating hard in his chest, all too aware of her bare arms against his warm, smooth skin, his lips only inches from hers. She remembered the way those lips had felt against hers.

"You scared me, too," he admitted just as softly. He, too, didn't move. He just looked at her.

The spell seemed to last forever, until a loud clap of thunder made Jess wince with pain.

"I'd better get you some ice," Rob said. He moistened his lips slightly, and his gaze travelled down to her mouth.

Lord, she wanted him to kiss her. Lightning flashed again, lighting his face.

"What color *are* your eyes?" Jess breathed.

He pulled away from her then, breaking free from her gaze. "Brown," he said abruptly, turning away. "I'll get you that ice."

He went out of the bedroom, fast.

After a moment, Jess stood up, holding on to the headboard with both hands to steady herself. Her flashlight was still on the floor. As she bent down to pick it up, her head swam and she couldn't keep her balance. She swayed and crumpled to the floor.

Rob was by her side in an instant, and he scooped both Jess and the flashlight up into his arms. She could feel the cold of the ice pack pressing against her bare leg. It was an odd sensation. His hands and arms were so warm, the ice so cold.

"I've got to go to Kelsey," Jess said.

"I know, sweet," he murmured, carrying her easily out into the living room. "Hang on," he added, as he opened the door onto the deck.

It was still raining hard enough to soak them both as Rob carried her the twenty-odd feet from his door to hers. He wrestled her kitchen door open and brought her inside, closing the door behind him with his foot.

He carried her swiftly into her bedroom, laying her gently on top of her bedspread. Grabbing a towel from the bathroom, he gave it to her so that she could dry herself off.

"I'll check on Bug," he said, leaving the flashlight with her.

The light from the flashlight was looking a little wan. It flickered, making the shadows of Jess's four tall bedposts jump and leap around the room. She struggled to sit up, wincing as she put the ice against her head. There were candles in the kitchen. But right now that seemed so very far away.

"Kelsey's fine—sound asleep." Rob came back into the room. "Jess, lie down," he said. "What do you think you're doing?"

"The batteries are running out," she replied, motioning toward the flashlight. "I was going to get some candles. And now that the wind's not blowing so hard, I want to open the windows. It's hot in here."

"I'll do it," Rob said. He moved toward her, gently pushing her back onto the bed. "Let me do it, okay?"

She looked up at him. He still didn't have his glasses on, but his eyes no longer looked blue. Must've been the light before, she thought hazily.

She closed her eyes, hearing him moving around the room, opening the windows. It had been a long time since someone had taken care of her, she realized suddenly. It felt nice, knowing that he cared enough to help her.

He was a good friend, she thought sleepily. Except she didn't want to be friends. She wanted . . .

She wanted to know more about him. And tomorrow she was going to ask him a raftload of questions that he *was* going to answer.

Jess drifted off to sleep, dreaming of snake tattoos and razor sharp knives.

Chapter Six

A persistent shaking woke Jess. She opened her eyes to see Rob sitting on the edge of her bed, leaning over her, candlelight playing across his handsome face. He smiled with relief.

"You scared me there," he said. "I thought for a minute that you weren't going to wake up, and I'd have to take you to the hospital."

She stared at him with wide eyes, taking in the candles on her bedside table, his tousled hair and lack of shirt, the tattoos of the snake and the sword on his left arm.

Rob frowned at her confused look. "Jess, do you remember what happened?"

"No," she breathed. Lord, what was he doing there, in her bedroom? Did he...? Did they...? And if so, why couldn't she remember? She recalled his tattoos. That was for certain. She'd definitely seen them before. As well as Rob's well-toned body...

"Do you know me?" he asked, his brown eyes searching her face.

"No," she said again. "I mean, I know that you're Rob Carpenter, but I don't know you very well at all."

There was relief in his eyes. Amusement and heat. He was leaning over her, with one arm supporting his weight, propped against the mattress, pinning her in place. If he leaned forward much farther, their lips would meet. She could see from his eyes that he was as aware of that as she.

"You hit your head," Rob said. "Do you remember that?"

It came back to her in a rush. His apartment. Thunder-storm. Windows open. Shadowy shape of a man. Big, gleam-ing knife...

"You had a knife...?"

"I didn't think it was you," he said quickly. "You always knock. You never just come in. I thought you were...someone breaking in. So, yeah—I had my knife out."

His knife. He said the words with such familiarity, as if he always carried a lethal-looking weapon. The blade of that knife had been long and deadly. Long enough to slit a throat...

Jess felt a shiver of fear. She was a little bit afraid of this man, she realized. Afraid, but also attracted.

"What were you doing, coming in like that?" Rob asked.

Jess moistened her dry lips. "I was in your place this after-noon," she said, "changing the AC filter. When it started to rain, I was afraid I'd left the windows open and..."

She gazed up into Rob's eyes. He wasn't wearing his glasses, and without them, he looked older and harder, and somehow, at the same time, more vulnerable. His perfect nose wasn't quite so perfect. It looked as if it had been broken at the bridge, maybe even more than once. And he had a scar she'd never noticed before, right underneath his right eyebrow. He looked dangerous in the flickering candlelight, with shadows dancing across his features. But he also looked tired. Not just physi-cally tired, but psychologically weary.

His gaze dropped almost longingly to her mouth. She could see his tension in the muscles that worked the sides of his jaw as he clenched and unclenched his teeth.

It wouldn't take much, Jess knew, for him to kiss her again, the way he'd kissed her in the parking lot of the Pelican Club. And this time there'd be nothing to stop them from carrying that kiss through to its culmination.

He pulled back then, putting more space between them, as if he could somehow read her thoughts. He probably could. Jess wouldn't have been surprised if everything she was think-ing was written clearly across her face.

But now that he wasn't sitting closer, his gaze was drawn to Jess's legs. She was wearing nothing more than an old T-shirt that barely met the tops of her high-cut panties. Her legs were bare and smooth and at that proximity, nearly impossible for him to ignore.

He briefly closed his eyes. "Is there anything I can get you?" When he opened his eyes again, he carefully kept his gaze on her face.

Jess shook her head. "Not unless you know where to get a spare air conditioner at—" she leaned forward to look at the glowing numbers on her clock radio "—two o'clock in the morning."

"No," he said with a laugh. It broke his concentration, and his eyes slipped down to her legs again. He wrestled his gaze back to her face. "It *is* kind of hot in here, isn't it? I know the power's been off for a while, but I'm also guessing that sometime this afternoon the AC finally broke down."

"Yeah. To the tune of five hundred dollars." He looked so good sitting there like that. He had the kind of lean, muscular body most men only dreamed of achieving, the kind of body muscle shirts were created for. Yet Rob never wore anything but long-sleeved shirts.

He wore them to hide his tattoos, Jess realized suddenly. Of course, that had to be it.

"Five hundred?" Rob grimaced. "Ouch."

Jess smiled ruefully up at him. "Ouch is right." She pushed herself up on her elbows. Her head still ached very slightly, but it was nothing like before. "You were supposed to go to Orlando," she said. "What happened?"

"The whole job's been delayed," Rob said. Beads of sweat had appeared on his upper lip, and he used the back of one hand to wipe it clean. "There's some problem with the contract, I don't know exactly what. I'm on hold for a while. It could be weeks or only a few days. For all I know, they could send me out to the site tomorrow."

This was insane. They were sitting here, both of them barely dressed, having a conversation that seemed on the surface to be extremely normal, almost mundane. But undercurrents of emotion and attraction and danger were flying around the room. Jess would have given nearly anything to be able to reach out and touch Rob's shoulder with her hand, to feel his smooth skin and hard muscles under her palm. She wanted him to pull her into his arms and kiss her. . . .

"Do you . . ." Rob stopped himself.

"What?" she asked.

"May I ask you a personal question?"

Jess nodded, caught in the intensity of his gaze. She couldn't begin to imagine what he was going to ask her. She could only hope.

"Do you have enough money to cover the cost of the repair?" Rob asked. "You know, for the air conditioner?"

Not the question she was hoping for. A combination of disappointment and pride made her lift her chin. "I'll handle it." It wasn't a lie. Somehow she *would* handle it. She'd pay in installments, or get an advance on her credit card.

Rob nodded, seeing right through her. "How about if I lend you the money? I've got a lot saved, and . . . well, you can take your time paying me back."

Jess felt a lump forming in her throat and the sting of tears in her eyes. It wasn't so much his offer that touched her—it was the fact that he had offered her a loan rather than a gift. Rob had money. She knew that. Five hundred dollars was nothing to him, a mere drop in the bucket. But he hadn't just blithely suggested he foot the bill. And in doing that, he *had* given her a gift—a gift of her pride.

"Thank you," she said softly. "I'll take you up on that offer."

It was the tears in Jess's eyes that did him in. Rob had managed to keep his distance up to this point by sheer force of will, but now it was clear he was fighting a losing battle.

He stood up. "I should go."

"Please don't." Her voice was low, her gentle southern accent a caress.

Rob could feel her eyes on his back, feel her watching him. If he turned around, if he looked into the midnight darkness of those beautiful eyes, he would be lost.

He stayed absolutely still, willing the waves of desire and need that were washing over him to subside. Desire, he could handle. Need, he could tame. But it was this other feeling—this *hope* that could destroy him. Hope that maybe he was wrong. That he *could* start something with Jess, something open-ended and permanent, something "happily ever after." Hope that somehow everything screwed up in his life would straighten itself out so that he could love this woman the way he so desperately wanted to.

Not a chance. There was not a chance in hell that any of that would happen. And if he started hoping, all he was doing was setting himself up to crash and burn.

He'd been living this life, this lie, long enough to know that there was no chance.

There was only bleak reality stretching on forever into the future, like two mirrors, each reflecting the other's desolation, creating an endless corridor of nothingness.

And, God, he wanted so badly to escape from that—even just for a little while.

"Don't go," Jess whispered again, and he knew that all he had to do was turn around. She wanted him to stay, to hold her, to make love to her. All he had to do was turn around, and he'd have his escape—at least temporarily.

"Oh, Jess," he said. "I wish . . ."

"What?" Her voice was breathless. "What do you wish?"

He turned around.

She was sitting on her bed, her long, slender legs gracefully arranged in front of her, her eyes wide and dark. Her hair was tousled from sleep, and the candlelight played across her beautiful face, giving her smooth skin a golden glow.

He was lost.

It took only two steps to bring him back to the bed, to her side. Holding her gaze, drowning in the darkness of her eyes, Rob sat down on the bed next to her.

"I wish . . ." he said, "this."

He pulled her into his arms and he kissed her, his lips feverishly seeking hers.

The night erupted in an explosion of heat as Jess hungrily opened her mouth to him. Yes, *yes,* this was what she wanted—Rob in her arms, in her heart. In her bed. She leaned back, pulling him down with her onto the bed.

His tongue swept inside her mouth, claiming her, even as his knees parted her legs. She clung to him, kissing him harder, running her hands down the smooth skin of his back as their legs intertwined. She could feel his muscular thighs through his pants, pushing against her. She heard him groan as she pressed her hips up to him.

She could feel his arousal, and she rubbed her body against him. He groaned again, and his hands swept underneath her T-shirt, exploring the smooth bareness of her skin, finding the softness of her breasts. His mouth left a fiery trail of kisses down her neck to the soft spot at the base of her throat, and she put her head back, welcoming him, wanting more.

"Stop me, Jess" he whispered, his breath hot against her neck. "Stop me now."

"I don't want you to stop." She reached for the waistband of his pants, and her fingers fumbled with the button.

He pulled back. "This is crazy—"

She looped her arms around his neck, not letting him go. "No," she said. "It's crazy to pretend this thing between us doesn't exist. *That's* what's crazy."

His eyes were hot, his breathing ragged. He kissed her again, hard and demanding, as if he couldn't bear to be apart from her for even a few seconds. And when he stopped, it was as if he had to tear himself away.

"I want to make love to you," he said hoarsely, "but I can't make you any promises."

"I don't expect any promises," Jess told him. She reached up and touched the side of his face, willing him to believe her. "Why can't we just see where this goes?"

His eyes were intense, his mouth tight. "What if it goes nowhere?" he asked.

Rob kissed her again, drawn by the sweet temptation of her mouth, mere inches from his. He felt her fingers in his hair as she angled her head, granting him easier access. He pulled back with a groan half born of frustration, half of anger at himself. When it came to this woman, he was so weak. "What if we only have tonight?" he continued, determined to make her understand, determined to give her a chance to end this craziness now. "What if you wake up tomorrow to find me gone?"

"I don't care."

Rob could see from her eyes that she didn't believe him. She was saying the words, but he knew her better than that. She did care. She *would* care.

"Jess, I can't give you what you want. The only thing I can give you is...pain." He closed his eyes, seeing blood, all that blood. Covering him, warm and sticky... God forbid it should ever come to that. He couldn't let it go that far. He wouldn't...

She kissed him—featherlight, gentle kisses on his face, on his mouth, and he opened his eyes to look at her.

She smiled, but her smile was so sad. "Love me tonight," she said softly. "We can worry about tomorrow when it comes. Please?"

There was such longing, such need in her eyes. She wanted him as desperately as he wanted her. And maybe, just maybe, she needed him now, tonight, to help chase away some demons of her own.

"Stay with me," she said, her eyes as dark and mysterious as the midnight sky, and full of her own secrets. "Just for tonight."

What loneliness had *she* suffered? What emptiness had *she* known? God, he knew all about being lonely. He knew that feeling, that hollowness in his chest, that burning ache that wouldn't go away.

He couldn't give her the promises she deserved, but he could make the loneliness disappear for just one night.

"Please don't go," she breathed.

"I'm not going anywhere," he whispered, and then he kissed her, lowering them both back on the bed.

He meant to take his time, to take it slowly, to make it last a lifetime—each kiss, each touch, each sigh. But the sensation of her body, so soft and pliant underneath his made his blood roar through his veins. He kissed her hard, harder, and his hands found the edge of her T-shirt and yanked it up.

She pulled free from their kiss long enough to help him draw her shirt up and over her head. Her body was beautiful—her breasts full, her nipples dark and taut with her desire. His rush of pleasure at the sight of her was so intense, Rob knew without a doubt that despite her begging him to stay, despite all his rationalizations, he was not here tonight for her. He was here for himself, for *his* pleasure. *He* was the one who needed his loneliness eased for an hour or two. What Jess needed was a man who could really love her.

But the sensation of her smooth, silky skin against his chest was overpowering. She kissed him then, a hard, fierce, demanding kiss that sucked all thought from him, leaving only their need and a wild, burning urgency to become one.

Jess was spinning.

It had been so long. It had been years since she had felt a lover's touch. Not that she hadn't had plenty of opportunities. Men had wanted to date her, to sleep with her, but she hadn't been interested. She hadn't realized it at the time, but she'd been waiting. Waiting for someone special. Waiting for Rob.

Now he was here, and Jess knew it had been well worth the wait.

Never in her life had she felt so desired, so needed. Never had she felt such an answering passion. His hands swept almost roughly down her body, kneading her softness, pulling her closer, even closer to him.

He slid one hand between their bodies, covering her, cupping her most intimately. Jess pressed herself against his fingers, and he quickly dipped his hand beneath the cotton of her panties. His touch was gentle now as he explored her softness and heat. Now it was Jess who wanted more.

She reached to pull down her panties, and quickly kicked them free. He pulled back slightly, his eyes sweeping the length of her naked body as he still touched her, harder now, deeper. When he met her eyes, he smiled, a hot, fierce smile at the pleasure she knew he could see on her face.

Dear heaven, she wanted him. *All* of him. "Do you have protection?" she asked, her voice breathless and husky.

"Yes."

She reached for him, and when she had trouble unbuttoning his pants, he helped her. He kicked off his shoes and his pants as he fell back onto the bed with her. His mouth latched onto the hard bud of one nipple, and she clenched her teeth, stifling a loud cry of pleasure that seemed to rip through her. His muscular body was hard against her, their legs intertwined, his hands exploring every part of her. She pulled at the waistband of his shorts, wanting nothing between them.

She felt something hard against his ankle, and as he pushed himself away from her to pull off his socks and shorts, she heard a clatter on the wooden floor. But she forgot it instantly as she heard the tearing of paper as he opened a condom that he had gotten, from where? His wallet, she guessed. His hot eyes raked her in the dim light as he sheathed himself. He came back to her then, and covered her with his body. Deeply, endlessly, he kissed her, and she felt herself melt.

It was at that moment, in a flash of understanding that seemed to illuminate the candlelit dimness of the room, Jess realized something with great clarity. She was falling in love with this man. He was still so full of mysteries, so private, even secretive. There were so many things she didn't know about him, so many unanswered questions. But that didn't matter. Nothing mattered except the fact that somehow, somewhere down the line, this thing that had started as friendship and attraction was turning into love.

Jess arched her hips up to him, aching for all of him. He touched her, kissed her, stroked her, carrying her to new heights of sensation, and just when she didn't think she could bear to wait any longer, just when she drew in a ragged breath to beg him to take her, he thrust into her.

"Oh, Jess," he said, his voice a whisper of pleasure, his breath hot at her ear.

They began to move together, slowly now, as he kissed her neck, his lips caressing her skin. She ran her fingers through his thick hair and down his powerful back, amazed at the way he could make her feel.

And the love that she felt for him, this love that seemed so new and fragile seemed to flare up around her, growing even stronger with every passing moment. She clung to him, lifting her hips so that he plunged even more deeply into her.

With a groan, he kissed her almost savagely, and began to move faster, each thrust harder and deeper than the last. His hands became rough, and Jess felt her own fingernails dig into his back as she welcomed the turbulence of his passion. Fiercely, she urged him on, with her mouth, with her hands, with her body.

"Jess!" she heard him gasp as the world exploded around her. Sheer pleasure knifed through her, and she had to bite her lip to keep from crying out.

And then Rob collapsed against her, holding her tightly, burying his face in her neck. She could feel his rapid heartbeat and unsteady breathing start to slow, and after a moment he rolled off of her.

His arms still encircled her, and she rested her head on his shoulder, sighing with contentment. They lay in silence, holding each other for a long time.

Finally Jess looked up to see him staring out into the darkness of the room. His gaze shifted down, and a smile softened his face. It was a small smile, a sad one, and Jess's heart lurched. No promises, she reminded herself. He'd made it clear that he could make her no promises.

She ran her fingers lightly across his chest, and he moved his hand, trapping her against him. "That was wonderful," she said softly.

Rob couldn't speak. To tell her that what they'd just experienced had been amazing seemed inadequate. To start talking about anything else seemed inappropriate. And the words that lingered on the tip of his tongue were unutterable.

I love you.

He could never tell her that. And even if he could, she would end up hurt—in the long run, she would feel lied to, cheated. Because his love was worth nothing. His love was meaningless, of no value.

Still, he could see that his silence confused her. He brushed her mouth with his lips, trying to tell her with a gentle kiss all the things he couldn't say.

It seemed to satisfy her.

Jess returned his kiss, then gently extracted herself from his arms. "I better go check on Kelsey," she said.

Her headache was almost entirely gone, Jess realized as she swung her legs out of bed and headed toward the closet to get her robe. That was good. She smiled, wondering if she should tell Rob that he was better than aspirin.

And then she stepped on something hard and cold.

Bending down, she picked it up, turning to look at it in the candlelight. It was seven inches long and thin, made of metal, with crisscrossed lines scored into it, as if it were some kind of handle. "Rob, what's this?" she asked.

He sprang off the bed. "Careful—"

A deadly, sharp-looking knife blade shot out from one end of the handle, narrowly missing her fingers. She fumbled it, lost hold, then jumped back to keep the knife from stabbing her in the foot. It landed blade down, stuck into the wooden floor, quivering slightly.

Jess stared from the knife to Rob. It was the one she had seen him holding earlier that night—the knife he'd held to her throat when he'd thought she was someone breaking into his apartment. It was bigger and sharper than she remembered. It looked deadly and seemed to shimmer with an aura of violence.

He pulled the knife out of the floor and released the catch. The blade slid back into the hilt with the quiet sound of metal on metal. "It's my switchblade," he said softly. He tried to make a joke out of it. "You carry a Swiss army knife in your purse. It's kind of the same thing."

"It's the same thing, plus four more inches of knife blade, which makes it pretty damn different. Isn't carrying that—" Jess stopped.

"Illegal?" Rob finished for her. He met her gaze steadily, as if daring her to comment. "Yeah. It's a concealed weapon. It's illegal."

But Jess didn't say a word. She just watched him, silently willing him to tell her more. But he turned away to put the knife inside one of his shoes, pushing them both out of the way. She watched as he sat down on the edge of the bed, elbows on his knees, as he lowered his head and ran his hands through his hair. When he looked up at her, she knew that he wasn't going to volunteer any more information.

She could see the tension in his neck and shoulders, and she climbed onto the bed behind him and began gently rubbing his back. He glanced over his shoulder at her, surprise in his eyes.

It was clear he'd expected the third degree, not a back rub. Still, there were questions that needed to be asked.

"Why do you carry it?" she asked quietly.

"I can't tell you that," he said, his voice so low she almost couldn't hear him.

"Okay," she said. The muscles in his shoulders were way too tight. She massaged him harder, trying to loosen them.

He pulled away and turned to look at her. "That's all? Just, 'okay?'"

Jess shrugged, forcing herself to smile at him. They'd just shared the most intimate physical act. Why wouldn't he share his secrets with her? "You said you couldn't tell me. So, okay. What am I supposed to do, Rob—whine? I don't think so. And using Chinese water torture isn't my style, either. I can't pretend it doesn't frustrate me, because it does. I hope that someday you'll tell me. Maybe someday you'll trust me enough to tell me *all* about yourself."

Rob reached for her, pulling her onto his lap and holding her close. *It's not about trust,* he wanted to tell her, but he couldn't. He couldn't begin to try to explain, because he could never tell her any of it. He felt her arms around his neck, holding him closely, comforting him—even though he wouldn't tell her why he needed her comfort.

He knew with a certainty that frightened him that he could continue this relationship with Jess for weeks, months, maybe even years, and she would respect his privacy and not demand answers to her questions. But she would be hurt. Every time he didn't tell her something, every time he couldn't answer one of her questions, she would think that he didn't trust her.

God, Jess's quiet understanding and gentle acceptance was exactly what he needed. And because of that, he had to end this now, before the temptation pulled him in too deep. Because that was exactly the kind of relationship that she *didn't* need.

She also didn't need him to tell her that their lovemaking had been a major mistake—at least not right now, not tonight. But he couldn't stay here with her. He couldn't bear the thought of sleeping with her in his arms, of waking up to her gentle smile and the welcoming softness of her body. The temptation would be too great. And each time he gave in and made love to Jess, the harder it would be to leave.

He had to get out of here. Now.

He gently disengaged her arms from their hold around his neck. "You better check on Kelsey," he reminded her. "And it's nearly three-thirty. I should go," he added, nearly choking on the words.

"Go?"

He steeled himself against the disappointment in Jess's eyes and nodded. "I'd like to stay all night," he said, and it wasn't a lie. He would've sold his soul to make things different, to make it possible to stay with her. "But I know you probably don't want Kelsey waking up to find me in your bed."

The disappointment in her eyes faded and she nodded. "Good point," she said. "It's kind of sudden to just spring something like this—like *us*—on Kel." She smiled. "Although I happen to know that she adores you. She'd like to see us together."

Jess stood up, and this time she made it all the way across the room to her closet. She slipped on her bathrobe and tied the belt. "I'm going to check on Kelsey," she said. "I'll be right back." She crossed to the door and when she put her hand on the knob, Rob spoke.

"Jess."

She paused, looking at him. He stood, his naked body strong and beautiful in the dim light. Shadows fell across his face, accentuating his cheekbones and his sensuous mouth. A lock of disheveled hair fell over his forehead. His brown eyes had a sad, haunted look.

"Only in my wildest dreams did I ever imagine we'd make love," he said.

Their eyes were locked, and slowly he moved forward, as if hypnotized. She turned as he pulled her toward him, cupping her face with his hands. He kissed her then, slowly and so sweetly. Jess felt her heart flip in her chest.

"If I don't leave now..." he whispered.

She nodded, understanding, feeling the familiar tug of heat and desire at his touch. If he didn't leave now, they'd make love again, and Kelsey would find them together in the morning. And then the little girl would no doubt start addressing wedding invitations.

"I'll see you in the morning," Rob said, quickly pulling on his pants and gathering up the rest of his clothes.

He opened the bedroom door and disappeared down the darkness of the hallway.

Jess heard the kitchen door open and then close as she tiptoed into Kelsey's room. The child's hair was matted with sweat despite the battery-powered fan that Rob had put in the window.

Kelsey shifted positions, still sound asleep, and Jess kissed her on the cheek.

Then she went back into her room, found her night shirt from the floor and climbed into bed.

It was the same bed she'd slept alone in for years, but it suddenly seemed much, *much* too big.

She lay awake, missing Rob's arms around her.

It was nearly dawn before she finally closed her eyes. Just as she was drifting off to sleep she was roused by a car engine. It was Rob's car, and he was pulling out of the driveway.

Jess sat up, suddenly wide awake.

Was he restless, unable to sleep—the way she was? Or did he have someplace to go, someone to see?

The aura of mystery that surrounded Rob like a cloak seemed to thicken, suffocating Jess with the uncertainty.

Who was this man she was falling in love with?

And where was he going at four o'clock in the morning?

Chapter Seven

The house had turned into an oven.

Jess awoke slowly, groggily, drugged both by sleep and the heat. It took her a moment to remember why the air conditioner wasn't working. And then it all came back to her in a rush.

Last night...

She'd made love to Rob last night. It had been wonderful. Exhilarating. Dangerous.

She saw a flash of Rob, his face lit by lightning, his eyes cold and menacing, a knife clutched in his hand....

"Mommy."

She shook away the memory, turning to see Kelsey standing in the doorway. "Morning, Kel."

The child's face was puzzled. "The clock in my room says four-thirty, but that can't be right, or the sun wouldn't be up so high."

"Power went out last night," Jess said. "We had a big storm."

Kelsey nodded, her unbrushed brown hair stringy in the heat. "Thought so," she said, satisfied the mystery could be cleared up so easily. Then she frowned again. "Your clock works."

"My clock has a backup battery," Jess said. As if to punctuate her words, the alarm went off. She reached over and shut it off. "Time to get ready for school."

"I *am* ready," Kelsey said patiently.

Jess looked more closely. Kelsey was dressed in clean shorts and a T-shirt. She even had her sneakers on and tied.

Jess swung her legs out of bed. "I'll get you some breakfast."

"I ate."

"Teeth?"

"Brushed." She bared her teeth as proof. "Can I play in the yard until the bus comes?"

"Hair," Jess said.

"Oops."

"Get it brushed, then you can go outside."

Kelsey headed out of the room, but turned back to her mother almost as an afterthought. "Rob's on the deck eating breakfast," she said. "He asked me to tell you he was out there."

Rob. Jess's pulse kicked into double time. "Thanks, Kel," she said, somehow managing to keep her voice even. He was back.

Jess dressed quickly, throwing on a pair of shorts and a halter top, splashing water onto her face, brushing her teeth and dragging a comb through her hair. And then, trying not to run, she headed for the back deck.

She made herself stop in the kitchen and pour a glass of iced tea, counting slowly to ten to catch her breath.

And then she pushed the screen door open.

Rob was sitting at the picnic table, reading the morning paper in the shade of the umbrella. He was showered and dressed, his sleeves carefully covering both tattoos. He glanced up, his eyes hidden by dark glasses.

Jess felt suddenly nervous and self-conscious. She should have showered before coming out here. She should've at least taken the time to put on some makeup.

"Morning," he said. A box of donuts sat on the table in front of him. He gestured to it. "Hungry? Help yourself."

Jess shook her head. "No, thanks."

She wanted him to kiss her good morning. She wanted him to stand up and take her into his arms and kiss her the way he'd kissed her last night. But he didn't move.

"Is your head feeling better?" Rob asked politely.

Jess reached up, lightly touching the bump with her fingers. "I'd forgotten about it," she admitted.

He nodded. "Good."

She set her glass of iced tea down on the table wishing he would smile at her—one of those soft, secret, "I remember what we shared last night" smiles that only lovers can give one another. She wished he would take off those sunglasses so she could look into his eyes and at least *guess* what he was thinking. "You're going to be late for work," she said, mostly to fill the silence.

He nodded again, looking out into the yard where Kelsey was playing on her swing set. "I called and told them that I wouldn't be in right away," he said. He turned and looked at her. "I thought it would be a good idea if we had a chance to talk."

Talk.

Jess wanted to feel glad that he wanted to talk. He was so quiet, so used to keeping his thoughts to himself. It *was* good that he wanted to talk, she tried to tell herself. But she couldn't shake the feeling that Rob was going to tell her something that she didn't want to hear. She squared her shoulders and sat down across from him.

"Okay," she said. "Let's talk."

He carefully refolded his newspaper and set it down on the table. "Maybe we should wait until Kelsey's bus leaves."

"Wow," Jess said, trying hard to keep her voice light. "The news is that good, huh?"

Rob was silent, turning to watch Kelsey climb the stairs to the deck.

"Carlos is waving at me from his yard," Kelsey announced. "Can I go wait for the bus in front of his house? His mom's out there, too."

Jess stood up. "Grab your schoolbag. I'll walk you down."

"See you later, Bug," Rob said.

Kelsey threw her arms around his neck. "Bye, Rob. Are you going to come home in time to play before dinner?"

Jess could see the muscles working in Rob's jaw as he returned Kelsey's hug. "I don't think so," he said. "Probably not tonight."

"Come on, Kel," Jess said, starting down the stairs.

This was bad. Whatever it was that Rob wanted to talk about, it was definitely bad.

Jess was silent as she walked to the neighbor's house, letting Kelsey chatter on. She exchanged pleasantries with the mother of Kelsey's friend, all the while thinking about Rob.

Rob—sitting back there on her deck, waiting for her to return so that he could hand deliver his regrets about last night. Jess had no doubt that he was going to let her down gently, but he *was* going to let her down. She could practically hear him now: "About last night ... It was a mistake, things got out of hand. I'm sorry...."

Sorry.

He was going to tell her that he was sorry about the thrilling perfection of the lovemaking they'd shared. But to Rob, it had probably been neither thrilling nor perfection. Apparently while Jess had fallen in love, he had fallen into a mud puddle of remorse.

Kelsey gave her a kiss goodbye, and Jess automatically kissed her daughter back. The little girl was gone then, racing around to the back of Carlos's house to check out his new puppy. And then there was nothing for Jess to do but walk back to her house—to Rob and his regrets.

She felt like a condemned woman, marching to the hangman's noose. She was more than half tempted to turn and run.

Somehow she was going to have to sit down and listen and pretend that Rob wasn't breaking her heart.

She climbed the stairs to the deck, and when she reached the top, he was sitting exactly where she'd left him.

Jess didn't bother to sit. She also didn't wait for him to speak. "You're going to apologize," she said flatly, crossing her arms. "You don't think it's going to work between us. Last night we got carried away, we let things get out of control, and now you're really sorry, but you have to be honest with me."

Rob looked away from her, out over the rail and down at the backyard. He didn't say a word.

"Am I right?" Jess persisted. "Please, tell me if I'm wrong—"

"No," he said, still looking away. "You're right." He turned and looked at her. "Jess, I don't want to lose your friendship." His voice was low, intense.

Jess felt both hot and cold. She wanted to run inside, to get away from this man, to throw herself on her bed and let herself cry and ache and hurt. But more than that, she wanted to know why. Why wouldn't he give their relationship a chance?

She sat down across from him, her hands tightly clasped together on the table in front of her. "I don't understand," she said quietly. "Please make me understand."

Rob took off his sunglasses and rubbed his eyes. He looked tired, bone weary, as if he hadn't slept at all last night. "I'm not sure I can."

"Try."

He shook his head, as if he couldn't find any words at all to help explain.

"Is it me?" she asked barely audibly, fighting the tears that welled in her eyes.

Rob looked up at her, his gaze suddenly sharp, focused. "God, no." He started to reach across the table for her hand, but stopped himself. "No, it's me. I can't . . . I can't give you want you want, Jess."

"How do you know what I want?"

He smiled then, a tight, sardonic twisting of his lips. "I don't, not really. But I *do* know whatever it is you do want, it couldn't possibly be me."

Jess felt anger, sharp and knifelike, sliding in among all the hurt. "And you're just going to make that decision for me?"

He faced her glare steadily. "Yes."

She lifted her chin. "I don't think so—"

"The decision's already been made," he said, almost gently. "What happened last night isn't going to happen again."

There was such certainty in his voice. He sounded so definite, so sure of himself. Jess felt her own conviction falter as the hurt again began crowding her anger out. But as she looked up into his eyes she saw something else. She could see a flash of that unmistakable heat. Unless she was absolutely mistaken, unless she'd totally misinterpreted what that fire in his eyes meant, he was sitting here, about to give her a classic "I think we should just be friends" speech despite the fact that he still wanted her.

"I just think . . ."

Here it came.

". . . we'd be better off in the long run . . ."

He had to look away. He couldn't meet her eyes.

". . . if we stayed friends."

Jackpot. But somehow she didn't feel very triumphant.

Jess didn't say anything. She just sat there, letting his words hang in the air between them. She waited until he glanced up at her before she spoke. "Is that really what you want?"

"Yes."

Jess stood up. She had to get inside the house before he saw her cry. "You want to be friends," she repeated. She laughed, a soft burst of air that had nothing to do with humor. "You mean like the way you've been avoiding me for the past few days?" She laughed again. "That was very friendly, Rob. And that was after only one kiss. After what we did last night, I'll be lucky if you send me a postcard from Kathmandu."

"I won't avoid you anymore, I swear."

Jess crossed her arms, holding herself tightly. "Maybe it would be better if you just moved out."

"Jess, I *won't* avoid you."

"Maybe you should," she said, and went into the house.

IT WAS HELL after it was over, after the need had faded. He felt sickened, remorseful, disgusting.

He recognized then that what he did was wrong. At those moments, he wanted desperately to be caught, to be stopped. But never enough to turn himself in.

More than once, his thoughts had turned to suicide. He had the knife—he could easily end this torment.

Oblivion would be so sweet, so peaceful. It would end this relentless nausea. It would stop the terrible dreams, the awful nightmares. Faces of women, eyes pleading, begging, accusing. Screams of terror, the salty taste of the warm spray of blood . . .

But then it would start again and the nausea and sickness would vanish along with any knowledge of right or wrong.

And the faces in his dreams became his trusted companions, his harem, his private fan club.

His nightmares ended—but for the woman who next caught his eye, the nightmare was only beginning.

WHAT WAS HIS NAME . . . ?

Pete.

The bartender from the Pelican Club.

The first time Jess saw him, he was driving past her house. She had just brought Kelsey home from Doris's day-care, and they were walking to the mailbox at the end of the drive to get the mail.

He was driving a dark blue sedan, and he seemed to slow slightly as he approached her little pink stucco house.

He was wearing sunglasses, so she might've been mistaken, but she could've sworn it was Pete.

But he didn't wave, and he turned his head as he went past, so Jess wasn't absolutely sure.

But then she saw him again, at the convenience store on the corner.

She was pulling in, to fill her tank with gas, and she saw him getting into that same dark blue sedan.

It was definitely Pete from the Pelican Club. He was wearing a dark T-shirt and jeans, and he looked as if he *still* hadn't shaved or combed his hair.

But this time, he looked up and she waved.

And when she got out of her car to pump the gas, he climbed back out of *his* car, and approached her.

"Hey," he said. "Jess Baxter. I thought it was you."

He was not a bad-looking guy. In fact, she might even call him handsome, if she went for the lean, angular-featured, stern-faced type. His T-shirt hugged his upper body, and his well-worn jeans clung to his thighs.

"Your name's Pete, right?" Jess said, selecting the least expensive gasoline from the pump and inserting the nozzle into her car's tank. The pumping gas made a quiet whirring sound.

"Yeah," he said. His pale gray eyes seemed to take in every detail—her aging car, her khaki shorts, the worn leather of her sandals, her faded cotton T-shirt, the way her hair curled damply against her face in the heat. "Do you live around here?"

There was surprise in his voice, as if he hadn't expected to run into her in this part of town. But as Jess glanced up, she knew with an uncanny certainty that Pete *was* the man she'd seen driving past just this afternoon. He was lying. He knew exactly where she lived.

"Yes," she said. "Do you?" Maybe he lived in her neighborhood, in the row of cheap apartments at the end of the street. Maybe that's why he was driving past. Maybe...

He shook his head. "No, I've got a bartending gig at a club up in Bradenton. I just got off the highway to get some gas."

Another lie.

"What a coincidence," she said.

"Yeah, small world." He glanced inside of her car, his sharp eyes taking in Kelsey and her collection of toy cars scattered across the back seat and the picnic basket and beach blanket up in the front. "Are you performing in any of the local clubs in the next few weeks?"

Jess carefully stopped the gas pump at five dollars and put the gas cap back on. She closed the little access door with a snap and turned back to Pete.

"Two weeks from Monday," she said, "I'll be at the Rose Café out on Bee Ridge Road."

Pete nodded. "I enjoyed your music."

"Thanks," Jess said, uncertain of what to do. No *way* was she leaving Kelsey alone in the car while she went inside to pay. Not with this man out here. But Pete started back toward his car just as the gas station attendant came out of the office.

"Maybe I'll see you around," he said with a wave.

"Maybe," Jess echoed. She handed the attendant a ten and watched as he peeled a five from his wad of bills and handed her the change. When she looked up, Pete and his dark blue car were both gone.

Still, she couldn't shake the feeling that she was being watched. Or followed.

Jess climbed into the car and turned back to look at Kelsey. "Maybe we shouldn't go to the beach for our picnic," she said.

Kelsey was not happy. "But you promised—"

"I know I did," Jess said, "and I'm sorry, but—"

"I already have on my bathing suit," Kelsey interrupted. "And you do, too."

Jess shook her head. She hated to admit it, but she was spooked. The beach would be nearly empty at this time of day. The thought of picnicking on a deserted beach was not a pleasant one.

Damn this serial killer, she thought suddenly. She'd never been afraid to be alone on the beach before. It wasn't fair that she should be scared now. And it wasn't fair that a near-stranger's casual interest should make her so paranoid that her daughter's evening would be ruined.

Pete wasn't the serial killer. It was crazy to think so. He was just a regular, normal guy. He probably got her address from the manager of the Pelican Club. He'd come out here to check her out, see where she lived. She'd caught him in her neighborhood, and he'd naturally told a white lie, covering his tracks. Ten-to-one odds were that he'd call and ask her out—probably that very evening. Still, despite her reasoning, Jess *was* spooked.

"Let's go back home," she compromised, "and call Doris. Maybe she and John will want to come on a picnic." Doris's husband was six feet tall and built like a refrigerator.

Kelsey nodded. "Did that man scare you?" she asked. "The man with the funny eyes?"

Jess glanced in the rearview mirror. Sometimes her daughter could be amazingly perceptive. "Yeah," she admitted. "He made me nervous, Kel."

"Me, too," Kelsey said. "Hey, look! Rob's home!"

Jess pulled into the driveway and sure enough, he was getting out of his car. Damn, this was bad timing.

"Let's ask Rob to come to the beach with us," Kelsey suggested, her brown eyes lighting with pleasure. "Can we, Mom? Please?"

Jess had been successfully avoiding Rob for the past several days, taking Kelsey out to dinner, to movies, shopping... anything in order to not be home when Rob returned from work. She hadn't even seen him some days. The hurt should have been lessening, but she felt a surge of fresh pain just at the sight of him.

"No, I don't think so, Kelsey," Jess started to say, but the little girl was already out of the car and running toward Rob.

Damn.

Jess followed more slowly, watching Kelsey dance around Rob with excitement.

"I don't know, I've got a lot of work to do tonight," she heard Rob say to her daughter.

He looked up, over Kelsey's head, and met Jess's eyes.

Nothing had changed.

That powerful bolt of attraction was still there. Maybe it was even more intense now—now that they knew what was possible between them, now that they'd made love.

And Rob felt it, too. Jess *knew* that he did. For one brief instant, he didn't hide the odd mix of emotions that crossed his face. She could see desire and loneliness, longing and a wistful despair. Then all of his defenses slammed into place, and all she could see was exhaustion.

But that small glimpse had been enough to rekindle a tiny flame of hope in her heart.

Maybe, just maybe, Rob was hurting, too. Maybe he missed her, longed for her, ached for her kisses, the way she ached for his.

And just maybe, if Jess was careful enough and patient enough, she could break through the wall of excuses he had erected between them. Maybe she could confront his reasons for keeping them apart. And maybe she could prove him wrong.

"Please come with us," Jess said quietly.

She could see the surprise on his face. After the last time they'd talked, the last time they'd even seen each other, an invitation to the beach was the last thing he'd expected from her.

He nervously ran his hand up and through his hair. Glancing from Jess to Kelsey and back, he cleared his throat. "Um . . . I don't think so . . ."

Maybe she could prove him wrong? Maybe the real truth was that she was a masochist and liked being rejected.

Still, she didn't back down. "Come on," she insisted. "It's just a *friendly* picnic."

Jess saw another flash of pain in his eyes, and he turned away again. "I'm sorry," he began. "But—"

She stopped him with her words. "You said you wouldn't avoid me," she reminded him. "Here's your big chance to prove you were telling the truth."

Rob turned and looked at her, his face expressionless. Then he nodded. "Let me get my bathing suit."

Chapter Eight

Rob sat in the sand at the edge of the water and watched the sun set.

Kelsey was playing in the shallow water, and every so often she ran to show him a particularly beautiful shell or pebble, then scampered farther up onto the beach where Jess was sitting on the blanket.

The early evening was still and quiet. Sounds of the gentle surf and calling seabirds were soothing, calming. He should have been able to relax. He should have started to feel the tensions of the week drain from him.

But Jess was sitting behind him, not quite twenty feet away. She was up on the beach blanket, wearing an indigo blue bathing suit. It was a bikini, and the sight of the clingy fabric barely covering her perfect, slender body would have raised the blood pressure of an indifferent man.

And Rob was hardly indifferent.

Coming out here like this was a mistake.

All evening long, he'd had to fight the urge to touch her, to put his arm around her, to brush her hair back, to cup the smoothness of her face, to touch the softness of her lips with his own.

She'd been right the first time, he realized. He was going to have to move out.

But not yet.

Not tonight. Tomorrow morning he was leaving for Orlando. He'd be gone for two weeks. A little time, a little space, a little distance. It could do wonders for *any* problem, no matter how large. At least he hoped so, because this particular problem was galactic.

The sand crunched to his left, and Rob looked up to see Jess standing behind him. She smiled and sat down next to him, careful to keep enough distance between them.

"It's almost time to go," she said quietly.

Rob nodded, squinting across the water at the red-orange globe of the sun as it began to sink beneath the horizon. He couldn't look at her. Not while she was wearing that bathing suit. He waited for her to stand up and pull on her T-shirt and shorts. Then he'd stand up, too, and get back into her funky little car and pretend that sitting inches away from her on the ride home wasn't killing him.

But Jess didn't move. She didn't start packing up the blanket and picnic basket. "So," she said instead. "Now we're friends. This is nice."

He risked a glance at her. She didn't believe that this was nice, or even that they were friends, any more than he did. This was as hard for her as it was for him—and for him, it was torture.

"You and Bug come to the beach often, don't you?" Rob asked. His question sounded stiff and stilted, like bad small talk at an awkward party.

But Jess answered honestly. "I love it here," she said simply. "Being on a beach watching the sun set is the next best thing to heaven."

He nodded. Yeah. "I love it, too." It seemed to be a simple statement—just a few short words—and Rob wondered if Jess knew how difficult it had been for him to make that admission. He *never* talked about anything he truly cared about. It was one of his rules. He never willingly gave up any personal information. And he never broke his rules—at least not before he'd met Jess Baxter.

Rob felt her watching him, felt her gaze traveling from his hair—which the wind and humidity had turned into a nest of dark curls—all the way down to his feet, stopping midway to examine the tattoos on his left arm. Here came the questions. Even for Jess, the world's least nosy person, his tattoos were too mysterious. He would've had them removed—if he wasn't so damn afraid of his medical records being traced.

"What made you decide to get a tattoo?" Jess asked just as he'd known she would, then corrected herself, "*Two* tattoos."

Rob wrapped his arms around his knees, still gazing at the sun. It looked as if it were being swallowed by the water. The sky was filled with gorgeous shades of pink and orange and red and yellow. "I was young," he said vaguely. "And probably drunk at the time."

"I've never even seen you drink," Jess said.

God, he'd already said too much. "That's because I don't drink anymore."

He glanced at her again. Her dark eyes weren't judgmental or damning or even pitying. They were compassionate and warm.

His eyes slid lower, to her mouth, to those lips that he'd kissed so desperately just a few days ago. She smiled sweetly, sadly. The impact of what he was giving up hit him again, harder than it ever had before.

"I *do* want to be friends with you," Jess said softly. "If you can't give me your love, at least allow me to be your friend."

Rob couldn't respond. What could he possibly say?

"Talk to me," she urged him. "I want to know who you are."

He couldn't even look at her. "I'm not even sure of that myself," he said, his voice low.

"Tell me something...tell me just one thing about...about your childhood," Jess said. "Tell me something...about your mother."

Rob sat silently for a long time. His mother. What could he possibly say? Maybe the truth. Could it really hurt to give this woman the smallest crumb of the truth? "I loved my mother more than anyone else in the world," he said. The word *mother* felt odd in his mouth. It had been so long since he'd talked about her to anyone. He picked up some sand and watched it trickle through his fingers before he glanced back at Jess. "She died when I was about Kelsey's age."

"I'm sorry," Jess whispered, and Rob knew that she truly was.

"You know, you remind me of her," he said, the words coming more easily now. "I don't mean so much the way you look, although she had hair about the same color as yours, and she wore it short, too. But...I'm talking about the way you love Kelsey. The way you talk to her as if she's a real person."

"But, she is," Jess said, somewhat surprised.

Rob had to smile. "See, that's what's so great about you," he said. "It doesn't even occur to you that some people might treat their kids like glorified house pets. My father was from the 'children should be seen, not heard' school. Except of course, when he was drunk. Then it was any child seen or heard was in danger of being—" He broke off, shaking his head. God, what was he telling her? "But you only wanted to know *one* thing."

Jess knew. He could see it in her eyes. She knew from conversations they'd had before that his father had hurt him. Too many times to count.

"I want to know everything there is to know about you," she said quietly. "Tell me about your father."

No way. Rob closed his eyes, remembering the sting of open fists, the suffocating darkness of closets—too many to count, the endless blur of fear and pain.

"Please?"

Rob forced himself to open his eyes, to look at Jess. "He was a beast," he said flatly. "He died a few years ago. There's nothing more to tell."

"It must've been hard, growing up...like that."

"I shouldn't have brought it up."

She was silent for a moment, gazing at Kelsey, who was turning cartwheels in the surf. "If I were you," she finally said, "I'd be pretty proud."

Rob couldn't hide his surprise. "Of what?"

"Of surviving. No, not just surviving—of turning out so...so solid, and, well...*nice*."

Rob had to laugh. "Oh, I'm *real* nice." He had to stop talking. He had to end this conversation, even if it meant standing up and walking away. But something kept him sitting there, gazing into the midnight darkness of Jess's beautiful eyes. "No, you're wrong. My father was a beast, and it's his blood in my veins."

She looked shocked. "You are *not* a beast."

"How can you be so sure?"

Jess didn't answer. She didn't even move—until Kelsey came splashing toward them.

"Make a wish!" the little girl shouted. "Quick—make a wish on the green flash!"

Jess turned and looked out toward the setting sun, and Rob followed her gaze. Most of the sun had disappeared from view, leaving only the very top curve above the horizon. "Kelsey's right," she said. "It's going to go. Watch for the green flash."

The mood was broken, thank God. "The what?" he asked.

Kelsey threw herself down on the sand, directly between them.

"The green flash," Jess repeated, leaning forward slightly to talk to Rob over her daughter. "Right when the sun disappears, sometimes there's a green flash in the sky. Haven't you ever seen it before?"

Rob shook his head.

Kelsey reached over and took his hand. "You have to make a wish," she said, "and it has a better chance of coming true if you hold hands. Mom says it's concentrated power—kind of like when orange juice comes in one of those little frozen cans."

The little girl's hand was cool and wet, and she gave his fingers a squeeze. She was holding on to Jess with her other hand.

"Do you have your wish?" she asked, looking up at Rob. "I do."

Jess leaned forward again. "It's an old family superstition," she explained with a smile. "Wishing on the green flash. Of course, the flash doesn't happen all the time—which makes your wish that much more powerful when it does."

Kelsey turned to Jess. "Mommy, do you have your wish?"

"Yes, I do."

Rob couldn't look at Jess. He wouldn't look at her. He *shouldn't* look . . . He couldn't keep from glancing at her, but when he did, she wasn't looking at him. She was gazing out across the water of the gulf.

"Here it goes," she whispered.

Rob stared out at the setting sun, watching as it actually moved, appearing to sink into the ocean.

I wish I could have this life, and stay here forever with this beautiful woman and sweet child. . . .

The ocean swallowed up the sun, and then, right when it was gone, there was a flash of greenish white light.

Kelsey squeezed his hand again, and Rob looked down into her round, freckled, smiling face. "Our wishes are gonna come true," she said, her brown eyes sparkling with pleasure.

Rob looked over the top of the little girl's head and met Jess's eyes. Would that he had the power to make his wish come true. But he didn't. The only ability he had was to hurt, to destroy. He only knew how to tear a life apart, not to build it. He felt tears sting his eyes, and as he gazed at Jess, he knew he wasn't able to hide his hunger and need.

"That would be nice, Bug," he whispered. "That would be really nice."

THE DARK BLUE SEDAN pulled onto Route 41 behind Jess's car.

It was four or five cars back, but she had been aware of it following her ever since she crossed the causeway leaving Siesta Key.

Kelsey had put her head down, and was fast asleep in the back seat. Rob was sitting quietly beside her, lost in his own thoughts.

A 7-Eleven was ahead, on the right-hand side. Jess slowed and pulled into the parking lot, into a slot directly in front of the store. "Mind if I pick up a loaf of bread?" she asked, quickly improvising an excuse for stopping as Rob glanced at her in surprise.

"I don't mind," he said.

In her rearview mirror, she watched as the blue sedan went sailing past.

If Pete the bartender was in that car that was following her, he would have stopped, wouldn't he? But he didn't. So it wasn't Pete. Besides, he didn't own the only dark blue sedan in Florida. *And* he was up in Bradenton right now, working.

She was becoming paranoid. Silently, she berated herself for letting her imagination get the best of her. "Sorry, what did you say?" she asked Rob.

"I said I don't mind," he repeated. At her blank look, he added, "That we stopped."

"Actually," Jess gave him a weak smile, "I probably have enough milk to last until Thursday when I get groceries. And it's less expensive at the Publix."

She backed out of the parking space and pulled back onto the road. Rob was watching her, his eyebrows slanted slightly together, as if he were trying to solve a puzzle. "Bread," he said. "You said you needed bread, not milk."

Had she? Oops. "Bread, milk..." Jess shrugged. "It's all running low. You know how it is, living with a six-year-old. I'm probably out of peanut butter, too."

He was still watching her. "Jess, what's going on?"

She checked her rearview mirror. No sign of the blue sedan. "Is someone following us?" he asked, searching her face, then turning around to look out of the rear windshield.

Jess glanced at him. "What?" she said with a laugh, "Of course not."

He wasn't buying it.

She sighed. Boy, was this going to sound really stupid. Now that the blue sedan wasn't behind them anymore, it even sounded really silly to *her*. "Do you remember the bartender at the Pelican Club?"

Rob shook his head, no, silently waiting for her to explain what the bartender had to do with any of this.

"His name was Pete. He was—" Jess searched for the right words "—kind of...odd. He had strange eyes—he was always watching, you know?"

"Everyone there was watching you," Rob commented. "You were on stage."

Jess ran her fingers through her windblown hair. "No, I mean he was watching *every*thing. Not just me." She glanced again into the mirror. There were only three cars behind her—all big and white.

"You think this guy's following you?" Rob asked, turning to look out the rear window again.

"Yes," Jess said. "No." She laughed in exasperation. "I don't know. This serial killer thing is making me lose my perspective." She shook her head. "I ran into Pete at the Lil' Peach on the corner—you know, the one by my house?"

Rob nodded. He was expressionless and silent, just watching and listening.

"That was after I thought I saw him earlier today, driving past the house," she continued. "And just now, I thought I saw his car again." She smiled ruefully. "The key word here is *thought*.'' She paused, but Rob still didn't speak. ''You think I'm nuts?''

He shook his head, no. ''I think you're smart to be careful.'' He frowned. ''Damn!''

''What?''

''I'm leaving for Orlando tomorrow. I don't like the idea of leaving you and Kelsey alone for two weeks.''

''Tomorrow?'' Jess repeated, trying to sound casually interested instead of disappointed. She'd seen the way Rob had looked at her on the beach. She hadn't missed the hunger in his eyes or the way his gaze almost seemed to caress her nearly naked body. Despite everything he'd said about being friends, she was under his skin. She knew she was. She was more sure than ever.

He'd shared some of the secrets of his past with her. Lord, she knew why he didn't speak of his childhood—why he seemed to want no connection to his family. His mother had died when he was a small child. His father had abused him. Her heart went out to the small boy that Rob had once been, and to the man that he'd become.

''The Orlando project's definitely starting tomorrow,'' he said. ''I have to be there by noon. I'll be on the road before you guys even wake up.''

Jess took the right turn onto her side street, slowing to pull into her driveway. She'd left the light on outside the garage, and she turned to look at Rob in the yellowish glow.

''We'll be okay,'' she said. ''We always are.''

''Maybe,'' Rob started to say, then stopped. He seemed to make a decision, looking directly into her eyes. ''Maybe you should call the police.''

The police? Jess shook her head. ''I don't know.'' It seemed so drastic. The *police*. . . ''It's probably nothing—I'd be too embarrassed . . .''

''You've read the newspaper accounts,'' Rob urged her. ''This guy stalks his victims. He follows them around—it's called trolling, remember?''

Jess nodded slowly. Rob's face was so serious, his eyes so concerned. He wasn't wearing his glasses, and with his hair still messed from the ocean wind, wearing his neon orange bathing suit and a Panama Jack T-shirt, with the head of his snake tattoo peering slyly out from under the left sleeve, he looked like a totally different person from Rob Carpenter, computer programmer. He looked more like the man who had made love to her just a few nights ago.

Jess gazed at him, caught in the intensity of his eyes.

"Promise me you'll think about calling the police?" he said.

She nodded silently. Yes. When he looked at her that way, she'd promise him damn near anything. "You really do care, don't you?" she whispered.

He was as lost in her eyes as she was in his, as unable to look away. "Yeah," he said. "I care." He moistened his lips, as if they were suddenly dry. "We're friends, right?"

Who was he reminding of that?

Jess couldn't help herself. She reached out, running her fingers through the soft, dark curls of his hair. "We can be friends," she said, her heart in her throat, amazed at her own daring, "*and* lovers."

Rob caught her wrist, pulling her hand away from him. "No," he said tightly. "We can't."

Rejection. Again. You'd think she'd have gotten used to it by now. But she hadn't. It hurt just as much as it had the first time.

"Why not?" If he would only give her a *reason*.

"I'm sorry." Rob opened the door and got out of the car, as if he couldn't bear to sit this close to her for another moment.

Jess swore under her breath, pressing the palms of her hands against her forehead and then running them down her face. It didn't make sense. None of this made any sense at all.

He leaned over so that he was looking in the open car window, but he carefully avoided her eyes. "Jess, I'm sorry—"

"I don't get it," Jess said. She was gripping the steering wheel so tightly, her knuckles were turning white. "When we're together, it's *so* great." She turned and looked at him, willing him at least briefly to meet her eyes. "You can't deny it."

"Jess—"

"I'm not just talking about sex," she continued, "although I don't understand how you could just walk away from what we shared."

"I'm sorry—"

"You keep saying that," she said hotly. "Don't tell me you're sorry. Tell me *why*. Dammit, Rob, I can *deal* with unrequited...attraction." She couldn't use the word *love*. She *wouldn't* be able to bear it if he knew... "If that's what this is about, just tell me. Tell me *something*!"

She could see her misery reflected in his eyes. But he didn't explain. He just shook his head. "You were right," he said, his voice low, tight. "I can't stay here. I have to move out."

Jess closed her eyes. "Oh, God."

"I'll get my things out of the apartment when I'm back from Orlando," he said.

"Rob, please—"

"I'll pay rent until you find another tenant," he said huskily. "Don't worry about that. And you can keep the security deposit, since I'm breaking the lease."

"I don't want your money!"

"I *am* sorry, Jess."

The hope that she had been harboring, the hope that had flickered to life in the past few hours that they'd spent together was snuffed, leaving her empty and cold. She'd honestly thought she could talk him into loving her. She'd foolishly thought she could turn him around. She'd hoped patience and time would bring them together.

She had been dead wrong.

THE NIGHT CLOSED IN, making him dizzy, giddy. He liked that feeling—it made the hurt disappear.

He'd been watching her for hours, lurking from closer than she ever would have believed.

She had the little girl with her. He knew the child, but when he got this way faces began to blur and names were meaningless. All the names, except for hers.

The little girl was too loud on the beach—her shouts hurt his ears.

He wanted to hold her beneath the waves until she was silent.

But now it was over and he was alone in the warm, suffocating darkness of the night.

There was another who lived nearby whom he'd been following, too. He knew that one's schedule, knew that she'd have been home for about an hour by now.

She'd just have finished her dinner and washed up her dishes.

She didn't know it, but she was waiting for him.

He'd be there soon.

Chapter Nine

Kelsey had just gotten out of the bathtub and into her night-shirt when the doorbell rang.

Jess peeked out the window before she opened the door. "Frank," she said, letting the tall man into the house, automatically glancing at the neighbors and waving to old Mr. Greene who was watching from the shadows of his porch. "This is a surprise."

Frank smiled at her, glancing around the living room.

At least it was clean, Jess thought, realizing how the slightly shabby sofa and well-used easy chair must look through a stranger's eyes.

Frank's gaze rested on the fireplace, his eyebrows slightly raised. Not too many homes in Sarasota had a fireplace, Jess knew, especially not a working one with solid brass andirons and fire irons. There weren't too many days cool enough to light a fire.

"Actually I'm here because Rob called me," Frank said.

Jess's hand tightened on the doorknob, but she carefully kept her face calm. "Well, come on in, make yourself at home," she said. "I was just about to tuck Kel into bed. If you don't mind waiting a minute or two..."

"No, no," Frank said. "Go right ahead. Mind if I turn on the ball game?"

Jess grinned. "I *did* say make yourself at home."

"It's the Sox against the Yankees," Frank said sheepishly, picking up the remote control. "I've been a BoSox fan for years."

Jess led Kelsey into the bedroom. She adjusted the air-conditioning vent, letting more cool air blow in. She pulled the sheet up to her daughter's chin and kissed her on the nose. "Good night, Bug," she murmured.

"That's what Rob calls me," Kelsey said.

Jess nodded. "I know. I like it."

"Me, too." Kelsey pulled Jess's ear down close to her mouth. "That guy was at the Pelican Club, wasn't he?"

"Yeah," Jess whispered back. "His name's Frank. He works at the same place Rob does."

"He's tall," Kelsey said. "And he likes baseball. Rob likes baseball, too."

"He does?" Jess couldn't keep the question from popping out.

"Yeah. When is Rob going to come back?"

"Not for a couple of weeks," she told her daughter. Now was *not* the time to discuss Rob's moving out. But she'd have to tell Kelsey sooner or later.

"I miss him," Kelsey said.

"I do, too," Jess whispered. She gave her daughter another kiss. "Good night."

She flipped the light off, and left the room, leaving Kelsey's door open about four inches.

Jess didn't feel like going into the living room and playing hostess. It wasn't that she disliked Frank—she didn't really know the man—but the past week had left her feeling emotionally scraped raw.

She'd heard Rob's car return late last night—well after 2:00 a.m. And, like he'd said, he was gone again when Jess got Kelsey up and ready for school.

Yeah, she felt wounded. And taken advantage of. She had never had a one-night stand before, and the thought that she'd so misjudged both Rob and the situation made her feel even worse. But maybe what she'd had with him *wasn't* a one-night stand. Maybe it was just a very, very brief love affair. One-night stands were had and forgotten. Somehow, she suspected it would be a long, *long* time before Robert Carpenter forgot about her.

Frank looked up, muting the television as Jess came into the living room.

"So what's a Boston Red Sox fan doing down in Florida?" she asked, forcing herself to smile.

Frank shrugged. "I go where the job sends me," he said. "And with cable these days, I can pick up the Sox just about anywhere."

"You said that Rob called you?" Jess sat down in the easy chair across from him, trying not to let hunger show in her eyes at the mention of Rob's name.

"Yeah, this afternoon," he said. "He asked me if I wouldn't mind staying in his apartment while he's away."

"He *did?*"

"Yes, ma'am," Frank said. "He told me you were afraid someone's been following you. He thought you might like having a man within shouting distance." He glanced back at the television. "I would have been over earlier, but something came up and I had to work late, so..." He shrugged. "Here I am. He said you'd be able to give me an extra key."

Jess tried to smile, but she knew it couldn't look very sincere. "I know he was worried, but it's really unnecessary."

Frank nodded, staring at the TV screen. The Red Sox were in the field, and they successfully completed a double play, but it didn't seem to register with him.

"You see today's paper?" he suddenly asked.

Jess shook her head. "No," she replied. "It's probably still outside. Why?"

"Well, the news, as they say down here in the south, ain't good."

Jess stood up and opened the front door. She pushed the screen and went outside. She grabbed the paper from where it lay on the lawn, and went back in. Leaning on the door to close it, she looked at the headlines—"Sarasota Killer Strikes!"

"Oh, not again," she said. Quickly she skimmed the article, then looked up in shock at Frank. "Oh, my Lord," she said. "This happened right on the next block over. Last night."

"The police think he's the same man," Frank told her, his face serious. "This makes his fourteenth time."

"'The victim was found with her throat cut,'" Jess read, revulsion in her voice, "'bound with a rope.' Do they give the woman's name?"

"I didn't get a chance to read the article yet," Frank answered.

"Dear Lord," Jess said, still reading. The police had identified the murder weapon as some sort of knife, probably a switchblade, at least five inches long. The coroner's report led them to believe he was right-handed, judging from the size and shape of the wound. Jess shuddered, holding her hand up to her own neck. "The police aren't releasing any information regarding suspects. I wish they would catch this guy."

"Sometimes they never catch them." Frank shook his head. "There's an awful lot of sickos out there, Jess. I guess that's why Rob wanted me to stay at his place, particularly since you seem to believe someone's following you. He thinks you fit the description of the victims pretty accurately, and I must say I agree. He thought you'd be safer with a man next door, but I realize that the decision's yours. I don't want to step on your toes."

Jess smiled weakly. What she *really* wanted was for Rob to come back.... "Well," she said slowly. "I do appreciate the offer, but I can't ask you to leave your own apartment. Rob told me you've got a nice place down by the marina."

Frank shrugged. "It's okay. And really, I wouldn't mind. I'm a big fan of yours—I'd like to be able to hear you practice. And I truly would love the company. It would be a nice change of pace. I've been living alone for way too long."

Jess looked at Frank carefully. His blandly handsome face was open and his smile seemed genuine. *What* is *it with you, Jess,* she scolded herself. *You spent too many years with Ian,* that's *what.* It was time she started believing her own words. A friendly smile was just that—a friendly smile. Nothing more.

"I don't know what to say," she said. "Except, welcome to the neighborhood."

"Evenin', Miss Jess."

Jess looked up in surprise, and the ball Kelsey was throwing to her bounced out of her hands.

"Oh, hi, Stan," she said, scooping the ball up and tossing it back to Kelsey.

Under the watchful eyes of his wheelchair-bound father, Stanford Greene was cutting the hedges that grew along the fence that separated their two yards.

"Looks like you've got a visitor," Stanford informed her, gesturing with his head toward the driveway.

Jess's heart leapt. Maybe it was Rob. Maybe...

It was Ian. He climbed out of his car and staggered slightly as he headed toward her. Perfect. He was drunk again.

"Kel, go inside," Jess said to her daughter. "Bonus TV time."

Kelsey was inside the house so quickly, the banging screen door was the only sign that she'd once been there.

Jess tried to brace herself as she waited for Ian to approach. It was going to be hard—she'd spent most of the day unable to keep herself from thinking about Rob. He'd been gone for nearly two weeks now. Until Rob came back and took his things from the apartment, Jess would be unable to move forward with her life, unable to fully recover from the pain of her broken heart.

Lately Jess was in a foul, black mood. Everyone and everything got on her nerves—even Kelsey. And Frank. Especially Frank. He came over every evening, without fail. He'd drone on and on about his day at work. Sometimes Jess didn't hear even a single word.

She felt guilty for being so impatient and annoyed with Frank. He was doing her a favor by staying in Rob's apartment. As much as she hated to admit it, she *did* feel safer knowing that he was there. And he'd gone out of his way to do her favors—he'd even lent her money to cover Rob's rent when the first of the month rolled around and Rob still was in Orlando.

"I was downtown," Ian said to Jess in place of a greeting, "and everywhere I turned, there were women who looked just like you. It was driving me half insane."

"I'm not interested in talking to you when you're drunk," she said evenly, moving toward the house.

Ian blocked her way. "But I'm interested in talking to you," he replied.

Jess tried to move past him, but he moved with her. She looked up to see both Stanford and his father watching with unabashed curiosity. Despite the audience, words like *court* and *deadbeat dad* and *restraining order* were on the tip of her tongue.

But Frank pulled into the driveway. He came out of his car, talking about the World Series. "You planning on watching the game tonight, Ian?" he asked easily.

Before Jess knew it, Frank invited *both* Ian and Stanford Greene up to Rob's apartment to watch the baseball game that had just started. "I'd invite you too, Jess," Frank said. "But I know you were planning to take Kelsey to the movies tonight."

She hadn't been, but she got the message.

She fixed a quick dinner of pasta, then took Kelsey to a seven o'clock showing of *Beauty and the Beast* at the local library. They'd both seen the movie several times before, but neither of them minded.

And when they returned home, Ian's car was gone.

As Jess got Kelsey ready for bed, she made a mental note to thank Frank for his intervention. He was a nice guy.

But he wasn't Rob.

Rob...

Jess knew that she had to put an ad in the paper, listing the apartment for rent, but she'd put off doing it. Taking endless phone calls and showing the apartment to strangers wasn't any fun. But she was procrastinating for another reason, too. Deep in her heart, she was hoping that he would return from Orlando, take her into his arms, kiss her, and tell her that he'd been wrong.

Dream on.

Jess kissed Kelsey good-night, then went out onto the deck to gaze up at the hazy stars.

A far more likely scenario was that Rob would return and he would avoid her like the plague. If he *did* run into her, it would be awkward and uncomfortable. He'd move his things out of the apartment as quickly as possible, and she'd never see him again.

She knew that was probably what was going to happen. So why did her foolish heart leap every time a gray Taurus drove past her house?

Even as she stood there, a car like Rob's turned onto the street. She could feel her eyes straining to make out the driver through the windshield, but it was too dark to see. The car drove past.

Why did she do this to herself?

Because she was a ninny, that's why. Because Rob had been gone for nearly two weeks, and according to Frank, the project in Orlando was nearly complete. He could return at any time.

And then he'd be gone for good.

Jess felt her eyes flood with tears, and blindly, she turned to go into the house—and ran headlong into Frank.

He caught her in his arms, to keep her from falling. "Hey," he said. "Hey, hey—are you crying?"

"No," she said, pulling away.

But he followed her. "Yes, you are," he said. "What's wrong?"

Jess shook her head, trying to wipe her tears away. "I'm fine."

"It's Rob, isn't it?" Frank said quietly, guessing correctly. It wasn't such a tough call—these days she was wearing her heart in full view on her sleeve. "You guys were...involved for a while, weren't you?"

Jess sat down on one of the deck chairs, hugging her knees to her chest. "Yeah," she said. "We were." She sighed. "Past tense."

Frank sat down on the chair next to her. He hiked up the legs of his pants, and his brown nylon socks showed. He looked faintly ridiculous sitting that way. "I'm sorry to hear that," he said.

"Me, too," Jess said. "I thought..."

"What?" he prompted.

She looked up into Frank's sympathetic hazel eyes. "I thought he was the one."

"The one?"

She smiled ruefully. "You know. That one special person I've been waiting for all of my life... God, it sounds so stupid when I say it out loud."

"It's not stupid," Frank said. He picked up a leaf that had fallen onto the chair and fiddled with it.

Jess closed her eyes, leaning her head back. "Thanks for helping tonight with Ian," she said. "You know, Rob thought I should get a restraining order and—"

"You know, Jess," Frank interrupted, "I was thinking. Maybe *I* could be the one."

Jess opened her eyes and looked at him.

He tore the leaf in half and let the pieces flutter down onto the deck. When he glanced up at her, his eyes were serious.

Jess chose her words very carefully. "It doesn't just work that way," she said. "It's not something that you can just decide to feel and then—"

"Why not?" Frank asked. He stood up, straightening his pants. "At least think about it," he added.

JESS AND KELSEY stood at the counter at the Sarasota Music Center, waiting for the clerk to notice them and ring up the strings Jess needed for her acoustic guitar. Looking into the glass-enclosed shelves by the cash register, Kelsey pointed to a collection of temporary tattoos, nestled among the Grateful Dead jewelry and the Nirvana bumper stickers.

"I want one of those," she announced.

Jess looked down and grinned. "Which one?" The dragon with gore dripping from its wickedly sharp teeth, or the skull with a snake entwined through its eyes and nose?

"The dragon."

Did she know her daughter!

"I don't think so, Kel. We're still too tight for cash this week."

Kelsey chewed her lower lip. "But it would look so good on you."

"On *me?*" Jess laughed. "Oh, no thanks—"

"Oh, *definitely,*" came an all too familiar voice. "But not the dragon."

Kelsey stood very still, seeming to shrink, and Jess braced herself, looking up at Ian's mocking face.

Naturally, because her ex-husband was the illustrious concert master of the SSO, the clerk came over immediately. "Can I help you, Mr. Davis?"

Ian leaned an elbow on the glass, directly on the sign that asked customers not to lean on the glass counter. "Yes. I'll take one of those tattoo things. Yeah, this one.'' He pointed down into the case. ''Put it on my account.''

The clerk handed him the small package and, with a flourish, Ian presented it to Jess. ''A rose for the lady,'' he said.

Jess didn't move. ''Charming, Ian,'' she said. ''Very charming.'' She bent down to Kelsey. ''Do me a favor, Bug,'' she said quietly. ''Go hang out right over there by the sheet music while I talk to Ian, okay? Stay right there, where I can see you.''

Kelsey nodded, and Jess watched her move out of earshot. She handed the sales clerk a ten-dollar bill for the guitar strings and waited until he walked to the cash register before she turned to her ex-husband. ''I've been waiting seventeen months for a child support check from you,'' she said softly. ''Believe me, if I had any choice, I wouldn't mention it, but the clutch is starting to go on the car again, and...'' Jess clenched her teeth, hating this humiliation. ''And here I am, resorting to begging, dammit.''

''Borrow the money from your new boyfriend,'' Ian said coldly, flipping the rose tattoo onto the counter in front of her.

''I don't care about the alimony payments,'' Jess stated. ''I never wanted that in the first place. That was your idea. But child support... Ian, she's your daughter, too.''

''Is she?''

Jess bristled. ''You know damn well she is. I was never unfaithful to you. *You* were the one who had the affairs, remember?''

''You were the one who kicked me out,'' Ian said. His icy blue eyes glittered. He leaned forward, and she felt his wild, long hair brush against her cheek as he whispered in her ear, ''You want money from me? Let me move back in. Get rid of the new boyfriend—what's his name? Frank?''

''He's not my boyfriend.''

''Give him half a chance and he *will* be,'' Ian replied. ''I've seen the way he looks at you—like you're to die for. And you know, maybe he's right.''

Jess flashed him a sour look and stepped away from him, taking her change and the bag with the guitar strings that the clerk had left on the counter. ''Come on, Kel,'' she called out, heading for the door.

"I saw the *old* boyfriend downtown this morning," Ian informed her mockingly.

Jess stopped short, her heart suddenly hammering in her chest.

"Good old Rob," Ian said in that same, sarcastic tone. "I was driving on Bee Ridge Road, going to the video store actually, and there he was, putting gas into his car at the Mobil station. *That* affair certainly didn't last very long, did it?"

Taking Kelsey's hand, Jess left the store.

Chapter Ten

Jess finished tuning her guitar, then looked around the small nightclub. It was spacious, airy even, with hundreds of potted plants hanging down in front of the walls of windows. The small stage was across from the bar. Tables covered with checkered cloths dotted the floor. Yes, this was a nice place. Terry Kitchen, the popular Boston folksinger that Jess was warming up for, actually had several CDs out on Urban Campfire records. This gig was very legitimate. And she couldn't wait to hear Terry Kitchen's set. That was one of the perks of doing a warm-up gig like this. Jess got to hear quality music for free.

As she slipped her guitar into the stand, she heard a voice call out her name.

From behind the bar, a familiar figure waved to her.

"Pete," Jess said in surprise. "What are *you* doing here?"

The bartender that she knew from the Pelican Club leaned on the bar as she approached. His mouth was upturned in a smile that didn't quite reach his eyes. His gaze took her in, as if memorizing her outfit. Blue jeans, black tank top, black cowboy boots, Navajo silver necklace.

"Moonlighting," he replied. "I know the owner of this club, so I asked to work tonight."

It had been weeks since she'd last seen Pete. She hadn't spotted his dark blue sedan following her since that day on the beach. Her earlier suspicions had been just that—suspicions. Pete wasn't the Sarasota Serial Killer. He was just a stern-looking guy who happened to like her music. And her running into him at the gas station *had* been a coincidence. Nothing more.

"How have you been?" Jess asked.

"Busy," he replied. "I've been out of town for a couple of weeks."

Jess's optimistic confidence took a serious nosedive. She hadn't seen Pete following her because he'd been out of town. Come to think of it, the serial killer hadn't struck in the past two weeks either....

"Can I get you something to drink?" he asked.

"No, thanks," Jess murmured.

"Your daughter here tonight?" he asked.

Jess shook her head. "She's at the baby-sitter's." She didn't want to talk about Kelsey. All of her suspicions were back, full force, and she didn't want this man even *thinking* about her daughter.

Rob had urged her to call the police, but she hadn't. When there had been no further sign that she was being followed, she'd forgotten. But what would she say now, if she called? "I think the Sarasota Serial Killer is tending bar tonight at the Rose Café?" That would go over *real* well.

"Excuse me," Jess said, moving away from the bar and Pete's disturbing gray eyes.

The club was filling up, and as she moved through the tables she saw several familiar faces. She stopped to say hello to a jazz piano player she knew from years back, and when she turned to continue on across the room, she came face-to-face with him.

Rob.

He looked uncomfortable, as if he'd hoped to sneak past without being seen.

"You're back," Jess said unnecessarily. He looked tired. And nervous. Thinner, as if he'd lost some weight.

"Yeah," he said. "I'm back. I'm ... actually here because I needed to talk to Frank. His voice mail said he'd be down here tonight."

In other words, he wasn't here to see Jess. She nodded tightly. "Well, don't let me keep you."

She turned away.

"Jess."

She stopped walking, but didn't turn to face him.

"You look good," he said.

She'd looked in the ladies' room mirror just a few minutes ago, and tired, lonely and sad had looked back at her. Not "good." She shook her head and headed for the stage.

IT WAS A MISTAKE for him to have come here. It was torture seeing her again.

He should have gone to the apartment and moved his stuff out. It was the perfect opportunity—Rob knew Jess would be out for most of the evening. He could have packed up his things and been gone—without running into her ever again.

Except something had drawn him here. Some strange force had pulled him out in this direction. It had nothing to do with needing to talk to Frank. In fact, despite what he'd said to Jess, he easily could have waited to see Frank at the office in the morning.

No, it was the idea of seeing Jess again that had led him here. So, okay. He'd seen her. He'd even spoken to her. She looked . . . fine. Had he really expected her to look devastated or even heartbroken?

He'd gotten what he'd come for. Now he should leave.

But just when Rob leaned forward in his seat to whisper to Frank that he was going, Ian appeared, sitting down at a table in the back of the room. Rob couldn't leave then. He knew how vulnerable Jess felt when her ex-husband was around.

And so he stayed.

Jess's set was a short one, and she was off the stage almost before Rob knew it. As he watched, she disappeared into the dressing room, and the lights came up slightly in the club.

Ian appeared at their table, like an unwelcome recurring nightmare. "Oh my goodness," he said to Frank in his crisp English accent. "What lovely flowers. For me?"

Rob glanced at Frank in surprise. Flowers? He hadn't noticed them before, but yes, Frank had a small bouquet of hot-house flowers resting on the table in front of him.

"No," Frank said. "They're *not* for you, Davis. They're for Jess."

"Ooh," said Ian. "Smitten, are we? Frank, you devil, you. You know just the way to a lady's heart, don't you? What's the occasion? Two week anniversary?"

Rob was staring at the flowers, only half hearing the conversation going on around him. Frank and Jess?

Rob stood up, his chair nearly toppling over in his haste to get away from the table. "Excuse me," he murmured, and blindly pushed his way to the bar.

He had no right to feel jealous. He had no damned right to feel anything at all. But he did. He felt . . . angry. Betrayed. Duped.

Here he'd gone and made the ultimate sacrifice. He'd given up paradise to keep Jess from getting hurt.

Dammit, he'd *loved* her. He'd desperately, passionately *loved* her—heart and soul, but only once with his body. Only once had he allowed himself to express his love physically. Only once, because he believed that this powerful love he felt was something she experienced, too. And he couldn't bear to lead her on and then leave her.

But—surprise! Apparently what Jess had felt for him was a little different. Apparently, she'd found him quite easy to replace.

He was numb. The Rose Café was crowded and hot, yet Rob felt flashes of cold.

"Can I get you something to drink?" the lean-faced bartender asked, his pale gray eyes seeming to look right into Rob's soul. "The special tonight's a strawberry margarita. It's like a frozen daiquiri, only with tequila instead of rum . . ."

Rob shook his head, turning away, pushing himself away from the bar. He had to get out of here.

And there was Jess. She was standing right in front of him, her guitar case in her hand. He'd inadvertently blocked her path.

"Excuse me," she said quietly.

He should have moved away. He should have let her pass. But he didn't move. "What'd ya do, invite Frank over for a little Chinese takeout?" he said, his voice sounding harsh to his own ears. Jess had to lean closer to hear him over the din of the crowd. "Did you invite him over for a little dinner and a game of Monopoly Junior? What'd ya do then, Jess, after Kelsey was asleep? Did you . . ." He used a word, an expression so crude, she jerked back a step, as if she'd been slapped.

"How *dare* you . . ." Her voice was no more than a whisper, her eyes wide with disbelief and brimming with unshed tears.

"Frank probably didn't know what hit him," Rob said. "All this time, Ian was right about you, wasn't he?"

"Is there a problem here?" the bartender's voice cut in.

"No," Jess said, holding her head high as she pushed past Rob and ran for the door.

Somehow she managed to hold it together until she reached the parking lot and unlocked her car. She pushed her guitar into the front seat next to her, and climbed in.

How could Rob say such a thing to her? How could he look at her that way, as if she were some horrible slug he'd found underneath a rock? How could his eyes look so cold, his face so cruel?

And then the tears came. She was barely able to see through the flood as she started the car.

How could she have been so wrong about him? The thought released another downpour. Jerkily, she pulled out of the parking lot and headed for the baby-sitter's, wiping her eyes almost continuously on her arms in order to see.

Had she fallen in love with a person who didn't exist? Had she mistaken this cold, angry, cruel, uncaring person for someone kind and gentle? Had she misinterpreted him, thinking he was a little shy and very thoughtful, when in reality his quietness was merely a mask for his hostility and anger? Rob had offered so little information about himself. Had she simply filled in all those missing blanks the way she'd wanted to, creating the perfect man, the one she'd dreamed about finding for so many years?

She began to cry harder, sobs welling up from deep inside her. She pulled over to the side of the road, took the car out of gear and wept.

It took many long minutes, but Jess finally got back in control. Taking a deep, ragged breath, she fished under the seat, looking for the box of tissues she knew was there. After she found it, she blew her nose noisily.

She turned on the interior light and glanced at herself in the rearview mirror and made a face. She wanted to stop at home and rinse her tear-streaked face with cool water before going to Doris's to pick up Kelsey, but it was already late. Every moment she delayed picking up Kel was digging further into the money she'd earned tonight.

With a sigh, she stepped on the clutch, and to her horror, she heard a far too familiar pop. Her foot pushed all the way to the floor, with no resistance from the little pedal.

The clutch had gone out again.

She put her head down on the steering wheel, half surprised that she didn't burst into tears. But of course she wasn't going to cry. She didn't have any tears left. She used them all up on Rob.

Lifting her head, Jess looked around, trying to figure out exactly where she was. She'd been driving on back roads, taking the quickest route to her neighborhood and Doris's house. There were no open-all-night convenience stores on this street, no gas stations. A citrus grove extended out to her left for Lord knows how many acres. And the tiny houses that lined the right-hand side of the street were mostly all dark.

The one house that had its porch light on was about seven houses down, and as she watched, the light went out.

Maybe a police car will drive by, Jess thought, but instantly knew it was simply wishful thinking. She'd been sitting in that same spot for going on a half hour now, and in all that time, only one car had passed her. It had been only a few minutes ago, and she hadn't thought to try to flag it down.

She was so tired, all she wanted was to climb into her bed and sleep for about three days straight. She rested her head on the steering wheel again—

The door to the car suddenly flew open, and before she had a chance to react, big hands grabbed her shoulders and yanked her out. One of the hands clamped down hard on her mouth, stifling her yelp of surprise and fear. She was pulled in, hard, to a very solid body, and she struggled, her fear mounting, but she couldn't get free.

"Are you *trying* to get yourself killed?" a voice whispered angrily in her ear, and she froze.

The hands released her, and she spun around to face Rob.

Her heart was pounding. It was only Rob. *Only* Rob? In a flash, she remembered all of her doubts and suspicions. Why had he grabbed her that way, covering her mouth so that she couldn't scream? What was he doing here? What did he want from her?

"Are you following me?" she asked.

"Don't you know there's someone who stalks this city, looking for defenseless women, ones who are *stupid* enough to be by themselves on a deserted street in the middle of the night?" he nearly spat at her. "I drove past and I couldn't believe it. You were sitting there with the light on inside your car! Dammit, Jess, you might as well have had a neon sign with an arrow, saying Easy target. Kill me."

His glasses had been knocked from his face in the scuffle, and he picked them up off the street and slipped them into his pocket.

"My car broke down," she said coldly. "The clutch finally went out."

She reached into the car and took her keys from the ignition, and her guitar from the passenger seat. She closed the car door and locked it carefully.

"Come on," Rob said. "I'll give you a ride."

"Go to hell," she said. "I don't want a ride from you."

He laughed. "Oh, come on. What are you going to do? Walk?"

Jess didn't answer. She began walking down the sidewalk, her shoulders stiffly set, her head high.

"Didn't you hear anything that I said?" Rob's voice rose with anger.

"I'm not afraid," Jess said, not even bothering to turn around.

He moved quickly in front of her on the sidewalk, blocking her way. "You're not afraid, huh?" he said. His handsome face was hard and stern.

He flicked his wrist, and suddenly he had a knife in his hand. The long blade glittered in the light from the one wan street lamp that was down on the corner.

He took one, then another menacing step towards her.

"Rob, don't," she said, backing away. Why was he doing this? Was he really angry enough to want to *hurt* her?

"Are you afraid yet?" he whispered.

Numbly, she nodded.

The knife hissed then, as the blade went back up into the handle. Rob flicked his wrist again, and it seemed to disappear, up his sleeve.

All her fear instantly transformed into anger. "You bastard," she cried, swinging her guitar case directly at his groin. He moved quickly, protecting himself with his thigh, and catching the case in his hands.

Jess let go of her guitar and began running down the street. Her only wish was to be away from this man, far away from him. She couldn't believe the stunt he'd just pulled—and at her expense.

Her breath sounded loud in her ears, and she glanced back at him. As she did, Rob's hand reached out for the waistband of her jeans. She tried to evade him, but his fingers grabbed the fabric. He pulled her, and she went down, onto the lawn. For a moment, neither of them moved. She lay there, feeling his breath, hot against her face.

"I'm sorry, Jess," Rob said softly. "I was trying to make a point, but I went too far."

Jess exhaled. "Let go of me," she said, her voice still and void of emotion. She twisted, so that she was lying face up, looking at him, too close to him.

Yet the weight of his body on hers brought back unbidden memories of the night they'd made love . . .

And Rob didn't move. "I'm afraid if I let go of you," he murmured in that same, gentle voice, "you'll run away from me again."

She looked up at him. His eyes were gentle, his face filled with sorrow and pain. "I'm sorry," he whispered again. "Please let me drive you home. Because I'd die if anything happened to you."

Jess caught her breath. This was Rob. *Her* Rob. The man she'd fallen in love with, the soul mate she'd given herself to.

She felt her body responding to his presence with a quickness that shocked her. Then with an even larger jolt of shock, she realized that he was responding to her nearness, too. She could feel his arousal hardening, lengthening, pressing down into her thigh. Still, he didn't move.

"I didn't sleep with Frank," she said. Suddenly it was very important that she tell him this. "I haven't been with anyone else in years," she added, fighting the hot tears that burned her eyes, hoping he wouldn't hear the way her voice shook.

Rob was silent as he looked down at her.

Jess met his gaze, her beautiful dark eyes shining with unshed tears. "Just so you know, I haven't been with anyone besides you since my divorce," she told him, her voice so soft he could barely hear her.

Rob closed his eyes as the full meaning of what she told him became clear. "But, why? Jess, you could have anyone you want."

"I don't want anyone else," she replied.

I want you. She didn't say it, but the unspoken words hovered in the air between them.

She took a deep breath. "There must be something really wrong with me," she continued. "You made it as clear as you possibly can without explaining why—you don't want me."

A tear escaped from the corner of her eye, sliding down toward her ear.

"I'm sorry," Rob whispered. "I wish I *could* explain . . ."

"I can't seem to learn," she said. "I can't stop myself from wanting you. And tonight alone, you insult me and scare me half to death, and all I can think about right now is whether or not you're going to kiss me. And whether or not you're going to take me home and make love to me."

She pressed herself up against him, and Rob inhaled sharply.

And then, God help him, he kissed her.

HE WAS A MACHINE.

It had been some time since he'd felt the need, but tonight it had suddenly sparked. Her eyes ruled his dreams, her lips, that smile, her long, delicate neck . . .

Yes, he was a machine.

It was late, but he knew where the clubs stayed open until nearly dawn.

It was worth the drive, because as he stepped through the main entrance into the dim, unnatural coolness, as the throbbing, pulsing music surrounded him, he was certain he would find her here.

She'd have short, dark hair, and a long, lovely neck. He smiled as he thought about her neck, and how he would touch it, kiss it. And drive his knife deeply into it.

Chapter Eleven

Doris smiled knowingly as Jess arrived in her rental car to pick Kelsey up at nine-thirty the next morning. But like last night, when Jess called her to ask if her daughter could sleep over, her friend only asked one question: "Honey, you sure you know what you're doing?"

No. Jess was not sure.

She'd woken up some time around 1:00 a.m. to find Rob gone from her bed. He'd left a note, a scribbled apology. This wasn't supposed to happen again, he'd written. He was sorry— he couldn't seem to stay away from her. This constant wanting, *needing,* was driving him crazy.

He wasn't the only one being driven crazy.

Last night had been wonderful. Incredible.

Last night had been proof that their first time hadn't been just a fluke. The love they shared *was* powerful and more passionate than any Jess had ever known. He'd filled her completely—emotionally and spiritually as well as physically. Jess was an independent woman. She would and could live without Rob and be completely whole. But when they were together, she felt a satisfaction, a happiness she'd never had alone.

Yet that was exactly how she'd woken up.

Alone.

She returned home from driving Kelsey to school to find her answering machine message light flashing.

The first message was from the nursery school where she was supposed to give a music class this morning. The entire three-year-old class had chicken pox. Could they please reschedule?

Then Frank's voice echoed out of the answering machine's speaker. He sounded stilted. He was going out of town for a few days—up to Atlanta on business. He'd call when he returned. He hoped she was all right, and he was disappointed that he didn't get a chance to see her last night.

The last message was from the garage where her car had been towed. The clutch had been repaired, but the mechanic had noticed that the brake pads were starting to go. Did she want those replaced, too?

The irony was too intense. Jess had rented a car to get to her gig at the nursery school. And now not only was the gig canceled, but her car was fixed and ready. Assuming, of course, that she didn't want to drop another two million dollars to get the brake pads replaced.

Jess leaned forward, resting her head on her folded arms on the kitchen table. She could handle financial disaster if only her personal life wasn't such a minefield.

Rob had made love to her so hungrily last night. Their joining had been wild. She liked it like that, though. She loved feeling so desperately needed, so passionately desired. She loved watching calm, quiet Rob lose control.

And afterward, he held her so tenderly, almost reverently. She'd fallen asleep in his arms.

Just once, though, she'd like to wake up in Rob's arms. Just once, she'd like to make love to him slowly in the early morning light.

The doorbell rang, interrupting her thoughts.

Maybe it was Rob. Maybe he'd come back from work to see her. Maybe...

Jess stood up and crossed to the front door. She started to unfasten the bolt when she realized that Rob wouldn't use the front door. He'd come to the back, to the kitchen door.

She glanced out through the peep hole and her heart nearly stopped beating.

It was Pete.

Jess leaned back against the door, double-checking the locks. My God! What should she do? Call the police?

The doorbell rang again.

"Ms. Baxter," Pete called out as if he knew she was right on the other side of the heavy wooden door. "May we have a word with you?"

We?

Jess peeked out through the peephole again. Yes, there were two other men standing slightly behind Pete. And Pete looked odd, and not just from the fish-eye effect of the peephole lens. He was clean-shaven, his hair neatly combed. And he was wearing a business suit.

"What do you want?" she asked, her voice low but clear. At least it wasn't shaking, the way the rest of her was. Damn, but that first sight of him had scared her.

Pete lowered his own voice. "We're FBI, ma'am. We'd like to ask you some questions."

FBI?

Jess peered out of the peephole again, and sure enough, Pete was holding up some kind of shiny metal badge. She unlocked the door and opened it a crack.

"May I see that?

Pete nodded, handing her the badge in its worn leather wallet.

Federal Bureau of Investigation it said. There was a picture ID card, identifying Pete as FBI agent Parker Elliot. Grungy Pete the bartender was really FBI.

"I was undercover when I met you at the Pelican Club," he said, answering her unspoken question. "And also at the Rose Café."

"Undercover?" Jess said weakly, handing the ID card and badge back to Pete. Parker. Whatever his name was.

"May we come inside, ma'am?"

Jess opened the door wider, letting them in.

"My name is Parker Elliot," Pete said, stepping into her living room and looking around. "I work with the Behavioral Science Unit in Quantico, Virginia. Do you know what that is, Ms. Baxter?"

Jess shook her head, no.

The stern-faced man wore his business suit with an ease and familiarity that had been missing when he'd dressed down as a bartender. He also looked far more comfortable with his hair neatly combed and his face cleanly shaven. Jess never would have guessed he was with the FBI. *Never.* Yet now it seemed so obvious. But what did the FBI want with *her?*

"May we sit down?" he asked.

She nodded, yes, and Parker Elliot sat on the edge of her couch's springy cushions. Jess lowered herself into the easy chair across the room. The two men who were with Elliot stood near the door, just watching and listening.

"The Behavioral Science Unit works to apprehend serial killers—men who kill in patterns, with regularity." Parker watched Jess steadily. "Ms. Baxter, how long have you worn your hair that length?"

Serial killers? Her hair...? Jess stared at him blankly. "What does *that* have to do with—"

"Some of the questions that I'm going to ask you are going to seem confusing, even strange," Elliot said, his pale gray gaze moving around the living room. "Please, just do your best to answer them, ma'am."

Jess was positive that this man missed nothing—the worn places on the couch, the stain on the rug where Kelsey had spilled a bottle of ink when she was three years old, the fact that the *TV Guide* was dated four weeks ago. Hell, he probably could tell that the last time she'd had a fire in the fireplace was Christmas Eve, 1990, just by the smell of the ash residue.

"We're here because a number of details seem to tie you to what we know about the killer—or the victims," Elliot continued.

Jess leaned forward, her eyes narrowing. "What?"

"You live in the same geographic area as many of the victims," Elliot explained, "and you fit the physical description of the victims almost exactly. But the reason we're here is that you often appear onstage at the Pelican Club—at the same restaurant three of the victims had been known to frequent."

Jess was aghast. "You don't think *I*—"

"No, ma'am," Elliot quickly interrupted. "You are not a suspect in this investigation. The perpetrator is definitely male. Each of the murders have been accompanied by sexual assault. Rape." He paused, his eyes taking her in, memorizing the details, the same way he'd seemed to memorize the room. She was wearing blue jeans that were a little bit too big. Her T-shirt was a muted floral print with a wide scoop neckline that had slipped down slightly, over one shoulder. Her bra strap was showing. Green. It was green. Jess was positive her green bra was going to be written up in some official FBI report. She self-consciously pulled the neck of her shirt back up over her shoulder.

"We *do* have reason to believe that the killer is someone you know," Elliot continued. "Maybe quite well, in fact."

Jess shook her head, fear making her stomach churn. Someone she knew? How could that awful person be someone she *knew*? Sure, she'd speculated about Rob and even Ian, with his recently increasing harassment. But she'd never honestly *believed* either of them could be a killer. "That's ridiculous. I don't know any serial killers."

"You wouldn't know he was a killer," Elliot said. "Unless you knew what to look for."

"Bloody gloves under his bed?" Jess retorted in disbelief. "A collection of the victims' body parts in his refrigerator?"

Elliot glanced at his two silent partners. "I know this is upsetting to you, Ms. Baxter," he said. "And yes, serial killers have been known to take . . . souvenirs from their victims. But the Sarasota Serial Killer doesn't have that particular habit." He leaned forward, resting his elbows on his knees. "In public, he would come across as very normal. Average. Only in private conversation might you notice certain odd behavior, if even then."

"So what are you asking me to do?" Jess said with a disbelieving laugh. "Give you a list of every man I know?"

"That would be a start," Elliot said.

He was serious. Jess was silent, staring down at the floor.

Elliot shifted in his seat, clearly picking up on her unwillingness to subject all of her friends and acquaintances to an FBI investigation. "Let me give you a brief psychological description of this man we're looking for," he said, "and you tell me if you know anyone who fits."

She met his eyes. "All right."

"He's white, male, twenty-five to forty-five years old, upper middle class," Elliot recited. "He travels frequently, keeps a low profile, blends easily into a crowd—"

"That could be just about anyone I know," Jess protested.

"There was a man," Elliot said. "You spoke to him right before you left the Rose Café last night. You seemed upset with him."

"Rob?" Jess laughed. The *idea* of Rob actually being the serial killer was ridiculous. Wasn't it?

Elliot fished a small notebook out of the inside pocket of his suit jacket and jotted a note with the stub of a pencil. "Rob's last name?"

Jess shook her head in amazement. "I can't *believe* this," she said. "Rob's *not* a serial killer."

"His last name?" Elliot persisted.

"Carpenter. I can assure you you'd be wasting your time checking into him."

"Is he your boyfriend? Former boyfriend...?"

"He's my tenant," Jess corrected him. "He lives in the apartment attached to this house."

Elliot's eyes seemed to pierce her. "For how long?"

"He moved in a few weeks ago."

That wasn't the answer Parker Elliot wanted to hear. He seemed disappointed and scribbled another note in his book. "That doesn't work," he said. "The killings started six months ago. Any other candidates? Former lovers? Anyone who might have a reason to be angry or obsessed with you?"

"My ex-husband, Ian Davis," Jess answered.

"We're aware of him," Elliot murmured. "He doesn't quite fit the type we're looking for, although there's no absolute rule." He frowned down at his notebook. "Tell me about your musical career. Any overly enthusiastic fans? Anyone you've noticed at every one of your performances? Anyone who's always there, maybe sitting in the back...?"

Only Rob.

Jess shook her head, no.

"Serial killers often feel inadequate, and as a result are paranoid. Someone or something is out to get them. As a result, for their supposed protection, they carry some sort of weapon." Parker Elliot was watching her very closely. "They also almost always come from a home with an abusive parent.... I'm striking some familiar chords here, aren't I?"

Jess shook her head. "No."

Yes. Rob carried a switchblade knife. Rob's father had abused him as a child.

But that was insane. Rob *wasn't* a serial killer. Not all abused children become serial killers. And as for his knife... Well, Jess couldn't explain away his blade, but there was surely *some* sort of logical explanation for it. There had to be.

Parker Elliot was watching her, his sharp gray eyes picking up every emotion that flickered across her face. "Tell me what you're thinking," he said.

Jess crossed her arms, leaning back in the chair. "I think you're on the wrong track."

Elliot nodded, glancing briefly at his watch. "Keep in mind what I said," he advised, reaching into his pocket and taking out a business card. He stood up, holding it out to her. "Call me if you can think of anything that might help us."

The business card had only his name and a phone number printed on it. There was no mention of the FBI, no official seal, nothing.

Elliot gestured to the men standing by the door, and one of them handed him a copy of the *Sarasota Herald* that he'd been holding under his arm. He snapped the paper open and handed that to Jess, too.

"Serial Killer Death Count: Fifteen," announced the headline.

"Another victim," Elliot said. "Fifteen women. God only knows the horrors they endured before he killed them." He held on to the paper for a second or two after she'd reached up for it. "I know you don't want to inconvenience your friends, Ms. Baxter, but keep in mind every day you delay helping us could mean another woman's life.

"I want to catch this man," he added, his voice soft but deadly. "I *am* going to catch this man. And I think you can help."

Jess stared blindly down at the newspaper.

"I'm going to have to ask you to keep our conversation confidential," Elliot continued. "If this man gets wind of our investigation, he won't stick around and wait for us to catch him."

Confidential? Jess looked up at him.

"I'm asking you not to tell anyone of this visit," Elliot said, his gray eyes nearly drilling into her with their intensity. "Not *any*one. Do you understand?"

Jess met his eyes steadily. Yes, she *did* understand. "I have no intention of lying to any of my friends."

"I'm not asking you to lie," Elliot said. "Just…don't bring the subject up." He flipped his notebook open again. "I need your phone number. It was unlisted."

"Don't tell me the FBI doesn't have access to unlisted phone numbers," Jess said.

Elliot gazed at her expressionlessly. "Of course we do," he said. "But it's much easier to get it this way."

Jess gave him her phone number and watched as he wrote it into his notebook. He was a lefty, she noticed, and that really surprised her. He seemed so totally right-wing, by-the-book, that it didn't seem possible he could have come out of the FBI agent mold with a deviation from the norm.

"Any other numbers where you can be reached? Work number?"

"No, I work at home," she said.

"Any plans to be out of town?" he asked.

Jess shrugged. "I don't have any gigs scheduled for the next few days, but I'll give you the number of my parent's beach house on Siesta Key. If a job comes up out there, that's where I'll be."

He wrote down that number, too, then shut his notebook, slipping both it and his pen back into his breast pocket. He fixed her with one last piercing look before he turned toward the door. "I'll be in touch."

ROB DROVE AROUND the block five times before pulling into the driveway.

It was late, nearly midnight.

He drove around for hours after work, trying to clear his head, trying to figure out what the hell he was going to do.

He knew he shouldn't go back to Jess's house.

He knew he should get a room at one of those cheap motels off Route 75.

He knew he shouldn't subject himself to any more of her sweet temptation.

Last night had been mind-blowing. He couldn't have stayed away from her if his life had been at stake.

But his life was worthless. It was Jess's life he was playing games with.

He'd decided, somewhere out near University Boulevard, that he would just never go back. To hell with his clothes and the other things he had in the apartment. He'd leave 'em. He'd leave it all—including his job. He'd leave town. Tomorrow morning he'd be nothing but a bad memory.

He'd send Jess some money to cover the rent for the rest of the year, and that would be that.

Eventually, she'd forget about him.

Eventually, he'd forget about her—yeah, like when he finally died. No, the truth was that her sweet smile and mysterious dark eyes were going to stay with him for the rest of his sorry life.

It wasn't fair—but it was the right thing to do.

So why did he end up back here in Jess's neighborhood, circling her house? Why did he pull into the driveway and cut the engine of his car? Why did he get out and walk up those wooden steps to the back deck?

Once there he had no choice. He had to knock on Jess's kitchen door.

The curtains moved, and then the door swung open.

She was wearing a bathrobe. Her hair was damp around the edges, as if she had just taken a shower. She looked otherworldly, angelic. Her dark eyes and hair were a perfect contrast to the white of her bathrobe. The neckline dipped down between her breasts, and he knew that she was wearing nothing else. She made no move to adjust the lapels. She just looked at him.

Rob could feel his hunger for her stretched tightly across his face, burning in his eyes, in his soul.

"I shouldn't be here," he rasped. Something was wrong with his voice—it wouldn't come out louder than a harsh whisper.

"Then why did you come?" she asked.

"Because I can't stay away."

He could see the gladness, the triumph, shining in her eyes, and he knew that he had given her false hope. He couldn't stay away tonight, but sooner or later he would have to leave.

She stepped back, letting him into the kitchen.

Rob could smell the faint scent of ginger. Jess and Kelsey had probably baked gingerbread after dinner. The kitchen smelled like home—a real, wonderful, lived in, delicious, loving home. It smelled safe and secure.

But that was just an illusion. There was nowhere Rob could go that was truly safe or secure.

Still, he followed Jess inside and watched as she locked the door behind him. She pushed the curtains back in place and turned to look at him.

She held out her arms, and he lunged for her. He kissed her, on the mouth, on the face, on her long, slender neck, pulling her in tightly to him.

"Oh, Jess," he whispered, delirious from the sensation of her soft body pressed against his. "Jess."

The belt of her robe was only loosely tied, and he yanked it open. He slipped his hands inside her robe, half-mad from the feel of her smooth, clean skin.

She moved away, clasping her robe together with one hand as she pulled him with the other down the hallway to the dimness of her bedroom.

She locked that door behind them, too, and opened her robe. It slid down, off her shoulders, and puddled onto the floor.

Jess was naked, and so beautiful Rob could barely breathe.

He had to touch her. His hands swept across her body and she kissed him and molded herself against him.

He'd never wanted a woman the way he wanted Jess. He'd never felt this uncontrollable desire, this feverish need.

He felt her hands unbuttoning his shirt as he fumbled with his belt and fly.

He had to have her *now*.

Somehow he remembered protection. Somehow he managed to cover himself with a condom before pulling her up into his arms and plunging deep inside of her.

He heard her cry out with pleasure, felt her legs lock around him as she threw her head back. She rode him wildly, meeting each of his desperate thrusts with a downward motion that drove him closer and closer to sheer annihilation.

He felt her release, felt it grow and consume her. She kissed him hard on the mouth, trying to muffle her cries of pleasure. Still she moaned—soft keening sounds from back in her throat.

It pushed Rob over the edge. He exploded in a flash of brilliant light, a mushroom cloud of sensation and pleasure, scorching him, burning him, branding him with Jess's scent, her smile, her liquid heat forever.

ROB CAME OUT OF THE shower, toweling his hair dry. "Your bathroom window was unlocked," he said to Jess.

"I had it open earlier today. Before it turned humid, it was cool enough to have the air conditioner off and—"

"You've *got* to keep the windows locked," Rob interrupted. "Especially at night. It's not safe."

"I thought it was locked," Jess said. "I'm sorry."

"Did you ever call the police about that guy—the bartender—you thought was following you?" he asked.

The bartender. Pete, who in reality was FBI agent Parker Elliot, who thought Jess was somehow linked to the Sarasota Serial Killer, who had warned her not to tell anyone, *anyone*, of his suspicions.

Short of an out-and-out lie, Jess didn't know what to say. "No," she said. "I . . . haven't seen Pete in a long time." It wasn't a lie, but it wasn't exactly the truth, either.

"When Frank gets back from Atlanta, I'm going to ask him to stay in the apartment again—until you find another tenant," Rob said.

Jess couldn't hide her surprise. "Frank Madsen?" she asked.

Rob wouldn't meet her eyes. "Yeah."

Jess was silent, remembering Rob's outburst of jealousy over Frank at the Rose Café.

"Frank will stick around if you want him to," Rob said quietly. "He's not a bad guy."

"My Lord," Jess finally said. "I can't believe you're doing this."

"I want you to be safe."

"I don't need a man around to be safe," Jess countered.

"It would make me feel better," Rob said. "Knowing that—"

"It would make *you* feel better?" Jess repeated. "You're the one who's walking away. If you're that worried about me, stay and 'protect' me yourself."

"I can't." Rob reached for his clothes, but Jess pulled them off the bed and held them, as if they were hostages, in her arms. He met her gaze steadily, and she could read sadness and resignation in his eyes. He was going to tell her goodbye again.

"I should go," he said quietly.

"You should stay." She couldn't keep her pain from cracking her voice. "Stay with me tonight."

He sat down next to her on the bed, as if he were suddenly weary. "I can't."

"All these things you say you can't do," Jess said. "I say that you can."

He turned to look at her and his eyes held a profound sadness. "I *can* stay the night," he conceded, "but I can't stay forever. I want to, but I can't." He closed his eyes briefly as if gathering his strength—or his courage. "Jess, I've done some terrible things. Things that can't be forgiven."

The Sarasota Serial Killer is white, male, twenty-five to forty-five years old, upper middle class....

Jess shook her head, willing the echo of Parker Elliot's voice from her head. Rob *wasn't* the man the FBI was looking for. He couldn't possibly be.

"Tell me," she said, her heart in her throat. What had Rob done that was so terrible?

"I can't."

Another "can't." "Yes, you can," she said in frustration. "Just open your mouth and *tell* me—"

"I *can't!*" Rob's voice rose in a flare of desperation and anger. Jess couldn't help but flinch. "I'm sorry," he said right away. "I didn't...mean to shout. I just...can't stand this any more than you can. It's killing me, Jess."

He travels frequently, keeps a low profile, blends easily into a crowd.... Parker Elliot's description was of Rob. It fit him perfectly.

Rob leaned forward, resting his elbows on his knees and his head in his hands. He held on to the top of his head as if to keep it from flying off. His shoulders were tense, his entire body tight. He looked miserable, a picture of anguish.

But he wasn't a serial killer. Jess didn't believe that. She *couldn't* believe that. Still, he *was* a man in pain. Whatever it was that he'd done in the past, it was clearly tormenting him. Jess felt her eyes fill with tears. Whatever it was that he'd done, how could he absolve himself unless he talked about it?

Jess touched Rob lightly on the shoulder. "When you're ready to talk about it," she said softly, "I'll be ready to forgive you."

He turned to her with a sound that was half laughter, half sob, and pulled her into his arms, burying his face in her neck. "God, what did I do to deserve you?"

Jess held him tightly, stroking the softness of his hair, rocking slightly, trying as hard as she could to comfort him and to take away his pain.

But he pulled back. "But that's just it, isn't it?" he said. His eyes looked red and tired. "I *don't* deserve you, so I have to give you up. I'm paying for my sins. I can leave and hate myself for the rest of my life, or I can stay and put you in danger."

"Danger?"

Rob gazed at her, as if debating whether or not to explain. "There are people looking for me," he finally said. "I can't let them find me."

Serial killers often feel inadequate, and as a result are paranoid. Someone or something is out to get them.

Jess's heart was back in her throat. Paranoia wasn't quite so easy to shrug off as those other, vague descriptions. For the first time, she couldn't simply dismiss the FBI agent's words.

"Who are these people?" she asked Rob. "Why do they want to find you?"

He just shook his head.

"You're a computer programmer, Rob. That's not exactly a hazardous job these days. I don't understand—"

"I've already told you too much." His voice was clipped, his face closed.

"Please—"

He stood up, his back stiff and angry. "Look, I'm sorry." He took a deep breath, letting it out slowly, as he rubbed his neck in an attempt to release his tension. "I'm leaving town," he said.

Jess felt as if she'd been punched in the stomach. "Another business trip?" she asked, hoping, *praying* she'd misunderstood.

But he shook his head, no. "I'm giving notice at work tomorrow. I'll leave as soon as they can replace me."

Jess's heart shattered. "Just like that?" she asked. "It's that easy for you to walk away?"

"No," he said. "It's not easy. But it would be far harder to stay. Jess, I can't explain."

Rob wasn't a serial killer. He was just a man with too many secrets—a man who had made her fall in love with him, someone who now was going to leave without telling her why.

"Why?" she asked, the word slipping out along with the single tear that rolled down her cheek. She wiped at the tear, but she couldn't make the question she'd asked disappear. It didn't matter. Rob wouldn't answer it anyway.

But he did. He turned to her, and with tears in his own eyes, he told her why.

"Because I love you," he said quietly. "I have to leave because I love you, Jess. I won't let you be hurt . . . or killed."

Hope flickered to life and began to thaw the frozen ache in Jess's heart. He loved her. Rob loved her, and Lord help her, she loved him. When there was love, there was always a way.

"Please," she said, holding out her hands to him. "Stay with me tonight. Stay with me . . . until you have to leave, until they replace you at work . . ."

He smiled, but it was another sad smile. "You think you'll be able to change my mind."

"I'm going to try."

Rob shook his head, his smile fading. "It's not a good idea."

"You think maybe I'll succeed."

"No. You'll be disappointed. I'll be gone and—"

"You'll be gone and at least I'll know I tried in every way that I could to convince you to stay," Jess declared. "At least I'll know I did all that I could, instead of just curling up and letting you walk away!"

Rob was silent.

"At least I'll have this time with you," she said, softer now. "At least I'll have the memories of that."

She could see the indecision on his face. Indecision and heartache.

"You told me you couldn't make me any promises," Jess continued, "but you were wrong. You can. You can promise me two things."

"I don't think—"

"Promise you'll stay here with me and Kelsey until you have to leave," she said. "Three or four days, Rob. A week at the most, right? That's not too much to ask, is it?"

He was silent for a long time. Finally he nodded. "No, it's not."

"Promise?" she asked.

"I promise," he said. "If you promise no more questions. No asking why."

Jess hesitated only a second. "All right. I promise, too." She paused. "The second promise is just as easy."

"That first promise isn't easy," Rob said hotly. "I can't promise you anything else."

"Promise me that if you *do* have to leave—"

"Jess, I'm going to leave. Whatever you think, you're not going to talk me into—"

"Promise me that if whatever you're running from, whatever this danger is that you're afraid of... Promise me that if it ever gets settled, if you're ever free... Promise you'll come and find me."

Rob pulled her into his arms and kissed her fiercely. "That's something I'll promise you with all my heart."

Chapter Twelve

Jess woke up with Rob's arms still around her. She didn't move for many long minutes, didn't even dare to open her eyes. She simply lay there, listening to the slow, steady rhythm of his breathing, feeling the warmth of his body pressed against hers, the weight of his arm thrown possessively across her.

Slowly, she opened her eyes. The shades were pulled down, and her bedroom was dim. But the morning light outlined the edges of the shades, and her digital clock switched from 8:16 to 8:17, a not-so-subtle reminder that the night had ended, and a new day had begun.

She had expected to wake up alone.

Despite his promise to her, she had expected him to sneak off like a thief in the middle of the night. And this time she had expected him to disappear for good.

Jess turned and looked at Rob. His face was serene and carefree in sleep. His long, thick lashes lay against his tanned cheeks and his lips were parted slightly. Lord, she wanted to kiss those lips.

What had he done that was so terrible? What had he done that made him so afraid? His face looked so innocent, so young as he slept. She tried to picture him robbing a bank, or burglarizing a house. She tried to imagine him in over his head, committing a crime through ignorance or desperation. But she couldn't do it. The images didn't fit.

What could he have possibly done?

The bedroom door swung open, and Jess turned, startled, to see Kelsey standing there.

"I have to get ready for the bus," Kelsey said, her wide, curious eyes missing nothing.

Jess put her finger to her lips. "Close the door," she whispered. "I'll be out in a minute."

She slipped out from Rob's arms without waking him, and pulled on her robe, opening and closing the bedroom door gently behind her.

Kelsey was in her own room, getting dressed for school.

Jess leaned in the doorway. "Kelsey, do you remember what I told you about other people's privacy?"

Kelsey nodded.

"That door was locked. That should have been a clear signal to you that I wanted privacy," Jess said sternly. She hesitated slightly, but then curiosity got the best of her. "How *did* you unlock it, anyway?"

Kelsey crossed to her dresser and picked up a paper clip that had been unbent most of the way. "I just stick this in the little hole in the doorknob," she said, "and the lock pops open."

Jess shook her head. Her daughter, the six-year-old lock picker. "Kelsey, you saw Rob in my room. You know he spent the night with me."

Kelsey nodded slowly.

"I love him," Jess said.

Kelsey nodded again. "I know," she said solemnly. "I do, too."

JESS PULLED HER ROBE more tightly around her as she watched Kelsey's bus drive away.

Turning, she closed the front door and locked it, then stopped.

Rob stood at the entrance to the living room, watching her. His hair was tousled, his face unshaved. He'd pulled on his pants, but nothing else.

He stood perfectly still, except for the rise and fall of his bare chest as he breathed. He wasn't wearing his glasses, and his brown eyes were guarded.

He had secrets he wouldn't share with her. But Jess had her own secrets, too. She wondered if he could see her secrets as clearly—shadowed mysteries and doubts lurking in her eyes.

"I have to go," he finally said.

Jess took a step toward him. "I was hoping...with Kelsey at school..." She nervously moistened her lips with the tip of her tongue and saw Rob's eyes drop down to her mouth. A flare of desire on his face gave her courage to go on. She closed the gap between them, moving so she stood only inches in front of him. But no matter how close she got, all those secrets—his and hers— would still be between them, keeping them apart. Even if they made love, it would be make-believe, their intimacies not completely honest. Still, it didn't make her want to give up that pretense of closeness. "I thought maybe we could make last night go on a little longer," she said. "I thought we could give ourselves this morning."

Standing so close to him was intoxicating. With each breath, she could smell his rich, male scent. She wanted to press herself against him. She wanted to close her eyes and forget about all of the secrets.

"I should be at work," he told her.

"Why?" she asked. "So you can type up a letter of resignation? Can't that wait?"

Their eyes met, and his were hot. Slowly, Jess untied her belt and slid her robe off her shoulders, just like last night. Rob's eyes swept the smooth expanse of her body. With a hand, he reached out and cupped one full breast, his thumb caressing the dark nipple that peaked to a hard bud quickly at his touch.

"I'm already late," he said, his voice husky. "What difference is another few hours going to make...?"

Jess closed her eyes, feeling his lips against hers, his arms around her. With her eyes still closed, she felt him lift her and carry her into the bedroom, placing her gently on the bed. At the sound of his zipper being pulled down, she sat up and watched him, wanting to remember the sight of his pants pushed off his muscular thighs, wanting to see the evidence of his desire for her.

He covered himself and came to her, touching, kissing, caressing, and she pushed him back on the bed, kneeling over him. She could see the pulse in his neck, feel the rapid beating of his heart as he gazed up at her. Did he know that she was hiding her own secrets from him? Did it show in her eyes?

Jess didn't believe that Rob was a serial killer. How could she be here with him, make love to him this way if she thought he was? But why, then, didn't she tell him about her visit from the FBI? Why didn't she tell him that his connection to her automatically made him a suspect?

His hands held her hips, moving her so he could enter her, but she pulled away. So much of her life seemed so crazily out of control, right now she wanted at least the illusion that she was in charge. Rob was going to leave, and when he did, he'd be able to walk away as quickly or as slowly as he wanted. Right now, *she* was going to set the pace.

Last night, each time they'd made love, it had been with explosive, barely restrained passion. This morning they were going to take their time.

She leaned across him, her lips, then her tongue, brushing the soft, round nipples in his muscular chest, making them spring to life at her touch. She could feel his erection against the softness of her stomach, pressing into her, seeking her.

Her mouth moved up his neck, gently, lightly kissing him, and he growled, low in his throat. He took her hips in his hands again, but once more she stopped him.

He looked up at her, and laughed, his smile still not hiding the sadness that never left his eyes. Despite the air-conditioning, sweat gleamed on his forehead, making his hair stick to his face. "You want to hear me beg, don't you?" he whispered, catching his breath as she touched him most intimately.

She smiled back at him. "It couldn't hurt."

He pulled her to him, cupping her face in his hands, bringing her lips to his, kissing slowly, deeply, filling her mouth with his tongue.

"Please," he breathed, his lips against hers. "Please, Jess. I can't wait another second...."

She moved then, on top of him, but slowly, oh, so slowly. She set a rhythm that was languorous, then smiled at the look of intense pleasure on Rob's face.

Like the night before, Jess wouldn't say the words, *I love you*. At least not aloud. But as their eyes met and locked, she was sure that he knew. And for those moments, all of the secrets between them vanished. Her heart merged with Rob's as completely as their bodies were joined, and she knew without the shadow of a doubt that he loved her as she loved him.

He pressed deeply up into her, filling her until they both cried out, their bodies racked with the turbulence of their release. Jess collapsed on Rob, and he clung to her, long after the rush of their pleasure had abated.

With a long sigh, she pushed herself up. He looked at her in silence. She just watched his face, memorizing every little flicker of emotion that appeared. He waited, motionless, as if he, too, were trying to burn her face into his mind's eye. Finally she spoke.

"If you leave," she said softly, but almost defiantly, "I'm going to haunt your dreams."

Rob closed his eyes, but not quickly enough to hide the pain that flashed there. When he looked back up at her, his brown eyes were filled with sorrow. "Oh, sweet," he whispered. "You already do."

WITH A SCREECHING of its suspension system and a hiss of the air brakes, the school bus pulled up to the front of the house. Jess looked up from her guitar, bracing herself for Kelsey to come bursting through the front door, shouting that she was starving and sweating to death and could she have an ice pop, please?

But Kelsey didn't come inside. One minute passed, and then two, and Jess set down her guitar and went to the front door.

It was a breezy day, and she had the air-conditioning off and the windows open. She looked through the screen door and saw Kelsey standing on the front lawn.

Talking to FBI agent Parker Elliot.

"Hey!" Jess said, her voice thick with indignation.

Elliot looked up from where he was squatting next to Kelsey.

Jess pushed open the screen door and came outside. "If you have any questions for Kelsey, you have to ask them in front of me. Isn't there some kind of law about that?"

"We're under certain time pressures, as I'm sure you can imagine," Elliot said, standing up.

"And that gives you the right to break the law?" Jess asked. She turned to Kelsey. "And you, young lady—have you forgotten our rule about talking to strangers?"

"He said he met me at the Pelican Club," Kelsey protested. "He said he *wasn't* a stranger."

Jess shot the FBI agent an incredulous look. But Parker Elliot didn't even have the good grace to look abashed.

"Go inside the house," Jess told Kelsey in a calm voice that belied the fact that her blood was boiling. "Get washed up, and get yourself a snack. I'll be in, in a moment."

"I wanted to talk to you," Elliot started, but Jess didn't let him finish. As soon as the door closed behind Kelsey, she lit into him.

"What could you have *possibly* been thinking?" she asked. "Don't you know how important it is that a child learns to stay away from strangers? Kelsey does *not* need to think that just because she meets someone once, that he's not a stranger—"

"What was I thinking?" Elliot said, his lean face hard. "I was thinking maybe this little girl knows something or has seen something that can help me catch the sonuvabitch who's been killing women in Sarasota for the past six months."

The serial killer.

Since Rob left for work late this morning Jess hadn't thought about much else besides Parker Elliot and his suspicions that the Sarasota Serial Killer was somehow linked to her. She stared at the FBI agent now, silenced by his vehemence.

When he spoke again, his voice was softer. "I apologize for overstepping the boundaries," he said.

Jess nodded. "Apology accepted." She turned to go inside.

"Ms. Baxter."

Jess looked back at Elliot. He was wearing a dark blue business suit. Again, as it was yesterday, his hair was neatly combed, every lock perfectly in place. Dark glasses covered his eyes.

He glanced at his watch. "I asked one of the Bureau's specialists to meet me here," he told her. "I want you to talk to her."

Jess started to shake her head. "You're wasting your time," she said. "I don't know anyone who could possibly be a serial killer."

Except Rob.

Now where did *that* thought come from? It had just popped into her head, unannounced. And it was ridiculous, too. Of course Jess didn't really think that Rob could be the man they were looking for, the man who had brutally murdered all those women. Not after last night. And this morning...

I've done some terrible things, Jess.

"I know that's what you believe, Ms. Baxter," Parker Elliot said evenly, taking off his sunglasses. "That's why I want you to talk to Dr. Haverstein."

His eyes were so piercing, Jess wished he would put the sunglasses back on. "Dr. Who?"

"Dr. Haverstein is a psychologist whose area of expertise involves serial murderers and their victims," he said. "I've asked her to talk to you, to give you a better picture of the man we're looking for. She should be here any minute. May we go inside?"

No. Jess didn't want Parker Elliot and his serial murderer specialist inside her house. She didn't want their questions and insinuations and suspicions. She didn't want to be forced to think about Rob and wonder what this awful thing was that he'd done. It was a thing so haunting he couldn't tell her, something so horrific that there were people after him, hunting him. Or so he believed.

It was driving her nuts. Why wouldn't Rob talk to her, tell her, *explain...?*

Meanwhile, Parker Elliot was standing there, waiting to be invited into her house. Jess knew that the FBI agent wasn't going to go away even if she shut her door in his face. He'd come back, probably with a subpoena, and then she'd have no choice but to talk to him.

"All right," Jess said. She opened the screen door, and Elliot followed her inside. "I need to talk to Kelsey first," she added. "Excuse me for a minute, please."

Kelsey was in the kitchen, sitting at the table, worry creasing her forehead. "I'm sorry, Mommy," she said. "But he said—"

"It's okay," Jess reassured her. "*This* time. But next time a stranger comes up to you, what are you going to do?"

"Say 'Excuse me, I need to get my mom,' and run and find you?" Kelsey said.

Jess kissed her daughter. "Correct for twenty points." She opened the freezer. "How about an ice bar?"

Kelsey nodded, but still didn't smile. "How come that man asked me about Rob?"

Jess froze, staring into the dark, coolness of the freezer. Her blood was running just as cold as the frozen treats she was touching. Parker Elliot had asked Kelsey about *Rob?* She forced herself to move, to breathe, to take out a Popsicle and close the freezer door.

"What did he ask you?" Jess asked, hiding the sudden tension that made her stomach churn. Elliot had asked about *Rob.* She tore off the paper wrapping and handed Kelsey the pop.

"He asked if Rob ever came over—if you and Rob were friends," Kelsey replied, searching Jess's face, her light brown eyes still so worried.

"And you told him yes," Jess said.

"Yeah." Kelsey's face was so anxious. She hadn't even given her pop one single lick. "Was that bad?"

Jess shook her head vehemently. "No, it was good, Kel. You told the truth. It's important always to tell the truth."

"I agree."

Startled, Jess looked up to see Parker Elliot standing in the doorway. "Please," she said coolly. "I'll join you in the living room in a minute."

He nodded and disappeared.

Taking a deep breath, Jess smiled at Kelsey. "We'll talk more later about strangers, okay?" she told her.

Kelsey nodded.

"Now, why don't you take that pop outside before it drips all over the kitchen floor?"

The kitchen screen door bounced shut, even before Jess had finished her sentence.

Taking a deep breath, she turned and went into the living room.

Parker Elliot was sitting casually on the couch.

Except Jess knew he was feeling anything but casual. There was an undercurrent of tension that ran through the man, and it never let up. He could create the illusion of being laid-back by putting his body in relaxed positions, but his eyes were always alert, always watching, picking up every little detail.

"You really think the serial killer might be...someone I know?" Jess couldn't bring herself to use Rob's name, even though Elliot had already asked Kelsey specifically about Rob.

Elliot nodded. "I certainly hope so," he said. "Because right now, you're the only lead we've got."

"If...someone I know...is the killer," Jess said, "then why hasn't he...killed me?"

"There could be a number of reasons," Elliot replied. "But I'm going to wait and let Dr. Haverstein explain. She'll be able to answer all of your questions."

"So that's why you're here?" she asked. "So this doctor can try to talk me into believing that a friend of mine is a serial killer?"

"I'm here because I think you have a solid connection to this man," Elliot finally said. "I want to find him before he kills again, Ms. Baxter. I think you hold the key to his identity. But to be perfectly frank, I'm aware of my limitations, and I feel Dr. Haverstein's presence will aid the questioning process."

"Nicely said."

Jess looked up to see a short, rather stout woman with graying hair smiling gently at her through the screen door.

"I'm Selma Haverstein." The doctor nodded at Parker Elliot as Jess rose to her feet and opened the door. "Hello, Parker dear."

Elliot started to stand as the older woman came inside. "Selma."

"Oh, don't stand. If I know you, you've been on your feet for the past thirty-odd hours." Dr. Haverstein put several paper bags on the coffee table and joined Elliot on the couch. "I brought some coffee and donuts with me," she explained as she began to unpack paper cups with lids from one of the bags. "Would you like some coffee, dear?" This last was directed to Jess.

Jess shook her head, no.

Dr. Haverstein was wearing a dress with a long, flowing skirt that reached almost to the floor. It spread around her on the couch like the gown of a queen. As Jess watched, she handed a paper cup of coffee to Elliot, then peeked into the smaller bag. "Jelly, cruller, cream-filled or honey-dipped," she said, turning to Jess. "You pick first, dear."

"No, thank you, I'm not hungry."

Dr. Haverstein looked at Elliot. "Did you have lunch?"

"I'll take the jelly donut," he said.

"You didn't, did you?" She sighed with exasperation, and looked at Jess as she said, "He's going to eat this on an empty stomach, and in about twenty minutes he's going to be very cranky from all that sugar. Just watch."

Elliot flashed Dr. Haverstein a smile. "If I get cranky, Selma, you have permission to say 'I told you so.'"

Selma gazed at Jess. The young woman really *was* as lovely as Parker Elliot had said, and she felt a flash of disappointment. Parker had used words like *gorgeous,* and *luminous* to describe her eyes, and Selma had thought perhaps the young FBI agent was infatuated with this girl. She sighed. No such luck. What she'd taken for romantic description had been mere facts. She was beginning to think maybe Parker *wasn't* human, after all.... Except they *had* spent an awfully long time last night discussing the color of Jess's underwear.

Selma smiled as she remembered Parker asking her what she thought about the fact that Jess had been wearing a green bra.

"You mean, like is she a member of the Green Bra Brigade?" she'd asked him back.

He'd looked at her blankly until he realized she was joking. Then he laughed. "Very funny, Selma. But I'm serious," he had said, waiting patiently until she'd finished chuckling. "I mean, red or black lingerie," he'd added, "implies a certain moral—"

She had swiftly cut him off. "Don't you *dare* go Stone Age on me, Parker dear. These are the 1990s. Women can wear whatever color underwear they want. Do you know why this young woman was wearing a green bra?"

"That's what I've been trying to get you to tell me."

"I'd guess one of two reasons. Either she happens to like green, or it was on the sale rack in the store. A bargain's a bargain, whatever the color."

Jess became aware that the older woman was looking at her, scrutinizing her, from the top of her short, dark hair, to her sleeveless red T-shirt, her worn-out denim miniskirt, her unstockinged tanned legs, red sport socks and white sneakers.

But Selma Haverstein's eyes were gentle, warm, and she smiled kindly at Jess. "You *are* very pretty, dear," she said. "How long have you worn your hair in that style?"

Jess looked at Elliot. "What is it with my hair?" she asked. "I've worn it this way, I don't know, two years? Maybe longer. Since my divorce, actually."

Dr. Haverstein nodded. "Uh-huh." She took a big sip of her coffee. "One of the reasons I'm here, dear, is because we know how very difficult it is for you to believe that a friend of yours could be a serial killer."

"Yeah, you're right," Jess said, crossing her arms. "I *don't* believe it. I *won't* believe it."

The doctor nodded again. "I'm going to start by describing a man I met once. He was handsome, strong, clean. He dressed well, he held down a job, did volunteer work for the community. People who knew him described him as friendly, maybe a little on the quiet side. What they didn't know about him was that every two or three weeks, he would follow a pretty young woman, charm her, drive her to a secluded spot, rape her and kill her." Selma took another sip of coffee. "Sometimes he'd kill her first, then have sex with the body."

Sickened, Jess closed her eyes.

"I want to talk to you this afternoon about your friend Rob," Selma continued.

No. Not Rob. Jess's heart was pounding and she felt herself start to sweat. Still, she forced herself to speak calmly. "Rob's *not* a killer. Not Rob."

Selma sighed and took a file from her briefcase. "That's what this other man's friends said. 'Not George.' I met him on death row, here in Florida. He confessed to countless murders. Perhaps you've heard of him—George Franklin? Also known as the Ocala Killer?"

"Of course I have," Jess said. "But—"

Selma opened her file. "Your friend Rob fits our description of the Sarasota killer pretty accurately," she said. "He's the right age, the right social class. He's not flashy or loud—he doesn't let himself stand out in a crowd. And according to your neighbors, even though he's only been your tenant for a few weeks, he's lived in the neighborhood for the past six or so months. He's been seen frequently at your performances...."

She paused, looking through her notes. When she looked back at Jess, she smiled kindly. "I know this can't be easy for you. But perhaps you can help fill out our file on him. Did he talk to you at all about his childhood?"

Jess hesitated. "His mother died when he was about six, and his father, I guess, wasn't...very nice."

Selma exchanged another look with Elliot and Jess knew that she had given them more fuel for their fire, despite her vague description of Rob's father.

Parker Elliot sat forward. "Serial killers generally come from abusive households. They grow up in an atmosphere of anger and violence."

"Rob hasn't told me *that* much about his childhood," Jess said stiffly.

My father was a beast, and it's his blood in my veins....

"Sometimes neglect is enough to trigger the social aberrations that—"

Jess glared at Elliot. "I'm sorry, I just don't buy it," she said, cutting him off. "All abused or neglected children couldn't possibly become serial killers."

"Good thing," Selma said calmly as she jotted down some notes. "Let's get back to Rob. Did he say anything else about his mother? Was he angry with her?"

"No," Jess said, annoyance in her voice and in her eyes. "He wasn't *angry* with her."

Dr. Haverstein looked up, her face crinkling apologetically. "I know. I'm sorry. I hate having to ask questions like that. It always makes me feel like a cartoon caricature of a shrink." She adopted a thick German accent. "'Vat did he say about his mutter?'" She smiled wryly at Jess, and went on in her regular voice. "This *is* important, though. Think hard. If you can remember what he said word for word, that's even better."

"He said he loved his mother more than anyone or anything—I can't remember which—in the world. He said..." She looked down at her hands.

"Go on," Haverstein urged. "Jess, you're not betraying him by telling us this. You're *helping* him. If he *is* the killer, he needs to be stopped. He *wants* to be stopped."

Jess took a deep breath, glancing over at Elliot. He was watching her steadily, sitting absolutely still, like a powerful animal about to pounce on its prey.

"He said I reminded him of her," she said. "That I wore my hair sort of the same way she did. But he said it was more than the way I looked—it was the way I treat Kelsey, the way I love my daughter."

Dr. Haverstein had stopped writing and was looking at Parker Elliot.

Elliot finally moved, glancing at Selma and nodding. "Bingo," he said.

Chapter Thirteen

"What?" Jess asked, looking from the FBI agent to the psychologist. "Bingo...what? Because I remind Rob of his mother, that makes you think he's the killer?"

Dr. Haverstein turned her warm eyes back to Jess. "A few more questions, then I'll explain. Tell me about your relationship with Rob."

Jess shifted in her chair. "I don't know what you mean," she hedged. "There's nothing to tell."

"You just said that you reminded him of his mother, whom he loved very deeply. Does Rob love you?" Dr. Haverstein's voice was calm, soothing.

"I don't see what that has to do with—"

"Oh, but it does." The psychologist nodded, wide-eyed. "If Rob has decided that you are an appropriate substitute for his mother—"

"Oh, come on," Jess said, skepticism in her voice.

Elliot cleared his throat. "Dr. Haverstein holds three different doctorate degrees," he informed her. "All of her studies have focused on serial killers—who they are, what makes them the way they are, how they behave. Maybe you should start listening to what she's saying, Ms. Baxter, instead of rejecting it out of hand because it doesn't fit the way you want the world to be."

Selma made tsking sounds at Elliot. "I *told* you the sugar would make you cranky, Parker," she said calmly. "Why don't you go away, dear, and stop glowering at us that way?"

"I'm not glowering, Selma."

"Maybe not externally," Haverstein replied with a sweet smile. "But internally you're in a positive snit. Go on. Shoo."

Parker Elliot stood up, his gaze lingering on Jess. He opened his notebook and wrote a brief note, then tore out the page, folded it, and handed it to Selma Haverstein. "I'll meet you back at the office." He looked at Jess again. "Thank you for your cooperation, Ms. Baxter. Again, I'd like to stress the importance of your keeping this information confidential. Don't tell anyone that you've been talking to us. Particularly not Carpenter. Do you understand?"

Don't tell Rob that he was the FBI's main suspect in the Sarasota Serial Killer investigation?

"I'm sure she understands, Parker," Selma stated calmly. "Goodbye, dear."

She waited until the FBI agent went out the door and closed it tightly behind him. Then she glanced at Elliot's note, folded it again and put it in her file.

"So. Rob loves you," she said to Jess.

Jess shook her head. "I didn't say that."

"You didn't have to. You also don't have to tell me that *you* love *him*. I can tell that quite clearly from the way you sit, the way you react when he's mentioned, from a dozen different things. What we need to talk about, dear, is sex."

Jess stood up and started to pace. "This is unbelievable. Do I *have* to answer your questions? Am I allowed to ask you to leave?"

"Well," Selma said slowly, "I suppose you could refuse to cooperate. At that point, Parker would get an order for you to appear in court, whereupon you'd be asked these same questions in front of a large group of people. It's easier for both of us this way."

"But answering these questions here like this," Jess argued, "just gives me the illusion of privacy. I'm well aware that every word I say is going to show up in some report that dozens, Lord, maybe even *hundreds* of people are going to read."

"I can't deny that," Selma admitted.

"I can't believe Rob is the man you're looking for," Jess insisted. "I'm sorry, I just don't buy it. He's *not* a killer. Maybe you should investigate my next-door neighbor. Stanford Greene. Or... or... my ex-husband. Ian Davis. *He's* been acting peculiar lately—and he's never been particularly stable to start with. Why don't you go check *him* out?"

"I'll make you a deal," Selma said, folding her hands over her pad. "Sit back down, and answer my questions, and then I'll tell you my theory. I'll tell you why, from just the little bit of information you've given me today, I'm more convinced than ever that Robert Carpenter is the Sarasota killer."

Jess sighed, then slowly sat back down. "It's a deal."

Selma took a deep breath, glancing down at her pad. "First question. When did you first have sexual intercourse with Rob?"

Jess shook her head, hiding her indignation under a very calm voice. "Shouldn't the first question be, 'Have I ever had sex with Rob?'"

"We already know that you have," the doctor said, with an apologetic smile. She took out the note that Elliot had given her and waved it at Jess. "Apparently Parker asked your daughter if Rob ever spent the night with you, if she ever saw him in your bed."

Jess closed her eyes. This was a nightmare. "What kind of man pumps a six-year-old child for information like that?"

"The kind of man who wants to stop a vicious serial killer," Selma replied calmly.

"It was just a few weeks ago," Jess said with a sigh, answering the psychologist's question. "The first time was just a few weeks ago."

Dr. Haverstein made a note on her pad. "Actually, that makes me change my theory a bit." She looked up. "But only a bit. Tell me about before that. He moved in as your tenant...when?"

"A few weeks before that."

"But you knew him from the neighborhood?"

"Yes."

"And it wasn't until he moved in as your tenant that he started making, um, shall we call them amorous advances toward you?"

"He didn't."

Selma looked up. "But..."

"*I* made the advances. I invited him out to the Key. I had a gig out there and—"

"The Key?"

"Siesta Key."

"When was that exactly?"

Jess told her the date.

Selma reacted. "How many days were you there?"

"We went out that evening, came back that night. But that wasn't when we—" Jess cleared her throat "—made love. That happened a few days later."

"You're aware that there was a murder on Siesta Key that same night?"

"Yes," Jess answered. "I read about it in the paper."

"I suppose this supports our theory about a copycat killer," Selma said, more to herself than Jess. "If Rob was with you all night..."

"He wasn't," Jess stated flatly.

"Oh, dear."

"We...kissed goodbye in the parking lot of the Pelican Club at around one, maybe a little later. He had his own car."

"Oh, dear."

"He's *not* the killer."

"I know you think that, Jess," Selma said in her best professional voice. "Please, try to be patient."

Jess sat back in the easy chair, gripping the armrests with her hands. She waited for Dr. Haverstein to continue.

"Then, how many days later did you and he...?" Selma let her voice trail off delicately.

"Three," Jess replied. "The night of the storm."

"There was another murder that night," Selma continued, reviewing her notes. "Did he stay with you *that* night?"

"No," Jess said shortly. "He didn't. The only time he's ever spent the entire night was last night."

"During which there *wasn't* a murder," Selma remarked. She made more notes on her paper, then looked up. "I don't suppose you'd want to go into specifics about the sexual act...?"

Jess put her head into her hands.

"No, okay, I understand. It would be helpful, however, to know...well, for instance...did he have problems maintaining an erection...or achieving orgasm?"

"No," Jess told her in a very choked voice, her hands still covering her face.

"Thank you, dear, I know that was very difficult for you," Selma said soothingly. "If it's any consolation, it's a point in Rob's favor. You see, serial killers often only achieve sexual release from the act of killing. But there's no absolute rule or standard, unfortunately. I've seen cases where the killer has an absolutely normal home life, a wife, children even. His family doesn't have a clue that he's on an extremely cyclical schedule of killing."

In a sudden flash of memory, Jess saw Rob as she'd seen him the night of the blackout, the night they'd first made love. He'd stood in the bedroom of his apartment, lit by lightning, his knife in his hand, his face contorted in almost inhuman rage....

"No," she said.

But she remembered him out on the street, the night that her car broke down. He'd flicked his wrist and his knife had appeared in his hand. He had stepped toward her, his eyes wild....

"No," she said again.

"It's important for you to realize that if Rob turns out to be Sarasota's serial killer," Selma added, "it's in no way a reflection on you, on the type of person you are. Do you understand that?"

"Rob's not the killer," Jess declared, but even to her own ears, her voice sounded less certain.

"Dear, you are *very* stubborn." Selma sighed. "All right, you want to hear my theory?"

"No." Jess clenched her teeth. "Dammit. Yes."

Selma Haverstein laughed. "I like your honesty, dear. Try to hear me out, okay?"

Jess nodded.

"When Rob was six, his mother died, in a sense deserting him. His father, as you said, was abusive, and we can only guess what horrors the child endured. It would be quite natural for a child, any youngster in fact, to grow to resent, and maybe even hate the mother who left him to a world of pain and suffering.

"Yet at the same time, there are feelings of guilt, for a child who loses his mother at the age of six would certainly be old enough to have vivid memories of the mother's love and caring. So the child grows up, beaten, perhaps even sexually abused, with feelings of worthlessness and self-loathing, and a great rage, a tremendous anger toward his mother, topped off with guilt about that anger that makes him hate himself even more.

"The child becomes a man, and his self-loathing grows. He feels inadequate, particularly in his relationships with women."

"Which brings us to six months ago," Dr. Haverstein said, "when Rob moves to Sarasota and meets you. You are, in a very real sense, his mother all over again. Naturally, he adores you, and even more, he despises you. Except now there's a twist. He wants you sexually. But you represent his mother, and, because reality and fantasy are so easily confused in the mind of a serial killer, perhaps you have even *become* his mother to him."

"I can't believe I'm sitting here listening to this," Jess whispered. "I just can't believe it."

"Every time he has strong feelings of lust for you, the cycle of self-loathing and anger starts, and he kills you."

Jess looked up, shocked.

"Not exactly you, of course, though at times it might seem like that to him."

"All those women who were killed," Jess said, her eyes wide with horror. "You think they were supposed to be *me?*"

"It's a little more complicated than that, but, in a sense, yes."

Jess felt almost light-headed and dizzy. "But that's just your theory," she finally said. "It's just a guess, right?"

Selma nodded. "But it *is* a pattern we've seen before."

Jess was silent.

"You need to think about all of this," Selma concluded, putting her file back into her briefcase and gathering up the coffee cups and the donut bag. "I'll leave you my card here on the table—call me anytime. Day or night. For any reason at all." Selma stood up. "I'll just let myself out."

As Jess watched, the older woman crossed to the door.

"Thank you again, for your cooperation, dear—"

"Do you really think it's Rob? Not someone else?" Jess stood up.

Selma turned slowly around. Her eyes looked so sympathetic and kind. "It's too early to say for sure."

"Am I . . . Do you think that I . . . might be in danger?"

"We can arrange for surveillance," Selma replied. "We can wire your house for sound. That way the agents who are watching will hear everything that goes on inside—"

"No," Jess said, hugging her arms to herself. It was odd, in this heat, to feel so chilled. "I don't want that. I don't want people watching, either."

"I'm afraid you don't have a choice about *that,*" Selma said apologetically. "We've already got a surveillance team following Rob."

"Oh, Lord." Jess turned away. She felt like crying. Or finding Rob and demanding that he tell her the truth. What had he done? What was he running from? He wasn't a killer. He *couldn't* be. Could he?

"You asked me if I think you're in danger," Selma said quietly. "I don't know, Jess. But I'll tell you one thing. If I were you, you wouldn't find *me* inviting Rob Carpenter into my house—or my bed—tonight."

Chapter Fourteen

Ian Davis.

Jess kept on coming back to her ex-husband's name.

She'd spent the entire afternoon making a list of serial killer suspects.

Because maybe Parker Elliot was right. Maybe the serial killer *was* someone Jess knew. But she knew many more men than Rob. Why should his be the only name on the list?

Jess had dropped Kelsey off at Doris's house, and now sat out on the deck filling a sheet of paper with names.

Ian was at the top of the list, along with creepy Stanford Greene.

All of the fathers of her twenty-seven piano and guitar students went down onto the paper. Lenny Freeman, the manager of the Pelican Club was there, along with her professor from that music theory class she took last year.

Frank Madsen was on the list, too. He was as ridiculous a suspect as Rob. As silly as just about *any* of the names on this list.

And as long as she was being absurd, why not Parker Elliot? An FBI agent would have the perfect cover. No one would *ever* suspect him of being a serial killer.

Yeah, right.

But there was Ian.

Seven years ago, when she'd first met him, Jess would have been wildly amused at the outlandish idea that the concert violinist might be a killer. Charming, mercurial, creative, handsome Ian Davis might have been temperamental and intense, but he was no killer. A lady-killer, perhaps, but that was very different. It was only after they were married that Jess started to see Ian's darker side, his depression, his jealousy, his deep fear of failure, his barely controllable anger. Such powerful anger. What she had always thought was creative intensity, artistic fire, was in truth a deeply burning rage. He was angry at the world. Mad at his domineering parents, furious at the conductors who held him back, disgruntled at the rules and laws that restricted him as if he were some ordinary, normal, *mundane* person, angry at Jess—always and forever angry at Jess.

He'd been angry at her for marrying him, for tying him down with a wife and a child despite the fact that he had courted her mercilessly, almost desperately, for months. And he'd been livid at Jess for divorcing him, for leaving him alone again. He claimed he still wanted her, but she knew it was far more likely that he only wanted what he could not have.

Ian's anger had moved closer to the surface over the past several years. He drank more and more often. His social facade and charm seemed almost brittle when Jess saw him, his trademark sarcasm more biting. He looked unhealthy and pale, as if he spent far too little time in the sun.

Was it possible that Ian had finally snapped? Had he lost all reason and turned to murder for his relief?

Jess had called the number on the card Parker Elliot had given her and told him about Ian. The FBI agent had listened politely. He'd said they'd look into it after they followed up on their current lead, but Jess had come away from the phone call with the idea that Elliot hadn't really taken her seriously.

What if it *was* Ian? Was she in danger? Was *Kelsey* in danger...?

"Jess."

She looked up, startled, to see Rob standing at the top of the stairs. "Hi." She quickly, guiltily, closed her notebook. "I didn't hear your car," she said.

He crossed to the table and sat down across from her. "That's because I didn't drive."

"Don't tell me you lent your car to Ian again."

"No." His voice was quiet, his face serious. "I gave notice at work and they asked me to turn my car in immediately. It was company owned."

"I didn't know that," Jess said. Did this mean he was free to leave? Panic made her heart start to pound. Had he only come back here to tell her goodbye?

"I still have to go in to the office for the next few days," Rob told her, "to make sure the files are up-to-date on the projects I was working on."

Jess nodded with relief. He'd stay at least another few days.

"But I'll be done by Friday at the latest," Rob told her. "And then . . ."

He fell silent, just gazing across the table at her.

What had he done, that he felt he had to leave like this?

But Jess couldn't ask. As much as she wanted to, as badly as she *needed* to ask, she couldn't. She'd promised Rob she wouldn't. No questions.

He couldn't be a serial killer, could he? She would somehow know if he was, wouldn't she?

Was it possible that these average brown eyes she was staring into belonged to a cold-blooded murderer? Was it possible that a man who could make love to her so impossibly tenderly could turn around and cut another woman's throat?

No.

Jess wanted to think not.

But everything that Parker Elliot and Selma Haverstein had told her undermined her confidence.

If I were you, you wouldn't find me inviting Rob Carpenter into my house—or my bed—tonight.

Was Rob a killer? The truth was, Jess wasn't one hundred percent certain that he wasn't.

"I can give you a ride to work tomorrow," Jess said, breaking the silence, "if you want."

Rob shook his head. "I can get a cab."

He knew something was different. He suspected that something was wrong. Jess could see questions in Rob's eyes.

"Where's Bug?" he asked.

"She's at Doris's for the afternoon," Jess said. "I have to pick her up in a few hours. Before seven."

He nodded down at the notebook that rested on the table in front of her. "What are you doing?"

Jess stared back at him. What was she doing? What could she tell him? "Nothing, really . . ."

"Are you writing a song?"

It would be easiest just to say yes. "Yeah," Jess said. It was easier, but it was also a lie. How had she ever become involved in this? How had she let herself become a part of this deceit?

She should demand answers from Rob. And if he couldn't give her those answers, she should let him go and be glad that he was leaving. There was no room for secrets and lies and deception in her life.

She'd had enough of that with Ian.

Ian.

Unless Ian had changed the lock on his condo door in the past few weeks, Jess still had the key to his place. At this time of year, her ex-husband had orchestra performances every evening. She could use the key, sneak into his apartment and search for . . . what? *Some*thing that would make Parker Elliot sit up and take notice. Some kind of incriminating evidence. A murder weapon. Bloodstains on his clothes. Lord knows Ian hated to do laundry. If he'd gotten blood on his clothes, it would be there still, in a pile on his bedroom floor.

Whatever the evidence was, when Jess found it, she'd know for sure that Ian was the serial killer. It was an awful idea—Kelsey's father a killer. But if he was, he had to be stopped.

ROB STARED AT JESS in disbelief as she rummaged through a junk drawer in her kitchen. "This is *nuts*," he told her.

"I'm not asking for your help." She paused from her search to glance up at him. "Although you're welcome to come along."

"To break and enter your ex-husband's condo to prove that he's a serial killer," Rob said flatly. "Jess, you've got to admit that the idea is a little out there—"

"It's not breaking and entering," Jess argued, finally unearthing a key on a Betty Boop key chain and holding it up for Rob to see. "Ian gave me his key."

"I don't think he meant for you to use it like this, with me tagging along as you search for evidence that will send him to the electric chair," Rob said. He followed her down the hall to her bedroom, and watched as she gathered up her purse and sat on her bed to slip a pair of sandals on her feet. "I think he probably had something else in mind."

Jess looked up at him then. Her brown eyes were so dark and so determined. "What if he's the killer, Rob?"

"Call the police," Rob replied without hesitation. He crossed toward her and lifted the receiver from the phone on her bedside table, holding it out to her. "Call them and tell them what you think. Let *them* check Ian out. That's their job. It's what they get paid to do."

Jess stubbornly crossed her arms. "I already called them," she said. "They don't believe me." With her chin, she gestured to the telephone receiver that Rob was still holding. "*You* call them. Maybe they'll believe *you*."

Call the police? No way. He couldn't. It would be too risky. Too dangerous. Rob's contact with the law was always from a distance, and it was going to stay that way.

With a muttered curse, he hung up the phone.

Jess stood up and started toward the door. "I'll be back soon—"

Rob swore again, louder this time as he reached out and caught her arm, swinging her around to face him. "What, really, do you expect to find?"

She gazed up at him, her expression unreadable, her eyes guarded. "Answers," she told him. "I want some answers."

Something was going on here. Why did Jess suddenly think that Ian was a killer? She knew something. "What's this about, Jess?" he said softly. "This is about more than just Ian, isn't it?"

"Please come with me," she whispered. "Please help me?"

She looked so worried now, so...scared. But of what?

"Of course," Rob found himself saying. "You know I'll help you."

JESS PARKED her car around the corner from Ian's condo—in front of the convenience store. Rob had been silent on the way over, and he was still quiet now. If he was having second thoughts about going with her into Ian's home, he wasn't voicing them. And, thankfully, he hadn't pressed the issue of why coming out here was so important to her. Because what could she tell him? *I want to prove that* you're *not a serial killer?*

Together they walked up the sidewalk that led to the front door of Ian's condo. The door was closed, but Jess could see into the living room through the little window on the top half. The only obvious sign of Ian was a half-eaten and probably fossilizing pizza lying out on the coffee table—and a half a ton of junk cluttering up the living room.

Jess rang the doorbell and waited. From several units down, she could hear sounds of a TV talk show. Someone else in the condo complex was playing an Allman Brothers CD much too loudly. She rang the bell again, but Ian's condo was silent.

Using the key on the Betty Boop chain, she unlocked the door. She glanced at Rob, but he was looking out at the street, as if making sure no one was watching them. Jess pushed the door open and stepped into Ian's home.

The place looked like a pigsty, and smelled like one, too. The pizza on the table definitely dated from some previous lifetime. There was a full ashtray next to the pizza and empty beer cans everywhere.

Rob closed the door tightly behind them, locking it from the inside. "I hope you know what you're looking for," he said, wryly surveying the rubble of junk and garbage piled around the living room.

The problem was, Jess *didn't* know what she was looking for. But she knew that she'd recognize it when she saw it.

She headed through the living room, to the back of the condo, toward the kitchen.

It was also a mess. As Jess walked in, her shoes stuck to the floor. Judging from the smell, garbage from longer than just the past week was overflowing the trash container. The sink was full of dishes and glasses. They were all dirty, most were disgusting. The counters and the small dining table were overrun with clutter of every kind.

But no knives covered with blood and gore.

Although, how could she be sure? How would she even notice such a thing in this mess?

Lord, how could she have lived with this man for all those years...?

Jess turned and found Rob watching her, his eyes gentle, as if he knew what she was thinking, as if he knew how difficult it was for her to be here.

"I used to...clean up after him," Jess said, looking around and shrugging hopelessly. "I'm sorry—I don't know why he doesn't hire a maid."

"Maybe he likes living this way," Rob responded quietly. "Maybe it gives him a real reason to feel sorry for himself."

Jess was silent.

"Besides, you don't have to apologize for Ian. You're not responsible for him anymore." Rob reached out and touched her shoulder.

It was the slightest, gentlest of caresses, yet it gave Jess a wealth of comfort. He was there and he cared.

"I *do* feel responsible," she said, "but not in the way you mean."

Rob followed Jess as she led the way back into the living room, toward the stairs that went up to the second floor.

"If Ian *is* the Sarasota Serial Killer—"

Rob shook his head. "Jess. Just because your ex-husband is nearly always rude and sometimes nasty doesn't mean that he's—"

"If he *is* the killer," she repeated, turning to face him. Standing on the first step put her almost at Rob's eye level. "If he *is,* then every time he kills one of those women, he's symbolically killing *me.*"

Rob's eyes looked shocked behind his glasses. *"What?"*

"Here's the theory," Jess said, turning and climbing the stairs. On either side of the steps, Ian had piled things that belonged upstairs. "For some reason, I don't know what or why, Ian snaps. He was never particularly stable, but say that something pushes him over the edge. His feelings for me—always confused and complicated, a kind of simultaneous love-hate thing, even at the best of times—go totally haywire."

There was a small landing at the top of the stairs with three doors leading off of it. Jess pushed one door open and found the bathroom. It looked as if it hadn't been cleaned since he'd moved into the condo, but other than that, there was no incriminating evidence of any kind.

"So Ian snaps," Jess continued, turning to look at Rob, "and now, instead of an unnaturally adversarial relationship with me, his ex-wife, he becomes absolutely obsessed. He comes to all my shows, he stops by my house at odd hours of the day and night, he calls, he writes, he follows me when I go shopping...."

"Does he really?" Rob asked.

"Sometimes," Jess said. The second door on the landing opened into Ian's music studio. In sharp contrast to the rest of the apartment, this room was spotless. Ian's violin lay open in its case near a music stand. He had a computer along one wall, attached to a keyboard rack that held several different synthesizers.

The synthesizers were tied in to a twelve-track recording system that Jess looked at enviously. He had a rack of compressors, effects boxes and equalizers that took up nearly another entire wall.

Ian hadn't had this stuff when they were married, and Jess knew she was looking at what had become of the child support payments she was supposed to have received from him.

"It's a big step from following your ex-wife around to killing women who look like her," Rob remarked.

"I'm not saying I understand why," Jess said, lightly running one finger along the polished wood of Ian's violin, "or even that this is anything more than a convoluted theory."

"How do you know so much about this?" Rob asked.

He was watching her again. Jess turned away from the questioning look in his eyes, staring down again at the decorative sound holes of the violin, her gaze slightly out of focus. What was she supposed to tell him? That she spoke at great length with an FBI shrink who believed *Rob* was the real serial killer...? *That* would go over *really* well. Or...

Wait.

Jess focused her eyes and for the first time truly *looked* at the ornate wood of the musical instrument that was directly in front of her.

Ian's violin.

What was Ian's violin doing here, in his condo, when he was supposed to be playing it tonight at Symphony Hall?

Unless...

Jess looked at her watch. Quarter to six.

Unless he hadn't left for downtown yet. In which case, he'd be back any minute to scoop up his violin.

Rob heard it the exact moment she did.

It wasn't a very big noise, but it was unmistakable. It was the sound of a key in the lock of the door at the foot of the stairs.

"Dear Lord, it's Ian," Jess breathed. "What do we do?"

"Hide." Rob grabbed her hand and pulled her, hard, across the top landing, and directly through the third door—the one that led into Ian's bedroom.

It couldn't have been any worse than the kitchen and the living room. It shouldn't have—but it was.

The shades were down and the room was dark and smelled damp—moist, like an animal's den. Rob quickly flipped on a switch next to the door and a bare bulb in the ceiling harshly lit the room. Piles of clothes were everywhere—except in the closet, which was empty. Ian's dresser drawers hung open at crazy angles, stuffed with even more clothes. Pizza boxes and beer cans littered the floor and an overflowing ashtray spilled onto a bedside table.

"In the closet," Rob commanded, giving Jess a little push in that direction. She hopped over a pile of books and newspapers and climbed inside. Rob turned off the light, and some-how—silently and without tripping over a single one of the obstacles on the floor—he joined her inside the closet.

It was dark in there. Very, *very* dark. It was also very close quarters. One of Rob's arms was around her, his body pressed tightly against hers. Jess could hear her heart pounding. She also heard the sound of metal on metal—Rob had taken out and opened his deadly-looking knife.

"Rob," she whispered. "What—"

"Shhh," he said, barely audibly.

She heard Ian then, his footsteps coming up the stairs.

Turn right, Jess prayed silently. Make him turn right and pick up his violin and head straight back down those stairs and out the front door.

Ian turned left, toward his bedroom.

The bedroom door opened with a spine-tingling creak, and Ian came in. He didn't flip on the overhead light. Instead he turned on a small lamp that was on the bedside table. The door creaked slowly closed. Jess could smell the smoke from his cigarette.

Rob's arm had tightened around her, and Jess looked up at him. His face was shadowy, but she could see his jaw was tightly clenched, his eyes narrowed as he listened intently. He was holding his knife as if it were an extension of his right hand. With his face such a picture of intensity, Rob looked absolutely capable of using that knife.

Something hit the back wall of the closet with a sound like a gunshot, and it was all Jess could do not to jump and give them away. Rob held her even tighter as a second thing hit the wall, and Jess realized that Ian, no doubt in a burst of neatness, had kicked off his sneakers, firing them into the closet.

And then, as quickly as Ian had appeared, he was gone. He left the light on, but the door creaked open and shut. There were several moments of silence, then the sound of his feet clattering down the stairs. The condo shook slightly from the force of the front door being slammed shut.

Only then did Rob move.

His knife hissed slightly as the blade disappeared back into the handle. Another swift movement sent it back into the holster.

Then Rob pulled Jess close, holding her tightly, both arms wrapped around her.

"Let's get out of here," Jess whispered. "This was a mistake."

Rob exhaled, as if he'd been holding his breath all that time. "Yeah," he agreed.

Jess stepped out of the closet, over the piles of junk on the floor.

Ian's waterbed was a rumpled pile of grungy sheets and stained pillowcases and...

Jess looked closer. There was a dangerously sharp pair of scissors open on Ian's bed. Razor sharp scissors, on a *water* bed... And there was also a packet of newly developed photographs on the bed. Pictures of *her*. She picked them up, leafing quickly through them. They'd been taken recently—pictures of her onstage, pictures of her and Kelsey in the backyard. There was even a picture of her driving her car.

Ian had been using the scissors to cut several of the photos. He'd painstakingly cut the backgrounds out of the pictures, leaving only Jess's face and body. And on several of the pictures he'd gone one step further—snipping Jess's head from her shoulders.

"Hey, Jess?" Rob's voice sounded strange, almost tight. Even though he was speaking softly, it seemed unnaturally loud in the stillness. "What were you saying about Ian being obsessed with you?"

Jess turned, and saw it.

Ian had put it on the wall on the other side of the door, so she and Rob hadn't seen it when they'd first entered the room. But now there was no way they could have missed it.

It was a collage, a huge ten-by-six-foot collection of pictures of Jess. There were hundreds of photographs, and all of them had had the backgrounds carefully cut away. And all of them had the heads removed from the shoulders. Ian had pinned all of Jess's heads on the top part of the wall. The collection of her bodies were on the bottom. It was weird, and more than a little scary.

"God," Rob breathed. "How long did it take him to do this?"

It was *way* outside of the realm of a normal, healthy bout of anger and bitterness due to a divorce.

It was clearly weird.

It was definitely obsessive.

It was exactly what Jess had been looking for, though Lord help her, she hadn't honestly expected to find it.

Jess took Rob's hand and pulled him out of the bedroom and down the stairs.

"Where are we going?" he asked.

"To find a pay phone," Jess answered. "To call Parker Elliot."

Chapter Fifteen

"Who's Parker Elliot?" Rob asked, watching Jess as she tried both to catch her breath and dial the phone number that was on the little white business card she'd pulled from her purse.

"He's with the FBI," Jess answered. She turned away slightly as someone on the other side of the line picked up.

The FBI?

Rob felt his blood run cold. Jess hadn't just said FBI, had she?

"Yes," Jess spoke into the phone. "I need to speak to Mr. Elliot, please." She paused. "No, it's very important." Another pause. "Tell him it's Jess Baxter, please. I think he'll leave his meeting to talk to me."

"Yes," Jess said again. "Mr. Elliot? I'm sorry for bothering you, but I've found out some information I'm sure you'll want to know." She paused, and shot a look at Rob. "No—no, it's not about . . . him. It's about Ian Davis—my ex-husband?" Jess lowered her voice as she gave this Elliot guy a description of the "artwork" they'd found in Ian's bedroom. She recited Ian's street address, then slipped her hand over the speaking end of the telephone receiver. "They're going to go check it out," she whispered to Rob.

They? Who were *they*? Were *they* really the FBI?

Rob watched Jess as she spoke again to the man on the other end of the telephone line. Her face was flushed. Her eyes were bright with excitement yet shadowed by grief.

Once upon a time, she had been married to Ian, Rob made himself remember. She'd imagined herself in love with the man, and no doubt she'd thought Ian was in love with her, too. Seeing those crude pictures, that strange collection of photos, that weird shrine—that had to have hurt.

Rob had always felt a little sorry for Ian. He found the concert violinist to be pathetic and sad. But now, after seeing those pictures on his wall, imagining the sheer number of hours it had to have taken to cut all those photos out, Rob had to wonder if maybe Ian wasn't also dangerously obsessed.

"Tomorrow," Jess said, hanging up the phone with a crash. "They're going to check it out . . . *tomorrow*." She threw herself down on the bench next to the pay phones and folded her arms across her chest. "Apparently, they're far too busy to get to Ian's house tonight."

She exhaled fiercely, jutting out her chin so the burst of air briefly lifted her bangs.

Rob sat down next to her. "Jess, who is this Elliot guy?"

She turned and looked at him, lightning bolts of anger still glimmering in her eyes. "Parker Elliot," she replied. "He's an agent with the FBI."

Rob forced himself to sit absolutely still. His expression didn't change, his face didn't give him away, but he couldn't keep his pulse from kicking into fifth gear.

"Do you remember Pete?" Jess asked.

"The bartender you thought was following you?" What the hell did *he* have to do with the FBI?

Jess nodded. "Pete wasn't really Pete," she told him. "He was Parker Elliot, an undercover Federal agent."

"My God," Rob said. The bartender had been an FBI agent. But that had been *weeks* ago. If the FBI had had any reason at all to investigate Robert Carpenter, then they might already know who he was, what he'd done. . . .

"Parker Elliot approached me a while ago," Jess was saying, "because he thought that I might have some kind of connection to the serial killer."

"Why didn't you tell me?" His voice sounded raspy, strained, but Jess didn't seem to notice.

She was looking away from him now, gazing down at her feet, clad in those enticingly bare leather sandals.

"You're not going to believe this," Jess said slowly. She glanced up at him and her eyes held embarrassment. "But…"

She smiled at him then, a sweet, self-conscious, lovely smile. Rob had a bad feeling in the pit of his stomach that the news she was about to share with him was not going to be good.

Jess continued. "The FBI—Parker Elliot—actually considered *you* their prime suspect."

Prime suspect.

Fireworks exploded in Rob's head as Jess's words took on meaning.

It was. All over.

He had to leave town, and he had to leave *now*.

But, how could he just leave Jess *now*? Ian was out there somewhere, in Sarasota, like a heat-seeking missile with Jess as his computer-programmed target. No way could he leave Jess right now. Not until tomorrow when Ian was brought in for questioning, and the FBI shrinks took a good long look at that bizarre collage hanging on Ian's bedroom wall.

No, Rob couldn't leave Jess alone tonight—even if it meant that he'd be caught.

ALL THROUGHOUT DINNER, Rob was tense and quiet.

As they cleaned up the dishes in the kitchen, Kelsey chattered away about the finger painting she'd done over at Doris's that afternoon, and the girl down the street who just had a baby brother.

"I'd like a baby brother," Kelsey said.

Jess looked up to find Rob watching the child sadly.

"I'd like you to have one, too, Bug," he said softly. He sat down at the kitchen table and took a deep breath. "Come here for a sec, Kelsey," he said. "Sit down."

Jess watched her daughter slide into a seat across the table from him. She saw the hope in Kelsey's eyes. Oh, Rob, she thought, be careful. . . .

"I have to go away," he told her. "I'm gonna leave in a couple of days." He looked up at Jess. "Maybe even tomorrow."

Tomorrow? Jess turned back to the sink, afraid of what Rob might be able to see on her face.

Kelsey was quiet for a moment. "Why?" she asked.

"Well," he answered slowly. "There's a lot of reasons, but the biggest one is because of my job. I'm going to have to live in a different city."

The little girl's eyes filled with tears. "I thought you loved us," she said in a very small voice.

Rob reached for her hand. "I do, Bug. I love you an awful lot." He looked up at Jess again and swallowed. "Both of you."

Kelsey pulled her hand away. "But you don't love us enough to have a job here."

He was silent, unable to respond.

"Which different city?" Kelsey asked.

"I'm not sure yet. Maybe Phoenix or Dallas. Or maybe Seattle. I don't know."

She nodded, hope in her brown eyes. "We can go with you."

Rob looked up at Jess. She said nothing. Leaving Sarasota was his decision, his choice. He was going to have to explain it to Kelsey.

"No, Bug, you can't," he replied.

Kelsey didn't move or speak for several long moments.

"I'm sorry," Rob continued, and she looked up at him, her eyes expressionless.

"No, you're not," Kelsey countered. "You're just like Ian."

She stood up and walked out of the room.

Rob closed his eyes briefly before looking up at Jess. "Ouch," he said.

"This isn't the first time she's been deserted," Jess reminded him.

"Man, both you guys really know how to hit below the belt."

Jess said nothing. She had promised herself that she wasn't going to beg him to stay.

They watched each other in silence. The small kitchen was filled with the heaviness of their unhappiness. It seemed to press down upon Jess, harder and harder with each passing second.

The sound of running water came from the bathroom as Kelsey began filling the tub for her bath.

"Why *can't* you take us with you?" Jess asked softly.

Rob ran his hands through his hair. "You don't want to live this way."

Jess was holding the dishcloth so tightly, her knuckles were white. "How do I know," she said, "when you won't even tell me what 'this way' is? What gives you the right to make that kind of decision for me?"

"Jess, you're going to have to trust me—"

"Why should I? You apparently don't trust *me* enough to tell me about whatever it is you're running away from!"

From the bathroom, Kelsey started to wail.

Jess ran toward the sound, pushing the bathroom door open with a crash. Rob was right at her heels.

"What's the matter?" Jess asked, with one quick look checking to be sure there were no broken bones, no blood, no bumped head.

Kelsey was sitting in the tub, face contorted, tears streaming from her eyes. "I left my drawing pad and my colored pencils out by the swing set," she cried, big sobs racking her small body. "And it's supposed to rain tonight!"

Jess sighed, looking at Rob. The toys left outside were just an excuse to cry. But if Kelsey chose to use this as a release for her emotions, that was fine with Jess. Kelsey was already taking the first steps toward getting over Rob. For Jess, it wouldn't be that easy.

She knelt down next to the tub, and pulled the plug. Kelsey's loud crying had changed to quiet whimpering. "Come on," she said. "Let's get you dried off. Then I'll go outside and get your things."

"I'll get 'em," Rob said.

Jess looked up from wrapping a big towel around her daughter. Fear rose inside of her. He was going to leave. Was it going to be now?

"I'll come right back," Rob stated as if he could read her thoughts. He leaned down and kissed her. "I promise."

She nodded then, moving out into the hall to watch him walk into the kitchen.

He turned on the porch lamp. It lit the deck and the stairs going down to the backyard, but the pool of light didn't extend onto the lawn where the swing set and Kelsey's toys lay. With one more look back at Jess, Rob went out and closed the door behind him.

The yard was dark, but there was light and movement out on the street in front of the house.

Cars. Three or four vehicles were out there, and as Rob watched, another pulled up. It was a police cruiser.

His blood ran cold. His time had run out.

He looked up at the light spilling out of the windows of Jess's house, realizing that he had told her a lie. He *wasn't* going to come right back. He was going to break his promise.

He could see her slender silhouette, moving about behind the shade in Kelsey's room.

He hadn't even said goodbye.

Rob turned, disappearing into the swampy woods at the edge of the yard.

JESS HAD RUBBED KELSEY dry and pulled a huge T-shirt over her head when a loud knock on the kitchen door made them both jump.

"Rob must've locked himself out," Jess said. She went quickly into the kitchen, and opened the door. "What happened . . ." she started to say.

It was Parker Elliot. He was surrounded by a crowd of other men in dark suits, along with several uniformed policemen.

"Good evening, Ms. Baxter," Elliot said. "Sorry to bother you this late."

"Is this the main entrance to Robert Carpenter's apartment?" a policeman asked, pointing to Rob's door.

"Yes," Jess said. "It's the *only* entrance." She turned back to Elliot. "What's going on?"

"I have a warrant here to search this entire domicile, ma'am," Elliot informed her. He handed her the warrant.

Jess looked down at the paper in her hands, but she couldn't seem to focus on it.

"I also have a warrant for the arrest of Robert Carpenter," Parker Elliot continued. "Is he here?"

Rob? A warrant for his arrest? No, they had it all wrong. Rob wasn't the killer. It was *Ian*.

Jess felt Kelsey press against her leg. "Go to your room, Kel," she instructed her daughter. "And stay there, okay?"

Eyes wide, Kelsey scurried back down the hall.

"Is there a key to this door, ma'am?" The policeman pointed again to Rob's apartment door. "Or should we break the lock?"

"Rob's not in there," Jess told him. "I'll give you the key, and you can look, but I can tell you right now, he's not inside."

She went into the kitchen to pull the key off the rack, and two of the FBI agents came in behind her, their guns drawn.

"Hold it *right* there," Jess bellowed, and they froze. "Elliot, are you in charge here?" she called through the screen.

Parker Elliot stepped into the kitchen. "Yes, I am," he said quietly.

"My six-year-old daughter is in her bedroom," she stressed. "I just told you that Rob's not inside. I will *not* have any guns drawn in my house while my daughter and I are here. Is that clear?"

"Yes, ma'am." Elliot nodded.

"Good," Jess snapped. "Here's the key to the apartment."

"Thank you," Elliot said. "Ms. Baxter, please get your daughter and come with me."

Jess stared at him.

"I can't allow my men to search the premises without their weapons drawn," he informed her, his gray eyes serious. "Just as you're concerned about your daughter's safety, I'm concerned about *their* safety."

"I don't understand what you want with Rob," Jess said, a note of desperation in her voice. "He's not the man you're looking for."

"Come outside," Elliot replied, "and I'll tell you what I can."

Jess quickly gathered Kelsey and brought her outside. Thankfully, the night was warm, and Jess got her daughter several sticks of brightly colored chalk from the garage. Kelsey was soon drawing on the driveway underneath the floodlight.

Jess stepped toward Elliot, drawing him farther away from the little girl. She looked toward the swing set. Kelsey's drawing pad and pencils were still there. And Rob was gone. He'd left. He said he wouldn't, but he'd left.

"Okay," she began, forcing back her disappointment and pain. "What's going on?"

"I have a warrant for the arrest of Robert Carpenter," Elliot said quietly, "for the rape and murder of Amelia Driscoll."

Jess couldn't speak. It was all she could do to stand, the world was spinning so quickly around her. "What?" The word came out a mere whisper.

"And we're hoping to find further evidence in his apartment to tie him to the murders of thirteen other young women in this city," Elliot continued.

"It's not Rob," Jess insisted. "It's *Ian*. I told you…I *called* you earlier. It's *Ian,* not Rob!"

He touched her arm. "Ms. Baxter, maybe you should sit down—"

She shook off his hand. "I don't *need* to sit down!"

Parker Elliot turned to one of his men. "Any luck contacting Selma Haverstein?"

"No, sir."

Elliot swore softly, turning back to Jess. "I'm sorry, Ms. Baxter," he told her. "I realize how difficult this must be for you. I wanted Dr. Haverstein to be here, but she's unavailable right now and we couldn't wait. You aren't going to want to hear this, but we have evidence that ties Robert Carpenter to the slaying of one of the victims."

"What evidence?" Jess demanded.

Elliot looked at her levelly. "Bloodstains in the trunk of the car Carpenter's been driving for the past seven months. Apparently, he turned the car in when he resigned this afternoon. The cleanup crew found the stains, notified the police—the police called our unit. We matched some fibers that we found in the car to the clothes Amelia Driscoll was wearing the night she was killed."

Elliot turned away as another agent approached him.

"The perpetrator's gone," the agent reported. "We've started dusting the apartment."

Parker Elliot swore again, stepping away from Jess to speak privately to the other agent.

One of the dead women had been inside Rob's car. Stains of her blood were found in the trunk. My God. My *God!* How could this be? It didn't seem possible. It was like a nightmare, only Jess couldn't wake up.

Rob wasn't the killer. He *wasn't*. But if he wasn't, where had he gone? If he wasn't, why had he run?

Her knees felt weak, and she sat down right on the driveway.

Every light was on inside and outside her house. Plainclothes agents and uniformed policemen swarmed around the place. Out on the road were more than a half a dozen marked and unmarked police cars—some of them with their lights spinning.

Up and down the street, neighbors stood on their lawns, watching. Next door, old Mr. Greene had been joined on his porch by both Stanford and Mrs. Greene. All three gawked unabashedly at the activity. This was better for them than TV. It was like "America's Most Wanted," or "Top Cops," only it was happening right next door.

"Where did Carpenter go?" Elliot demanded of Jess, his gray eyes glittering in the garage spotlight. He crouched down on the asphalt, right next to her.

"I don't know," she answered honestly.

He didn't buy it. "The surveillance team reported Carpenter returned home with you and Kelsey at around 7:00 p.m.," he said, his voice clipped, impatient. "He was here. No one saw him leave. Where did he go?"

"I *don't* know."

Elliot nearly pierced her with his gaze. "Did you tell him about this investigation?"

She couldn't lie. "Yes."

"When?"

"Just today," she replied. "This evening."

"And now he's gone," Elliot said tightly. He stood up in one quick, fluid motion. "When did he leave the house?"

Jess stared up at him. "What time did you arrive?" she countered.

"Eight-thirty," he answered.

"Rob left at 8:25," Jess said. "He went outside to get something Kelsey left on the swing set."

"Five minutes." Elliot shook his head, his lips tightening. "If you'd told us that right away, we might have caught up with him. I should charge you with aiding and abetting."

He started to walk away, then turned to look back at her. "I hope for the sake of your conscience, Ms. Baxter, that another woman doesn't die tonight."

Chapter Sixteen

Jess pushed the shopping cart out into the parking lot and loaded her bags of groceries into the trunk of the car.

Look at her. She was functioning. Whoever would guess that she'd found out last night that the man of her dreams—who intended to leave her forever in some twisted act of selfless love—was wanted by the FBI for brutally murdering more than a dozen innocent young women.

He didn't do it.

That's what was holding her together. It was her total conviction that Rob was not capable of murder. He was not the killer. He couldn't be.

The obvious answer had come to her in the middle of the night.

Ian had borrowed Rob's car.

Of course. That *had* to be it. It all came back to Ian.

Jess had called Parker Elliot at three o'clock in the morning with that information. His voice had sounded alert and awake when he'd answered the phone, and she could hear voices in the background, as if his office were busy despite the late hour.

He'd taken her news about Ian calmly—a little *too* calmly. In fact, it was clear that he didn't believe Ian Davis had anything at all to do with the murders. Rob was still his number one suspect.

He'd made an appointment for ten-thirty in the morning to pick Jess up and bring her to the FBI headquarters where she could talk to Dr. Haverstein.

Jess knew that Elliot hoped the psychologist would be able to talk some sense into her. Jess hoped she'd be able to convince Selma Haverstein that Rob wasn't the man they were looking for—*Ian* was.

But until ten-thirty, Jess had the option of sitting in her house and wringing her hands, or getting on with the day-to-day chores of her life. It was Thursday. She had groceries to pick up.

And right now she had to get those groceries home before the ice cream melted.

The street in front of her house was still packed with large, dark cars, so unobtrusive that it was obvious they were unmarked police cars. A silver-gray Acura Legend sat in the driveway. Elliot's car, she guessed. Had to be.

She pressed the automatic door opener, and drove the car into the garage without stopping. She cut the engine and gave the remote control another push, and the door began to slide noisily down.

Lord, she thought to herself, please help me get through this day. And please help them believe me. Rob is *not* the killer. He *can't* be.

The garage was dim and moist, and she rolled up the windows of the car so the musty smell wouldn't penetrate. She turned to gather her purse from the passenger seat when she heard a sound.

Startled, she glanced into the rearview mirror, and in the dimness of the back seat was a shape . . . with two eyes.

Jess opened her mouth to scream, and a hand clamped down over her mouth.

"Jess, it's me!"

Rob.

With a sob of relief, she flung her arms around him, pulling him as close to her as she could in the little car.

"Oh, Rob," she gasped. "Are you all right? Where have you been? Where did you come from?"

She pulled back slightly to examine his face. He looked dirty and exhausted, his eyes red-rimmed with dark circles underneath. He was pale beneath his tan, and in the dim light, his skin looked almost gray. He'd torn the sleeves off his white shirt and the fabric itself was stained with perspiration and dirt.

"I hoped you'd be at the supermarket this morning," he said tiredly. "Even though it's Thursday, I still wasn't sure you'd be there. But I found your car in the lot and hid in the back. Jess, do they really think I killed all those women?" His forehead was creased in disbelief.

Jess nodded.

"Why?" Rob asked, frowning harder. "What evidence do they have?"

"They found bloodstains in the Taurus...in the trunk," she said. "And some fibers or something in the car. Fabric, I think, from one of the victim's clothes."

Rob sat back, his face hard as he thought.

"Rob, you should turn yourself in. You're innocent, it's obviously a mistake. You know, *Ian* borrowed your car—"

He looked up at her then, meeting her eyes. "I can't turn myself in."

"Why not?"

He looked away, not answering her question. "I'm sorry." He swore softly but explosively. "I know I shouldn't have come here, Jess, but I...I didn't have anywhere else to go. I've been shot—"

"What? Oh, Lord—" Jess scrambled out of the car, pulling the back door open. "Where?"

He pointed down to his left leg. "It's not bad, just a nick, but the bitch of it is, when the bullet hit me, it knocked me off-balance and I tore the hell out of the ligaments in my ankle," he said. "I can barely walk. I need a place to hide for a few days...."

She could see the bloodstains on the thigh of his jeans. He'd used the sleeves from his shirt as a makeshift bandage, and blood had long since turned them brown.

Shot. He'd been *shot*.

His gentle hand on her hair made her look up at him.

"It's not that bad," he repeated.

She swallowed. "Is the bullet...?" She couldn't finish the question, but he answered it anyway.

"No, it's out."

What was she going to do? Harboring a fugitive, that was bad news. If they found him, she could go to jail....

Start with the little problems, she told herself. We'll work our way up to the big ones. Right now, he needed to get cleaned up, get some food and some rest.

"Come on," she said. "I'll help you inside."

He carefully pulled himself out of the car then leaned on her heavily as she helped him into the basement and then up the stairs, into the house. His face was tight, his teeth clenched, and she knew that he was in worse pain than he was letting on.

She brought him directly into her private bathroom, and helped him sit on the commode. His forehead was wet with sweat, and the muscles in his jaw were tight. But his brown eyes were filled with thanks as he looked up at her.

"Where are your glasses?" she asked, taking a clean towel and a washcloth from the linen closet.

"I don't know." Rob shook his head. "Gone."

"Can you see well enough without them?" Jess found a package of gauze bandages under the sink.

"Yeah, it's not a problem."

Pulling her Swiss army knife from her purse, Jess extracted the tiny pair of razor sharp scissors from the handle and began cutting the bandage from Rob's leg.

"Who shot you?" Her voice shook.

"I don't know. Some guy in a dark suit. I'm assuming he was FBI. His backup was late, or I'd probably— Oh, *God!*"

Rob's knuckles went white as Jess pulled the final layer of bandage off his leg.

"I'm sorry," she murmured.

"I'm okay, I'm okay," he said, but his face had gone a shade paler, and he had to wipe his forehead to keep the sweat from running in his eyes.

The bullet had torn a ragged line in his jeans, and bits of the denim had been embedded in the angry-looking wound. This was going to take more time to clean than she had. She glanced at her watch. Ten-fifteen. Damn.

"I'm supposed to meet one of the FBI agents at ten-thirty," she told him worriedly. "You know, there's about twenty agents in your apartment and outside the house. As glad as I am to see you, it seems kind of crazy for you to be here."

Rob managed a tight smile. "I'm probably safer here than anywhere else in the city. They've already searched your house, and I knew they wouldn't check your car coming *in*. I mean, who in their right mind would come *back* here, right?"

Who in their right mind, indeed.

"Look, I can take care of this," Rob continued. "The less you actually help me, the better anyway. Go on, you've got groceries that need to go in the fridge. We can't do anything that looks suspicious. And buying a gallon of ice cream and then letting it melt in the trunk of your car is *definitely* suspicious."

Jess stood up uncertainly. "Rob, I still think you should turn yourself in." Her voice grew stronger with her conviction. "I mean, they were *shooting* at you. You could've been killed—"

"No." He said it quietly, but absolutely.

Discouraged, Jess turned away.

"You have to promise me something." His voice stopped her.

She looked back at him. His face was lined with pain and his eyes burned almost too brightly in his face.

"Promise me that if somehow they find me here, you'll tell them that you hid me only because I threatened you," Rob said. "Tell them I threatened to hurt Bug. That way they can't send you to jail for helping me."

Jess didn't move, didn't speak.

"Please, Jess," he implored softly. "I've never asked you for anything...."

He'd never asked her for anything? Lord, he'd asked *every*-thing of her. He'd asked her to live without him....

"All right," she said softly. "Don't make too much noise while I'm gone. Take a shower, but do it now, while I'm still here, otherwise some smart FBI agent is going to wonder why the water's going on and off in an empty apartment."

Rob nodded.

"Keep your ankle elevated," Jess continued. "I'll get you an ice pack before I go. You can rest in my bed—I'll turn down the sheets. Try to sleep, you look like you could use it." She looked at her watch again. "You've only got eleven minutes to use the water, so hurry, Rob."

She crossed to him, leaning down and kissing him on the lips. "And at least *think* about turning yourself in."

She left, closing the door tightly behind her.

JESS WATCHED the city streets roll past from the quiet comfort of Parker Elliot's car. The windows were tinted slightly, giving the bright day a softness.

She glanced across the car at the FBI agent who had picked her up at home just minutes ago. He drove with both hands on the steering wheel, like a race car driver, exuding an air of utmost confidence and efficiency. He was impeccably dressed, his hair carefully in place, his eyes hidden behind a dark pair of aviator sunglasses.

Jess tried to picture him at home, with a wife and family, but simply couldn't. "Are you married, Mr. Elliot?"

He glanced over at her, giving her a long, cool, appraising look. She fought the urge to give her shorts a swift tug downward. "No," he said.

She *could* picture his fellow FBI agents wheeling him, like a robot, into a closet at the end of each day, and taking him back out in the morning.

"Any children?"

Elliot looked at her again. "I just said I'm not married."

"Well, I'm not married, either, and I have a daughter."

"No children," he answered curtly.

"Do you live in Virginia?"

"Yes."

"Do you live in the city or the country?"

"Suburbs. Why the questions?"

"I feel at a distinct disadvantage. I haven't had the opportunity to read *your* file, as I'm sure you've read mine. What's your favorite color?"

"I don't have one."

"It figures. Where did you grow up?"

"Connecticut. Why, 'it figures?' "

"A guy with your taste in clothes doesn't care about colors."

"I guess right now there's only one thing I care about," Elliot said, signaling to pull into the parking lot of one of Sarasota's few tall office buildings.

"Catching Rob," Jess stated. She leaned forward to look up at the building. "Where are we?"

"My unit has temporary office space in this building."

He parked in a spot marked Reserved by the front door, and unlocked the car doors.

As Jess opened her door, she was hit by a wave of humidity that the car's air-conditioning had concealed. The damp, hot air surrounded her, pressed down on her. Lord, she thought, please don't let him ask me directly if I know where Rob is.

Elliot led her into the lobby, and into a waiting elevator. He pushed the button for the twelfth floor.

The elevator door opened, and Jess felt the gentle pressure of the tips of Elliot's fingers on her back as he gestured for her to go ahead of him.

"Selma's office is down here, to the right," he told her, leading Jess to a heavy oak door. "We're supposed to go right in."

He opened the door, and Jess went ahead of him into a tastefully decorated, homey office. A large wooden desk sat on one side of the room, on the other was a plush sofa, several easy chairs and a rocking chair. The walls were covered with a pleasant flowered wallpaper, and the curtains matched.

The room was empty.

"We're a few minutes early," Elliot said. "And Dr. Haverstein usually runs behind. A great *deal* behind. Hopefully, we won't have to wait too long."

"I'm here, Parker. Don't be making nasty comments about my timekeeping habits. I am fully armed with knowledge of your own imperfections—enough to launch a full-scale counterattack." Selma Haverstein's voice was teasing as she swept into the room, a warm smile on her pleasant face. She was wearing a long, dark blue dress covered with small, gold-colored, stylized suns and moons. It was a dress Jess might've expected to see on one of the artists in Siesta Village, not on an FBI psychologist. "How are you today, dear?" This last was directed toward Jess.

"I'm still pretty upset about all this," Jess admitted.

"Aha," Selma remarked. "Honesty. Did you hear that, Parker? With Jess as a fine example, I'll admit that, yes, at times I tend to be rather...inexact when it comes to keeping appointments. The same way that, at times, *you* can be rather..."

"Rude," Elliot supplied, crossing his arms. "Like right now, when I'm obviously in a hurry, and you're obviously not."

"*Brusque* is a much nicer word, dear," Selma said, patting his arm.

"If we're done wasting time," Elliot drawled, "I'd like to take Ms. Baxter upstairs to the office and begin this interview."

"Actually," Jess said, "I was hoping to have a word with Dr. Haverstein." They both turned and looked at her. "Alone," she added.

Parker Elliot headed for the door. "Bring her upstairs, please Selma, when you're finished."

Dr. Haverstein nodded, and waited until he went out the door and closed it tightly behind him. Then she smiled at Jess. "Would you like to sit down?"

Jess shook her head, no. "I just wanted to tell you that I still don't believe Rob is the serial killer."

"You think it's Ian Davis." Selma perched on the arm of one of her big easy chairs. "Your ex-husband. I know. Parker told me that you found something disturbing in Ian's condo yesterday. Parker also said you called him late last night and told him that Ian had borrowed Rob's car." Selma sighed. "Jess, don't you think it's a little too convenient for Ian—the awful ex-husband—to turn out to be the villain in the piece?"

"You don't believe me," Jess said flatly. "I guess that means Elliot hasn't gone out to Ian's to verify my story."

"He's been a little busy with other matters," Selma responded.

"Trying to pin the serial killer's murders on Rob."

"Trying to prove that Rob is the killer," Selma gently corrected her.

"Well, he's not."

Selma leaned forward slightly, her kind eyes suddenly quite sharp. "Dear, has Rob Carpenter tried to contact you?"

Jess answered without hesitation. "No." It wasn't a lie. He hadn't *tried,* he'd succeeded.

"Yet you're absolutely certain that Rob is innocent."

"Yes." At least 99.9 percent certain.

If Selma could see that tenth of a percent of doubt in Jess's eyes, she didn't comment on it.

"Why don't we go upstairs and talk to Parker," Selma urged. "He's got some new information he wanted you to know about."

Jess shifted impatiently. She didn't want to hear about any new information incriminating Rob.

"I'll make a deal with you," Selma offered. "You go up there and listen to Parker. After you listen to him, if you *still* want us to check into Ian Davis, I'll personally see to it that we get a warrant to search his house *and* that we call him in for questioning."

Jess held out her hand. "Deal."

HE WAS DROWNING, choking, and he knew when he opened his eyes, he'd be covered in blood.

Her blood.

So he wouldn't open his eyes.

But her scream echoed through him, trapped in his head, ringing against the inside of his skull. Over and over and over, and he knew it wasn't going to stop until he opened his eyes.

Blood.

Everywhere.

Pouring out of her.

How could she still be alive when so much of her blood was on the ground?

Her eyes looked up at him with fear, with pain, with disbelief.

He turned away, closing his eyes, unable to watch her die.

She screamed again, his name this time. "Rob!"

It cut through him like the blade of a knife.

But that wasn't his name... How did she know... He opened his eyes in shock.

It was Jess lying there, Jess covered with blood, *Jess* looking at him with her beautiful dark eyes as her life leaked away.

He shouted, pulling himself up out of the dream, surfacing in the dim light of her bedroom.

"Jess!" he cried, turning to look for her.

But he was alone in the bed.

And the blood on the sheets was his own.

UP ON THE FOURTEENTH floor, the temporary office of the Behavioral Science Unit of the FBI was silent. The empty office was big, with six or seven desks, each with two computer terminals, twice as many telephones, and several large conference tables covered with files and papers. Maps covered one whole wall, the largest being a street map of the city. There were red pins at the murder sites.

Also adorning the walls were scores of eight-by-ten black-and-white photos of the victims, taken from various angles. Jess swallowed, and kept her eyes carefully averted.

Ian had loved to watch slasher movies, and the violence had always sickened Jess. In some ways, these photos were less graphic than the scenes in those movies. But the women in the photos weren't lying in pools of special effects blood. The women in the photos weren't going to stand up and take a shower, washing the gore off them when the director yelled "Cut!"

Those women were dead. Totally, irreversibly dead. And Selma Haverstein and Parker Elliot thought Rob had killed them because of his twisted feelings for *her.* . . .

"Where is everybody?" she asked, and it came out a whisper.

"They're all over at Rob's apartment," Selma replied cheerfully. "Or out on the street. *Or* down at the lab. That's on the thirteenth floor. For luck, you know."

Movement from the other side of the room caught Jess's eye, and she turned to see Parker Elliot standing in the open doorway of a private office. He had a telephone tucked under his chin, but he waved, motioning for them both to come in.

As Jess sat down in a hard plastic chair across from his desk, Elliot hung up the phone. "How did Carpenter pay his rent?" he asked, not bothering with a greeting.

"Cash," Jess answered. She glanced at Selma.

"No checks, no credit cards, no paper records? It figures."

"Why?" Jess watched as the FBI agent lowered himself into his chair. He swiveled his computer monitor to a better angle, and adjusted his modem.

"They're verifying it now. . . ." Elliot said, distracted, keying something into the computer. He looked up at Jess and then at Selma Haverstein. "I can't believe the team didn't run an identity check on Carpenter before this. I'd just assumed it had been done. Apparently, so did everyone else...."

The computer beeped, and Elliot looked back at the screen, a frown furrowing his brow as he read intently for several moments. Then he shook his head, and laughed humorlessly.

"Still don't think Robert Carpenter's our man?" he asked Jess.

She shook her head. "No, I don't."

"Maybe this'll help convince you, Ms. Baxter," he said, turning the computer monitor to face both Jess and the psychologist. They leaned forward to get a closer look. "I just ran a full identity sweep on Robert Carpenter, middle name unknown, using the social security number he'd given his employer, and look what I found.

"The man doesn't exist. There is no such person. His social security number is fictional." He shook his head. "Damn, why didn't someone do this three weeks ago?"

Jess stared at the computer screen, but the words upon it merely repeated what Elliot was saying.

"So Robert Carpenter is an alias," Selma stated. Jess could barely make out the words over the roaring in her ears. "How do we find out who he really is?"

"There's where we have a problem," Elliot said. "It's the same problem we've had all along. Whoever he is, he's never been arrested and he's never been in the military. We don't have his fingerprints on file. In fact, out of the six different sets of prints we came up with in Carpenter's apartment, not a single one was on file." He paused, then dropped the bomb. "But we did make a match to the prints we've found in all of the victims' apartments."

"Jess, are you all right?" Selma asked, her voice coming as if from a distance.

Jess was still staring at the computer.

Fingerprints.

Matched.

Rob's fingerprints matched the prints from the victims' apartments....

She saw him, on top of her as they made love, his eyes hot with passion, with love.... She heard her voice crying out his name as the world exploded around her. Rob...

No, not Rob. His name wasn't really Rob.

Rob Carpenter was a made-up name, an alias.

For whom?

In her sudden whirl of thoughts, she remembered Rob telling her, *My father was a beast, and it's his blood that's in my veins....*

Jess, I've done some terrible things, things that can't be forgiven....

I have to leave because I love you, Jess. I won't let you be hurt...or killed....

"Oh, Lord," Jess breathed, her voice shaking. "It can't be true...."

"Parker, get the girl some water," she heard Selma say sharply. Then more gently, Selma said, "Jess, I know what a shock this must be...."

Jess stood up. "I have to go."

Selma pressed a pamphlet into Jess's hands. "Read this, dear. Maybe it will help you to understand—there was no way you could have known that Rob was so...troubled." She sighed. "And if Rob should approach you, or call, or contact you in any way," she continued, "it's imperative that you notify the authorities. If you don't want to call Parker, dear, call me. However, if my theory is correct, I'd bet big money that Rob is long gone."

Selma's words seemed to swirl around Jess. Rob. Long gone.

"If he *does* return, and he *is* the killer," Selma added, "then he probably only came back for one reason—to kill *you*."

Killer. One reason. Kill *you*.

Woodenly, Jess turned toward the door.

"Wait for Parker, dear, he'll drive you home."

But Jess didn't want to wait. She walked out of the office, past the walls plastered with the horrible, gruesome photographs. She walked out into the hall, over to the elevator and pushed the down button.

Outside the building, she continued to walk, aimlessly heading south and west. She walked all the miles down to the quay, and finally she stopped walking. She sat for a while, just looking out over the water.

No matter how she tried to figure it out, she couldn't ignore the fact that Rob was using an assumed name. Even taken by itself, apart from the damning fingerprints, having an alias suggested some degree of criminality.

As she sat there, she realized she was still holding the pamphlet Dr. Haverstein had given her, outlining the profile of the serial killer.

Slowly, Jess opened it.

Number one was ritualistic behavior. Well, according to Selma, the ritual was part of the killing. Each of the women killed had applied thick makeup to their faces, and had a length of rope tied to their ankles. What it meant, no one but the killer knew, but it was definitely some kind of ritual.

Number two was pretense of sanity. Well, yeah, sure, Rob seemed sane enough. But so did everyone else she knew. So how do you tell the serial killers from the rest of the people? You don't. At least, often enough, not before it's too late.

Number three was compulsive personality. Excessive cleanliness was mentioned. Jess thought of the difference between Rob's kitchen and her own. No fair, she thought. Rob didn't have a six-year-old daughter. But still, he was neat almost to the point of obnoxiousness....

Number four was inability to tell the truth. According to the pamphlet, serial killers not only attempted to provide people around them with the information that those people wanted to hear, but they also were unable to perceive the difference between reality and fantasy. Truth was whatever they wanted it to be, *when*ever they wanted it to be.

Great. That meant if she went and asked Rob if he was a serial killer, he would perceive that she wanted him to tell her no, so he'd say no. So whether he was, or whether he wasn't, the answer would still be no....

Number five was suicidal tendencies and-or paranoid thinking. Rob had the second half of *that* one covered, from the mysterious people who were out to get him to the money he kept hidden in the freezer.

Number six was alcohol or drug-abusing parents.

Number seven was physical or emotional abuse as a child. *My father was a beast....*

Jess put down the pamphlet.

She could remember the look on Rob's face after they made love.

She could see the way his mouth curved, at first just a bit at the edges, then more and more until his face broke into a genuine smile.

She could see his eyes hot with desire, warm with love, even icy with anger.

But she couldn't, not for the life of her, picture him raping a woman and slitting her throat.

She simply could not imagine it.

There must be some kind of mistake.

Pushing herself to her feet, Jess found a pay phone, slipped a quarter in the coin slot, and dialed the number on Selma's card.

As the older woman picked up, Jess didn't even bother to identify herself. "I still don't believe it's Rob," she said.

Selma sighed. "Jess—"

"Did we or did we not have a deal?"

"Of course we—"

"Then get a warrant, and search Ian's condo."

Selma sighed again. "All right, but—"

"I need to speak to Mr. Elliot," Jess continued. "I have some questions for him."

"I'll connect you right away."

There was a brief pause, then the FBI agent's voice came on. "Elliot."

"You said there were six sets of fingerprints found in Rob's apartment."

"Jess, tell me where you are, I'll come give you a ride home." His voice was oddly gentle, but she couldn't let the surprise of his unexpected kindness distract her.

"Just answer my question, please."

"Yes, that's right. Six sets."

"How can you be sure which of those six sets are Rob's?"

Elliot was silent for a moment. "We can't," he finally answered. "One set of prints was that of a child. We're assuming those belong to your daughter. One set is yours." He laughed shortly. "You probably won't like this, but we took your prints off a glass in your kitchen."

"I hope you intend to return the glass," Jess said.

"We already did."

"So that leaves four sets of fingerprints," she concluded. "One of the sets you've matched to the killer's."

"Yes. What exactly are you driving at, Ms. Baxter?" Parker Elliot sounded impatient.

"You *can* call me Jess," she told him, "and drop the Ms. Baxter crap."

She could almost see him bristle on the other end of the phone. "I'm just trying to be polite—"

"You're *just* trying to intimidate me, Elliot, so cut it out. You called me Jess a minute ago."

"I did?"

"Yeah. You slipped and actually acted human."

He gave a short bark of laughter. "You sound like Selma," he said. "All right, *Jess,* get to the point of this phone call."

"Four people were in Rob's apartment," Jess said. "Four people, four sets of fingerprints. But if those four people walked out of that apartment and stood in a line, you'd really have no way of knowing which of them was the murderer. Not unless you took their fingerprints."

Elliot laughed again. "I get it," he said. "You're still working hard on denying that Carpenter's the killer. Okay." He took a deep breath, exhaling loudly. "We'll go with this for a while. We have four sets of prints, four men. And you're right. Any one of those four could be the man we're looking for. We're assuming it's Carpenter because of the evidence we found in the car that he'd been driving."

"What if," Jess continued. "What if I told you that I could name the men that the four sets of prints belonged to, and what if I told you that each of those men at one time or another borrowed Rob's car?"

Elliot suddenly became very, very silent. "Go on," he finally said.

"Rob is one, my ex-husband Ian Davis is two, Frank Madsen, a friend of ours who worked with Rob and stayed in his apartment for a few weeks is three, and Stanford Greene, who lives next door is four," Jess concluded. "And you're right. I don't think Rob's the one you're looking for. I think it's Ian."

"The ex-husband?" He swore softly, on a sigh. "All right. Give me Davis's address. I'll go by there and check his place out. And we'll pick him up for questioning."

Jess felt the hope she was carrying around in the pit of her stomach start to expand. "So you think it could be Ian . . . ?"

Elliot sighed again, even softer this time. "It's a nice theory, Jess, but unfortunately it doesn't offer an explanation for Carpenter's lack of proper identification. You know, it's not exactly legal to use an assumed name and social security number. Whoever he is, he has something to hide," he said. "My money's still on Carpenter being our man."

"But you'll take Ian's fingerprints," Jess persisted, "and compare them to the killer's?"

"We will."

She closed her eyes. "I *know* it's Ian."

Elliot sighed again, and when he spoke, his voice had lost its hard edge. He sounded remarkably compassionate. "If it's Ian," he asked, "then why is Rob the one who's running?"

HE WAS GOING TO have to change. Too many people were afraid. Too many people knew what to look for.

Too bad.

He liked the rope. He liked it a lot.

Maybe just one more time . . .

He closed his eyes, drifting off to sleep again.

Jess.

She was always there in his dreams. She smiled radiantly, her face lovely, so lovely. . . .

But suddenly the smile wasn't for him. She was turning, walking away. . . .

He felt the rush of panic. Don't leave, he wanted to shout, but she just kept walking. He tried to run toward her, but he felt as if he were surrounded by molasses. He could barely move, barely breathe. . . .

He screamed again, and it came out a strangled moan.

She turned.

But her face had changed.

She wasn't Jess. She was his mother. She was so big, so angry, her eyes impossibly red with rage, towering over him. . . .

"You can't have her," his mother taunted. Laughing harshly, abrasively. He wanted to cover his ears the way he had when he was a boy.

But the blade was in his hand. He could feel the cold smoothness of the metal.

"She'll never be yours," she said, her face mocking. "You worthless piece of—"

He struck.

The sound of the blade slicing was so familiar, the hiss of her windpipe, the spray of warm blood on his face. . . .

Her eyes began to glaze as the life left her body. But still she smiled, now lovingly, tenderly. And spoke.

"Kill her."

Chapter Seventeen

Slowly, Jess unlocked the kitchen door, and let herself inside.

It was quiet as dusk drew near. She could hear the kitchen clock ticking, the second hand pounding its way around the dial.

Ian was the killer. It *had* to be him.

Not Rob.

Still, she left the kitchen door open.

Parker Elliot was going to stop by after he went over to Ian's and checked out his sick idea of wallpaper. And in the meantime, there were still several other FBI agents finishing up their work in Rob's apartment. If Jess screamed, someone would hear her.

But that was ridiculous. She wouldn't have any reason to scream. It wasn't Rob. It was Ian.

But Parker Elliot was convinced Rob was the killer.

Rob.

She didn't even know his real name.

Her heart in her throat, Jess moved quietly through the apartment, and pushed open her bedroom door.

It was darker in there with all the shades pulled down. She let her eyes adjust, and saw Rob lying in the middle of her bed. He lay on his back, one arm thrown carelessly over his head, legs twisted in the sheet.

He breathed slowly, steadily, his face relaxed.

He looked so young, so innocent, even with the tattoos on his arm. Maybe especially *because* of the tattoos on his arm...

He *couldn't* be a killer.

She crept past him, into the bathroom, where his clothes were lying on the floor.

His jeans were caked with dried blood, and his socks and underwear were filthy. She carried them carefully into the laundry room that was just off the kitchen, and tossed everything into the washing machine. There wasn't time to wash it separately.

Back in the kitchen, she washed her hands, then picked up the phone and quickly dialed Doris's number.

Her friend answered on the second ring.

"Hi, it's me," Jess said. "Sorry I'm calling so late. How's Kelsey?"

"She's fine. She's teaching my two-year-old how to color. They're both happy, and I've even managed to get some of my work done around the house," Doris said.

"I need to ask you a huge favor," Jess said.

Doris laughed. "How huge?"

"Well . . ."

"How late do you want her to stay?" Doris asked, making it easy. "Can't be past eleven, I've got a class over at Ringling School of Art in the morning."

"Eleven is no problem," Jess responded, glancing at the clock. It was six-thirty. "It'll probably be more like nine-thirty or ten."

"You're lucky she's an angel," Doris said.

"I know. Doris, thank you. You're an angel, too."

Jess hung up the phone and got out her big spaghetti pot. She started filling it with water.

She wasn't hungry. In fact her stomach felt tight, almost sick with anxiety. But she wanted to give Rob something to eat before she . . .

Kicked him out.

She closed her eyes, the sick feeling in her stomach getting stronger. That's what she was going to do. She was going to kick Rob out of her house at a time when he needed her the most.

But he couldn't stay here. Not with Kelsey here, too.

He wasn't the killer.

She believed that with almost all of her heart.

But what if, just what if she was wrong?

For God's sake, she didn't even know his damned *name*.

She might've been willing to risk her own life, but not her daughter's.

So she'd feed him, make sure his clothes were clean, and she'd drive him over to the beach house. He could stay there for a few days. At least until his ankle got strong enough to walk on.

She put the pot of water on the stove and turned the gas up high, then got the sauce and a pile of fresh vegetables from the refrigerator.

She turned the radio on to the country station and set the volume low enough so it wouldn't wake Rob, then fell into a pattern of cutting. Summer squash, cauliflower, broccoli, green beans, snap peas. She moved slowly, taking her time, afraid that if she slipped and cut herself, the sight of her blood would take away her last bit of control. Finally, she put everything together in the vegetable steamer, and turned it on low.

As the water for the pasta began to boil, she heard the washing machine complete its cycle. She poured nearly an entire box of little pasta shells into the pot, stirred it once, then went back into the laundry room.

The dried blood on the jeans hadn't washed out, but the stain looked more like dirt now. She wasn't sure what to do about the hole. . . .

A knock on the door made her jump, and she stuffed the jeans into the dryer and turned it on before she went out into the kitchen.

It was Parker Elliot.

He stood on the other side of the screen, looking in at her. She resisted the urge to glance nervously back at the hallway that led to the bedroom where Rob was sleeping.

"May I come in?"

Damn, thought Jess, but she opened the screen door, and he stepped inside.

Elliot sniffed appreciatively at the aromatic spaghetti sauce that was bubbling on the stove. "I just spoke to Selma," he reported. "Ian Davis wasn't home when I went over to his place. We've got a warrant out for him now."

He was watching her closely, his sharp gray eyes not missing the sudden paleness of her face. Jess sat down heavily at the kitchen table.

"He could be anywhere," she said.

"I'll leave a man out in front of your house tonight," he assured her. "At least until we locate Davis."

Jess put her head in her hands. "Lord, I wish this would just be over."

"I've been wishing that for a long time," Elliot said quietly. "I started wishing that the day I opened the file and read the first murder reports from the Sarasota Police."

Jess looked up at him, watching as he lifted the lid off the pot of spaghetti sauce and stirred it with the spoon that was out on the counter.

"I'm going to nail this guy," he vowed. His voice was deceptively soft, but his eyes were as hard as rocks. "I'm going to see him burn. But, you know, it never ends. I'll go back to Quantico and find seven new files on my desk. Seven new killers working overtime. My team will help me pick one, and we'll spend six months tracking down that—"

Elliot used a word Jess didn't expect to hear, coming from him. It seemed so emotional, so heartfelt, so spontaneous. He apologized instantly.

"I'm sorry," he said. "I must be more tired than I thought. In this job, I've seen the worst mankind can dish out. Still, I'm constantly appalled at the things people do."

He looked down at the kitchen floor, and for a moment, Jess could see the weariness in his face.

"Parker," she began. "Maybe Selma's right. Maybe you should take a vacation."

There was no mistaking the hope in his eyes as he looked up at her, and inwardly she swore to herself. He wanted her to invite him to stay—for dinner, and maybe even more.

"I can't ask you to stay," Jess said softly.

Elliot hid his disappointment with a curt nod. "I know." He turned to the door. "I'll call you after we apprehend Davis."

"Thank you, I'll feel better knowing you've caught him."

He nodded again and left.

Jess sighed, and remembering his warning about Ian, locked the kitchen door.

The timer buzzed, so she turned off the pasta, and poured it into the colander that was perched in the middle of the sink.

Then she went to wake up Rob.

Already awake, he looked at her as she pushed open the door. She stood in the doorway and watched him.

"You really draw them like flies, don't you?" His voice was soft.

"What?" Jess asked uncertainly.

"You know," Rob said. "Men." He painfully pulled himself up, holding on to the bedpost so that he was sitting in the bed. He looked mysterious in the dim light. Shadows fell across his face, and outlined and defined the strong muscles of his bare chest and arms. "That guy was FBI, right?"

Silently, Jess nodded.

"I can understand how it must've driven Ian nuts," Rob continued. "Wherever you go, men fall all over themselves to help you, to try to be near you—"

"I don't ask for it," Jess interjected, her chin out in defense. "I treat everyone exactly the same—"

"Jess, I know, I'm not accusing you of anything," Rob said, his voice gentle.

Jess's heart felt squeezed. Nearly every word that sprang to her lips, everything that she wanted to say to him was an accusation. And yet she could barely look at him without wanting to feel him lying against her. She wanted him to kiss her, hold her....

"I washed your clothes," she managed to say. "They're in the dryer now. And I made you something to eat."

He nodded, his face still in the shadows. "After that, I'll go."

"I'll drive you to my parents' beach house on Siesta Key," she whispered, not looking at him. "It'll be empty until next weekend. That should give your ankle enough time to heal...."

Rob didn't speak for a moment, watching her. She hadn't moved from the doorway, hadn't come closer. Her head was bent now in misery.

"Jess, I love you," he said, pain in his voice. "I never meant to hurt you this way."

"Tell me what you're running from," she pleaded, her voice low.

He shifted his weight, and she looked at him. Suddenly spooked by the shadows, she flipped on the light. He looked down, eyes shut against the sudden brightness. He was silent, not answering her question.

With the light on, she could see the lines of strain on his face, the pain that was etched about the corners of his mouth. She could see where his leg had bled through the bandage and the sheet. She could see the tension in his shoulders and neck. She could see the muscle working in his jaw.

And then she couldn't see anything, blinded by her own tears. Angrily she wiped them away. "*Damn* it," she said. "Tell me. At least tell me your *name*. Your *real* name."

As she watched, he nodded, very slowly, very slightly, still looking away from her.

"Connor Garrison," he said.

"Connor," Jess repeated, her voice only a whisper.

He looked up at her then, and she gasped.

Blue.

His eyes were blue. Not just any old blue, but nearly turquoise.

"Oh, Lord," Jess breathed.

All this time, he'd been wearing contact lenses to make his eyes look brown. His name wasn't Rob, it was *Connor*. His soft brown eyes were really brilliant blue.

She looked at his brown hair, then down at the hair on his arms and legs. It was noticeably lighter. "Your hair's really blond," she stated. It wasn't even a question.

But he answered it anyway. "Yes." He looked up at her, miserably. "I'm sorry," he said.

"Tell me why."

He shook his head.

"Please?" The tears had appeared again, and she pushed them impatiently away.

But still he was silent.

She held his gaze several long moments. His blue eyes were beautiful, such an unusual shade, and she could easily picture his hair golden instead of brown. He had been good-looking before, but with those extraordinary eyes he was startlingly, breathtakingly, *noticeably* handsome.

With brown contact lenses and his hair a nondescript shade of brown, with his glasses on, hiding the handsome lines of his face, with his understated, average, yuppified clothes, he could blend into any crowd. He could hide.

"Who are you hiding from?" she asked, her voice shaking.

He didn't answer—*wouldn't* answer.

She spun on her heels and went out into the kitchen, into the laundry room. She pulled his clothes from the dryer, welcoming the burning heat from the jeans' brass rivets on her hands. It cut through the numbing anger that had enveloped her.

Back in the bedroom, she threw the clean clothes at his head, then stormed back into the kitchen. She piled a plate with pasta, vegetables and sauce, and carried it back to the bedroom. Suppressing an urge to throw *that* at him, too, she put it down on the bedside table, and turned to walk out.

He caught her wrist.

She looked at his hand pointedly, but he didn't let go. Please, Lord, she thought, don't let him feel the way my pulse speeds up when he touches me....

He didn't release her until she met his eyes.

They were so soft, so remorseful.... So blue.

"I'm sorry," he whispered.

She turned and left the room, closing the door tightly behind her.

JESS STARED DOWN into her own plate of pasta as she sat at the kitchen table.

Connor Garrison.

Did he call himself Connor? Con for short?

But it didn't matter.

In a few minutes, she would drive him out to the Key, and then she'd never see him again.

She could hear him moving around in the bedroom, getting dressed, she supposed.

Without warning, the front doorbell rang, and Jess jumped. In the bedroom, Rob was still.

It rang again.

Slowly, Jess stood up and went to the door. She opened it, keeping the chain on.

She sighed with relief. It was only Frank.

There was also a man, a stranger, standing on the front walk, down by the sidewalk.

Jess took the chain off and opened the door.

"Everything all right?" the man called. He was the FBI agent Elliot had left to watch the house. Jess could see the dark shape of his car out on the street.

"Yes," she replied. "Thanks."

A wind was starting to pick up, and Jess glanced at the night sky. She could see only a few stars directly overhead and to the east, and they were hazy from high clouds. The rest of the sky was black, stars covered by the storm front rolling in from the gulf.

"Heavy rain's coming in," Frank said. "Yes, sir! I beat it into town by just a few hours."

Jess stepped out onto the porch. "Frank, I'm sorry about the other night."

He shrugged and smiled. "That's okay. I got beeped and had to get right back to the job. We wouldn't have had time to talk anyway. Can I come in?"

Nervously, she glanced down at her watch. Five after eight. "I don't know, Frank, I've got to go pick up Kelsey from the sitter's...."

Frank opened the screen door as if he hadn't heard her. "I was shocked when I heard about Rob," he said, going into the living room. Helplessly, Jess followed him into the house. "I mean, I *knew* he had some problems, but—"

"Rob *isn't* a killer!"

"His picture is in all the papers. The drawing they made doesn't look very much like him at all."

"I haven't seen it," Jess said, crossing her arms.

Frank sat down on the sofa, but Jess stayed standing. "You're lucky they've managed to keep you out of it," he continued. "Not a single one of the papers mentions you."

"Why would the newspapers want to mention *me?*"

Frank took off his sport jacket and loosened his tie. When he glanced up at her, his pleasant face was apologetic. "You know how reporters can be. Anything sensational or titillating... And Rob living next door to you—" He broke off. "But I didn't come over here tonight to talk about Rob. I came over...well, to find out if you've, you know, thought about that conversation that we had. Maybe we could have dinner tomorrow night—you know, make it a real date.''

Jess slowly sat down in the easy chair. ''Please Frank, can we talk about this another time?''

He looked at her, his eyes wide and earnest. ''A simple yes or no is all I'm looking for.''

She took a deep breath, and closed her eyes. ''Then, no, Frank. No, I can't go out with you. Not now.''

He sighed. ''That's too bad.''

''I'm sorry—''

''Me, too.''

''I don't have time to explain right now,'' Jess said gently. ''But really, Frank, it's not you. You're very sweet—''

''It's Rob, isn't it?'' There was a spark of anger in Frank's normally serene eyes.

Jess shook her head. ''No—''

''Don't lie!'' Frank's voice rose. ''I'm not stupid, Jess. I know you were close to him before. I just hadn't realized how close you'd gotten again.''

''Frank—''

''Two weeks, I stayed with you. I took care of you, I made sure that you were safe. I never touched you, even though I wanted to. God, I wanted to... You're so beautiful, Jess....''

There were tears in Frank's eyes as he reached for her hand. But she stood up, moving away from him. Lord, she'd suspected he had a crush on her, but she had no idea the extent of it.

''It's not fair.'' Frank pulled himself to his feet, his voice getting louder.

Jess nervously moved a few steps back. He was so tall.... ''Frank, I'd like to talk about this, but not right now. I have to get Kelsey, and—''

''There's nothing to think through,'' Frank nearly spat the words out. ''I lose. Again.''

''I'm sorry—''

''No, you're not—''

''If she says she's sorry, she's sorry.''

Frank froze, looking over Jess's shoulder.

Slowly, Jess turned to see Rob standing in the doorway. He'd put his brown contact lenses back in, and was wearing his jeans.

He'd found one of her oversize T-shirts in her dresser, and the big, old hooded sweatshirt in her closet, and wore them in place of his ripped shirt. He hadn't shaved, and the two-day growth of beard on his face glinted almost reddish in the living room light.

"Well, well," Frank said. "Look who's here. I should have known you'd be lurking around somewhere."

"Sit down, Frank," Rob instructed calmly.

Frank had four inches and probably seventy-five pounds on Rob. He took a step forward, menacingly. "No."

Rob barely moved his fingers, and suddenly his knife was in his hand, blade open. He took a step toward Frank. "Yes."

Frank's eyes were on the knife as he backed up and sat down on the couch.

Rob came farther into the room, his movement smooth and sure. Jess frowned. She'd *seen* his swollen ankle and the sprain had been a nasty one. By all rights, he shouldn't even be able to put his weight on it.... Rob moved closer, and Jess could see a film of perspiration on his face. He was in serious pain.

Realization hit her. He didn't want Frank to know he was hurt. He didn't want Frank to tell the police he'd been injured. And they could count on Frank going straight to the police after... After what?

What on earth were they going to do with Frank while Jess drove Rob to the beach house?

"Get some rope," Rob ordered her.

She stared at him blankly.

"I said, get some rope, dammit." His voice rough, he brandished the knife in her direction.

Jess stared at the knife, then back up at Rob. "Rope?" she asked faintly.

"Rope," he repeated, giving her a look that Frank couldn't see. Please, his eyes said, imploring her, begging her, their softness belying the edge in his voice. "So I can tie Frank up."

Jess understood. This was part of Rob's plan to be sure that she wouldn't be accused of helping him escape.

"I think there's some out in the garage," she said, glancing at Frank. He was sitting quietly, his eyes watchful.

Rob nodded. "Get it." His eyes hardened as he looked back at Frank.

Jess headed for the door to the garage, but Rob's words stopped her.

"And if you try to leave, or escape . . . I'll kill him."

She glanced back at him, and the look on his face was so strange, so terrible, she could almost believe it.

But he's just pretending, she told herself, as she turned on the garage light. He's just playacting. Isn't he?

A rope was hanging on a hook on the garage wall, next to a length of orange outdoor extension cord, and a roll of speaker wire. Jess pulled the rope down. There was about ten feet of it. It was nylon, sturdy and bright blue, the kind of rope used for grappling or mountain climbing.

She carried it into the living room and handed it to Rob.

"Get a chair from the kitchen," he ordered her, and silently she complied.

"Sit there," Rob told Frank, pointing at the chair.

Frank didn't move.

Rob grabbed Jess, hard, pulling her against his chest, holding the blade of his knife dangerously close to her throat. She gasped, her fear not entirely feigned.

"Move!" Rob said.

Frank moved from the couch to the kitchen chair, his face expressionless.

Rob let go of Jess, pushing her away from him with enough force to make her stumble. He tossed the blue rope down at her feet.

"Tie him."

Jess's fingers were shaking as she pulled Frank's hands behind the back of the chair. She started to tie them together using the only knot she knew—a square knot, but Rob stopped her.

"Use a slipknot," he commanded. Then, because she hesitated, he impatiently told her how.

She put Frank's hands in the loop, and pulled, tightening it.

But not tight enough. Rob reached down and jerked the rope hard enough to make Frank flinch from the pressure.

"You don't have to hurt him," Jess protested.

Abruptly, Rob pushed her aside, holding his knife in his teeth as he secured Frank to the chair.

Frank's hazel eyes looked at Jess worriedly. "You're going to die," he said. "Just like the others."

Jess shook her head. "No."

"Yes, sir."

With a big heave, Rob turned the entire chair around, so that Frank was facing the television. He turned the TV on, flipped to the sports channel and cranked the volume. A baseball game was on, and the announcers' lazy voices were at a near deafening volume. If Frank tried to shout for help, he wouldn't be heard.

Jess was relieved. She hated the thought of having to gag poor Frank.

Rob grabbed her arm roughly. "Come on."

She took one last look back at Frank. Now that Rob's back was turned, he was struggling, trying to get free of the ropes.

His face was frightened, eyes wide, nostrils flared. She saw his mouth form her name before Rob pulled her down the hall to the garage.

Chapter Eighteen

Out in the garage, Rob leaned heavily against the car, putting his head down and favoring his injured leg. He closed his eyes and swore softly and steadily, finally letting his pain show.

The switchblade had disappeared—back up his sleeve, Jess assumed.

She moved closer, and he opened his eyes, looking at her. "I'm sorry I had to be so rough," he said. "But—"

"I know," she interrupted. "We should get going. If Frank manages to get free ..."

"He won't," Rob stated. "Not the way I tied him."

His face was pale, with beads of sweat on his upper lip and forehead. He wiped his face with his sleeve.

Where did you learn to tie someone up like that, Jess wanted to ask. Where did you learn to act so ruthlessly, so cold-bloodedly matter-of-fact about taking a prisoner?

Silently, she opened the car door and helped Rob into the back seat. She covered him carefully with her beach blanket.

Then she got into the car, closed her eyes briefly, and pushed the remote control that opened the garage door.

A turn of the key, and the engine roared to life. She backed out of the garage, turning around in the driveway. Praying that they wouldn't be stopped by the FBI man, she pulled onto the street.

Oh, no, the FBI agent got out of his car, motioning for her to stop. If he got close enough to look in the back seat, he'd surely see Rob....

Quickly Jess rolled down her window, leaning out slightly. "I'm going to pick up my daughter from the baby-sitter's," she called to him.

He waved, moving back to his car.

Thank God, Jess thought, and tried not to speed as she drove out of the FBI agent's sight.

For fifteen minutes, they drove in silence. Jess made their way across town, turning frequently to take smaller side roads. There weren't many cars out even though it was still early. Everyone was staying home on account of the storm's imminent arrival.

The wind was much brisker now, and a large gust tugged at the chassis of her car, blowing them slightly to the left until she compensated for it.

Just as suddenly as the wind gusted, it died down, and the release of the pressure on the car made Jess swerve slightly to the right, hitting a pothole with unexpected force.

She heard a muffled exclamation from under the beach blanket.

"You all right?" she asked, glancing again in the rearview mirror. The road behind them was empty. They weren't being followed. "We're clear, if you want to sit up."

Rob pulled back the blanket. "I never noticed what an incredibly nonexistent suspension system this car has until now."

"So sit up."

"I prefer bumpy to apprehended, thanks."

"But we're *not* being followed."

"Why take a chance?" Rob asked.

Jess shook her head. "If *that* was my philosophy, I probably wouldn't be in this car with you right now."

Rob was silent.

"I would never hurt you, Jess," he finally said, very quietly.

From out of nowhere, Jess could feel the tears welling up in her eyes, and she willed them away. You will *not* cry, she told herself fiercely. You were doing so well up to this point....

"I didn't think you would," she said, downshifting as she approached a red light. "Can't you tell me—" her voice broke, and she struggled to get it back in control. "*Won't* you tell me one thing, just *one* thing about . . . Connor."

She heard him sigh very softly.

She couldn't keep her voice from shaking slightly as she made the right turn onto the causeway that led to Siesta Key. They were only a few minutes from the beach house now.... "Tell me..." she said. "Tell me what you did for a living when you were Connor Garrison."

He didn't answer for a solid sixty seconds. And when he did speak his voice was low. Jess had to strain to hear him. "It's not important."

"What?"

Louder now. "I was insignificant. I worked in an office, in the mail room. It was meaningless. But my roommate Chris, now, *he* had a job. He made more money in a week than I made in a month. He was a deliveryman. He worked for his uncle, he told me. I didn't ask any questions, which was pretty stupid, but I was young, God, I was barely twenty years old. Then one night Chris was in a bind and he needed me to help him make his deliveries. That was when I found out his Uncle Frank was head of a crime syndicate. Chris was distributing cocaine, and I was helping him. I was helping him run drugs."

Jess felt sick. Crime syndicate. Drugs. Parker Elliot had been right. Rob—*Connor* was a criminal.

He sharply drew in a breath in pain as they went over the edge of the driveway and the car bounced. "Back then I was saving every cent I made," he said, as Jess pulled to a stop outside the beach house. "I had this dream. I wanted to travel, and write books about exotic places. Well, I got the traveling, but I haven't written a word in over eight years. Check to make sure we weren't followed. Please?"

She dragged her eyes up to the rearview mirror. No one behind them. Getting out of the car, Jess walked to the edge of the driveway and looked up and down the street, trying to be casual. There were no other cars in sight, and the shrubbery and bushes shielded them from the neighbors' view. She opened the door and looked at Rob...*Connor*.

Connor Garrison—the drug runner.

She helped pull him out of the car. Lord, he was heavy. He managed to bump his injured ankle on the car door, and he stood there for a moment, balancing on one leg, swaying slightly from the pain.

The wind was stronger coming in off the water, and a large burst swirled around them. Jess was afraid the gust would knock Rob over, and she put her arms around him.

He held on to her tightly, and she could hear his heart pounding in his chest, even over the roar of the wind and the rising surf.

Lightning crackled out over the gulf, way in the distance, and thunder rumbled ominously.

The hell of it was, Jess thought, she loved him. Connor or Rob or whatever he wanted to call himself, brown-eyed, blue-eyed, green-eyed . . . It didn't matter.

She loved him.

So he'd made a mistake when he was twenty—that was how old *she'd* been when she'd married Ian. And talk about mistakes . . .

She could forgive Connor for his mistakes. She *did* forgive him.

Could she forgive him for the brutal murders of fifteen young women?

Never.

But he wasn't the killer. She was more convinced of that than ever. Selma Haverstein was wrong. Elliot was wrong.

This man may have broken the law, he may have made some mistakes, but he was no killer. In her heart, she'd known that all along.

"Come on," she urged. "I'll help you get inside."

With his lips pressed tightly over clenched teeth, he nodded. And together, they wrestled him through the kitchen door and into the house.

He leaned up against the kitchen counter and loosened his hold on her shoulders.

But Jess didn't let go of him, wouldn't let go of him. She held him tightly, arms wrapped around his waist, pressing her body close to his.

"Jess," he said softly, with such wonder in his voice. His arms went back around her, slowly, tentatively.

She looked up at him, letting all of her love for him show in her eyes. He inhaled sharply as he saw her face.

Pulling his head down toward hers, Jess kissed him.

It was a perfect kiss.

Slow and sweet, with an undercurrent of passion, it was filled with a love that would stretch beyond eternity. It carried a promise of things to come, of a lifetime of sharing—

It was a promise neither of them could keep.

He slowly, jerkily, pulled away from her, as if that single act cost him all that he had left.

"I love you," Jess said simply, and his eyes filled with tears.

He'd taken out his brown contacts, Jess realized. His eyes were brilliant blue and they held more than a trace of desperation.

It was time to say goodbye.

Jess let go of his hand, reaching down to pick up her purse. She opened it and took some money from her wallet.

"Here's eight hundred dollars," she told him, holding it out to him. "I know it's not a lot, but I know your money was all in your apartment and..."

Rob looked down at the bills in her hand, knowing with a flash of disbelief that she'd emptied out her savings account for him. For *him*. What had he done to deserve this woman's love?

He'd given her nothing but evasive answers and half-truths, and still she loved him enough to make such sacrifices for him.

"Take it," she whispered.

"No." He shook his head. "Thank you, Jess, but I've got enough money. I never use banks. I had cash hidden all over your house—most of it in your garage. So I've got plenty. I even left some behind for you. It's in the top drawer of your bedside table... I wanted you to have it. And, if the FBI doesn't find it, there's still some cash in my apartment. It's inside the control panel of the microwave." He smiled at the look on her face. "Yeah, they'll probably find it. But if they don't, I'd like you to keep it."

Slowly, she put the crisp hundred dollar bills back in her purse. "I don't want your money."

"Consider it the rent I owe you. You can pay Frank back."

Frank. They both thought of him at the same time. He was tied up in Jess's living room, his hands and feet uncomfortably bound together....

"I should go," Jess whispered. "It's getting late. I have to pick up Kel . . . and untie poor Frank...."

Outside, lightning lit the white beach as the storm moved even closer. The wind knocked over an aluminum-framed beach chair out on the deck and they both jumped.

Jess's eyes were dark pools in her pale face. Rob could see uncertainty and sadness on her face, and he longed to see her smile. But there was nothing left to smile about. The only thing left for them was the pain.

Rob knew without a doubt that a very large part of him was going to die when she turned and walked out that door. He also knew the longer their goodbyes lasted, the more her leaving would rip into him, tear him open—and there'd be no chance of recovery.

And he knew without a doubt that she would feel the same.

He leaned forward, pulling her face toward him, kissing her fiercely, his lips hard and unyielding. She barely had time to respond before he pushed her away.

"Go," he said, his voice harsh.

"Rob—"

"Please, Jess. Go, and don't look back. Go home and untie Frank, and fall in love with him. He's a good man. He can give you all the things that I can't—"

"I don't *want* Frank! I told you that before—"

"This FBI agent then! What's his name?"

"You mean Parker Elliot?"

"*Elliot,* yeah—"

"Come on!" Jess said, angry. "I'm not going to be able to just *forget* you, as if you never existed. . . ."

"Jess, you've got to move forward—"

"No—"

He slammed the palm of his hand down on the kitchen table with a deafening crash. "Yes, dammit. Jess, will you please leave! *Now!* Quickly, because this is killing me!"

She grabbed her purse and fled toward the door. But when her hand touched the knob, she stopped and looked back. "You made me a promise," she said softly, tears overflowing and streaming down her face. "You damn well better keep it, Connor."

And then she was gone.

He heard her car whine as she backed out of the driveway. He heard the tires squeal in her haste to get away.

Outside the window, lightning flashed and this time the thunder was a deafening roar. The skies opened up and it rained, large heavy drops that hit the roof with enough of a racket to raise the dead.

Yeah, he'd promised Jess he'd come back and find her when he was done running from his demons, when he was finally free. But he'd never be free. All his promise had done was give her hope. And he'd have to carry that with him, too, on top of all his guilt and regrets. Every night before he went to sleep, he'd have to live with more than just his burning love for her. He'd have to live with knowing she was thinking about him, waiting for him to walk through her door.

Waiting for something that could never be . . .

He put his head in his hands, knowing that he had finally paid the ultimate price for his sins.

Chapter Nineteen

Selma Haverstein walked into Elliot's office without knocking.

"I'm done," she announced. "I've interviewed both of them."

Elliot had taken off his jacket and tie, and rolled up his sleeves. He stood up as she entered, and she saw he'd even untucked his shirt from his pants. His hair stood on end, as if he'd run his fingers through it repeatedly.

The effect of his disarray was charming. Selma had a sudden clear vision of Parker Elliot at age ten on his way home from church. But seeing him like this was also disturbing. The man was obviously exhausted. She suspected he hadn't slept in days. And she knew he wouldn't sleep until they caught the Sarasota Serial Killer.

"And?" he said, one eyebrow raised expectantly.

"And nothing."

He sat down behind his desk, his disappointment obvious. He ran a tired hand across his eyes. "Yeah, I knew that." He sighed.

Selma leaned over the desk, her face worried. "Parker, dear, I think you should call Jess. When I spoke to her on the phone before, she was so absolutely sure her ex-husband was the killer."

"There's something you're not telling me, isn't there?" Elliot's eyes narrowed as he looked across his desk at her.

The older woman sighed, her normally cheery round face full of anxiety. "I have a feeling that Jess knows where Rob Carpenter is."

His eyes were instantly flinty. "And you waited until *now* to tell me that? *Dammit,* Selma . . ."

"It's only a *feeling,* Parker. I have no evidence to base it on, no facts. . . ."

"I'll take one of your feelings over ten facts any day," Elliot said shortly. He turned around, searching for his jacket on the back of his chair. It had fallen off, onto the floor. He found it and quickly pulled his little notebook out of the breast pocket. As he flipped through the book, he picked up the telephone, stuck it between his ear and his shoulder, and dialed four quick numbers.

"Yeah, lab? You make a match on either of those two sets of prints I sent down earlier?" He paused, listening for a moment. "Yeah, thanks."

He hung up the phone, staring at the page in his notebook where he'd scribbled Jess's telephone number. "I've got two numbers for Jess," he said. "And I'm damned if I can remember which is her home."

Selma moved behind his desk to look over his shoulder. "That second number is out on Siesta Key. She told me she sometimes works out there and stays over someplace—her parents' beach house, she said. Try the top number first."

Elliot already had the phone back against his ear. "It's busy," he stated. He disconnected the line and dialed another number.

"Yeah," he barked. "Get me through to Johnson." He glanced at Selma. "He's sitting out in front of Jess's house—Yeah, Johnson, this is Elliot. Look, I need you to get a message to Ms. Baxter for me." Silence. He frowned. "What time was that?" He looked at his watch. "Okay, look, if she comes back, bring her down here, and don't take no for an answer. Thanks."

He met Selma's eyes. "She left her house over two hours ago—to pick up her kid at the baby-sitter's. Why don't I believe that?"

"Maybe you should try the other number," she urged. "In case she's there."

He nodded and dialed.

HE SAT VERY, VERY STILL, anticipating, playing it through over and over and over in his mind.

He could feel the spray of blood, hear the sigh of her windpipe....

He could picture her eyes dark with fear and pain.

Yes, sir.

He didn't mind waiting.

This was going to be *very* good.

JESS COULDN'T TELL if the windshield wipers weren't working right, or if the blur was simply from the tears she couldn't keep from falling.

She pulled into Doris's driveway at ten minutes after ten and wiped her face with a tissue, then loudly blew her nose. She took a deep breath, hating to face the bright lights and Doris's inquisitive eyes.

Just do it, she thought. Do it and get on home.

ROB STEPPED OUT of the shower and stared into the bathroom mirror. For the first time in over eight years, he allowed himself to look, *really* look into Connor Garrison's blue eyes.

But something was different. Gone was Connor's cocky, devil-may-care attitude. Instead, the blue eyes held caution, reserve, determination to survive. Eight and a half years on the run will do that to a man, he supposed.

Eight and a half years...

He'd only been Rob Carpenter for one of those years, yet he already mourned the loss of this particular identity more keenly than any before. He'd changed his name and his job and his past six different times, and he'd never felt as if he were leaving anything behind. He hadn't even felt this bad when he'd turned his back on his life as Connor Garrison.

Maybe because when he gave up his life as Connor, he'd really had nothing important to give up. His apartment had been a rat hole, despite the amount of money he paid in rent each month. He had no family—his father didn't count—and his neighbors wouldn't have hesitated to turn him in for the mob reward that was posted on him, dead or alive.

What, really, had he given up?

A silly dream of being a great writer. Big deal.

His freedom.

Freedom to live his life without constantly looking over his shoulder, without being afraid that someone would recognize him and try to collect that reward.

Freedom from guilt. He closed his eyes against the sudden vision of Janey, lying in a pool of blood, fear and disbelief in her eyes as she bled to death in his arms....

He shook his head, erasing the picture.

That was why Rob Carpenter had to disappear. That was why he had to give up Jess, even though it was killing him to do it. Because there was no way he would ever let her die like that. No way.

Sure, maybe she and Kelsey could go with him. He'd make sure they'd be safe. But a life on the run was no life at all. He knew that too damn well.

The phone rang, suddenly, shrilly, cutting through the sound of the rain and the rising wind.

Rubbing his wet hair with a towel, he limped painfully into the kitchen, and stared at the phone.

The house was supposed to be empty.

Jess's parents were out west somewhere visiting relatives or something, weren't they?

So who would be calling?

Jess?

His heart beat harder.

But he didn't dare pick it up.

After four rings, the answering machine clicked on, and Jess's recorded voice spoke. "Hi! We're not here, leave a message at the beep!"

"Jess, this is Parker Elliot," came a man's voice. Lightning crackled and thunder boomed, and Rob stepped closer to the answering machine so he could hear. "Please call me. It's imperative that we talk." There was a moment of silence, as if Elliot were listening to someone else speaking. "Yeah, uh, Jess, Selma thinks I should just leave this message, so... We pulled both Ian Davis and your neighbor, Stanford Greene, in for questioning, and neither of their prints matched our killer's. That pretty much leaves Carpenter—"

A woman's voice took over the phone. "Jess, I think you know where Rob is, and dear, it's important that we talk to you as soon as possible. Please call." She left the number.

There was a click as the line was disconnected. The answering machine beeped and was silent.

Rob stared at the telephone.

There was something wrong. There was something *very* wrong.

What was it Jess had said about the evidence the police had against him? Blood in the back of his car and some fibers. Right. And fingerprints. Whoever the killer was, he'd been inside his apartment.

Jess said there were six sets of prints from the apartment, and one of them matched the killer's. Kelsey's, hers, and four others. His. Ian's. Stanford's.

And Frank's.

Oh, God.

Frank.

KELSEY WAS ALREADY asleep, so Jess borrowed an umbrella from Doris and carried her daughter gently out to the car. She put Kel into the back seat, managed to get a seat belt around her small waist, then let her sag, like a rag doll, until she was lying across the seat. She covered her carefully with the blanket, aware that the rain falling on her back and legs was cold.

Lightning struck nearby, with a loud roar of thunder sounding almost simultaneously, and she hurried back to return the umbrella.

The rain fell faster and the wind gusted, blowing the water horizontally, and directly into her face. She was soaked as she got into the car, and she sat there for a moment, just dripping.

Finally, she started the car and headed for home.

ROB HUNG UP the phone. Busy. Her line was busy.

Quickly, he dialed another number.

"Yeah, hi, I'm at 2786 Midnight Pass Road, and I need a cab right now," he said.

"I'm sorry sir," a nasal voice replied. "All of our taxis are tied up at the moment. We can get someone out there in . . . ninety minutes."

He swore. "Please, it's an emergency— It's a matter of life and death."

"If it's an emergency, sir," the voice said calmly, "call the police."

He hung up.

Call the police.

If they put him in prison, he was a dead man. But he'd gladly trade his life for Jess's.

Thunder roared again, and he quickly pushed the message button on the answering machine, fast-forwarding until he found the telephone number the woman had left.

He punched the numbers into the phone.

A man answered, his voice tired. "Yeah."

Rob's mouth was dry. "Is this Parker Elliot?"

"Yes, who's this?" The voice was sharper now, more alert.

"Look, I need your help. Jess is in trouble. She's heading back to her house, and the killer's in there, only she doesn't know it's *him* and—"

"Who *is* this?"

He closed his eyes. "It's Rob Carpenter."

He could hear the mad scramble on the other end of the phone. There was a click, and a woman's voice came on. It was the same woman who had left part of the message for Jess.

"Rob? My name is Selma . . ."

"Please, you've got to help me. He's going to kill her—"

"*Who* is going to kill her?"

"Frank Madsen. He's in her living room. Please, don't let her go home."

Elliot spoke. "Where are you?"

"That doesn't really matter, does it?"

"Rob." Selma's voice was soothing. "We can help you, dear, if you just tell us where you are."

They didn't believe him, he thought, feeling a surge of panic. "Look, Jess thinks her ex-husband is the killer, but he's not. Stanford's not, I'm not, so that leaves *Frank*. And—" He broke off, staring at the telephone, realizing that he'd virtually handed them his location. It wouldn't take Elliot long to realize he'd overheard the message on the answering machine at the beach house, if he hadn't figured it out already....

Oh, God...

"Talk to me, Rob," Selma said. "We want to help you."

ELLIOT GOT DOWN to the parking lot and out to his car in less than forty-five seconds, talking on his cellular phone the entire time.

The adrenaline that coursed through his body felt good, *really* good. They had that bastard now. He'd painted himself into a corner and there was no way he could escape.

He spat out the orders, setting up the roadblocks, calling in the local and state police to help, calling any available units out to Siesta Key.

Hell, he called the unavailable units. Why bother keeping Johnson out in front of Jess's house when they had the killer's location pinpointed on Siesta Key?

Elliot pulled out of the parking lot into the driving rain, his tires squealing on the wet pavement.

JESS STOPPED at the side of the road as the rain became so heavy that it obscured her vision. Impatiently, she tapped the steering wheel with her fingers, wishing that she was home, hoping that she'd be able to persuade Frank not to call the police until the morning. She didn't think she could handle the countless questions, the inquisition that was sure to follow.

What was she going to tell them when they asked her where she dropped Rob off? What was she going to say when they asked her why she didn't call the police immediately, why she picked up Kelsey and drove all the way home first?

Because I was afraid, she thought. A good answer, as long as she didn't finish the sentence. Afraid of what? Afraid that Rob would be caught.

The rain lightened marginally, and she slowly pulled out into the street.

At this pace, she'd *never* get home.

She slowed as headlights raced toward her, and she thought she recognized the oversize FBI car that had been positioned outside her house. Where the heck was *he* going in such a hurry?

Unless, maybe they'd caught Ian....

Please God, she thought, staring hard at the road through the relentless rain. Let them have caught Ian, and let this all be over.

ROB'S HEAD WAS SPINNING. It wouldn't take the FBI long to set up roadblocks across the two bridges that connected the Key to the mainland. There was no way Rob could get there before they did. Especially not without a car, not with only one good leg.

There was just one thing he could do, and he prayed it would work. Because if it didn't, Jess was dead. And he was, too. He put the telephone receiver back to his ear.

"2786 Midnight Pass Road," he told Selma, in as calm a voice as he could manage. "That's where I am."

"Hang on a second, Rob," he heard Selma say, and after a short moment, she was back. "That was very brave, dear."

"Look, I wouldn't have told you where I am if I was the killer, right? So *please,* get someone over to Jess's house. Don't let her go in there alone. Selma, I don't want her to die."

"I don't want her to die, either, Rob," she said. "Is she there with you?"

He cursed, frustrated. "No! *Dammit,* I just told you. She's on her way home. You're wasting time!"

JESS PULLED INTO the driveway. The FBI agent's car was gone. It must've been the one she saw heading west so quickly on Bee Ridge Road.

She pushed the remote, pulling the car into the garage and closing the door after her.

Kelsey was fast asleep, her fingers curled into fists, pressed against her cheeks.

I'll untie Frank, Jess thought, before I bring Kel inside. God forbid she wakes up to find a man tied up in the living room.... *That* would be a hard one to explain.

Jess made sure the blanket covered Kelsey completely, then, leaving the car window open a crack, she went into the house.

THE RADIO CRACKLED in Elliot's car as he sped toward Siesta Key, going much too fast, considering the wind and rain.

"Yeah," he said shortly.

"We have an address for the perp," one of his team members told him. "2786 Midnight Pass Road. We've verified that the property is owned by Bill and Nadine Baxter."

"Is Jess with him?"

"Selma's not sure."

"She get him to confess?" Elliot asked.

"Not yet, but she's working on it."

"Just have her keep him talking," Elliot said. "That's all I want."

"PLEASE, ROB, just stay calm," Selma said.

"I *am* calm!" He took a deep breath, running his hands through his hair. "Look, I'm going to give it to you in a nutshell, all right?"

"I'm listening."

"Almost nine years ago, a friend of mine, my roommate, was a runner for a crime syndicate up in New York. He made deliveries. Of drugs. One day I . . . messed things up, and suddenly there was a million dollar contract on my head. The bosses wanted me, dead or alive. I started running and—"

"What did you do?"

"What?"

"You said you messed things up," Selma said. "What did you do?"

"I dumped a ten million dollar shipment of cocaine into the Hudson River."

Selma laughed. "You're kidding."

"No, ma'am, I'm dead serious. So was my friend's boss when he found out what I did."

A clap of thunder made the house shake.

"This is taking too long," Rob said. "When is Elliot going to get here?"

There was a moment of silence on the other end of the phone. "You *want* Parker Elliot to get there?"

"I *want* to go help Jess. God, this is killing me. If she's over there, alone with him . . ."

FRANK'S EYES were closed, and Jess stepped over his legs to turn off the television.

His eyes opened slowly, and he stared at her blankly for a moment, as if trying to remember where he was.

"Hi." She smiled. "I'm going to untie you, okay?"

He smiled back at her. "About time."

"I'M NOT THE KILLER," Rob insisted. "Selma, you've got to believe me."

"I'm not sure what to believe," she said carefully.

"Look, it can't hurt to cover all the bases, can it?" he said, persuasively. "Send someone over to Jess's. Please!"

"We've already got a man out there," Selma admitted. "Tom Johnson. He's sitting out in front of Jess's house. Elliot told him to stop Jess, and bring her downtown for some questions. She won't even get inside her house, Rob."

He slumped into a chair with relief. "Thank *God*," he said. "Thank you, Selma."

JESS STRUGGLED to untie the knots in the heavy nylon rope. "I'm sorry this is taking so long," she apologized.

"Why don't you get a knife, and cut it?" Frank said.

"It would be pretty hard to cut this rope," Jess replied. "My knives just aren't that sharp. I'm afraid I'd slip and hurt you."

Outside the window, lightning flashed, followed by a resounding crash of thunder.

The lights flickered slightly, and Jess looked up in alarm. "Oh, great, that's all we need. A blackout."

"This is crazy weather, isn't it?" Frank remarked.

Jess finally worked his hands free, then moved around in front of him, and started untying his feet.

He rubbed his wrists gingerly, and she looked up at him. "Frank, I'm really sorry about...well, about not wanting to go out with you. The time's just not right for me and..."

He shrugged. "I guess I really didn't expect you to."

The lights flickered again, and Jess looked up at them. "Don't you *dare* go off," she said, but they flickered again and went out.

She swore under her breath.

"What's the matter, Jess?" Frank murmured. "Don't you like the dark?"

Jess stood up. "No," she replied. "I don't. And I can't get this untied if I can't see the knot. Wait here, I'll light a candle."

Slowly, she felt her way into the kitchen.

"I keep a candle in the cabinet," she said, loud enough for her voice to carry into the living room. "Here it is." She pulled the candle down from the shelf. It was a taper candle stuck into a traditional candlestick, but the wax had melted and it was shaped like a sideways S. She searched through her junk drawer, looking for a book of matches. "Boy, wait'll you see this candle. Remember when the AC broke down last summer? It got so hot in the house, all the candles drooped. And Kelsey's crayons melted into one giant block...."

She gave up searching for the matches and switched on the front burner of the gas stove. It lit, and she held the end of the candle to the flames. She switched off the gas, and holding the candle, turned toward the living room.

Frank was standing in the doorway, holding the blue rope in his hands.

Jess jumped. "Lord! Frank! You scared me! How did you get that knot untied?"

The light from the candle played across his bland features. "I'm good with rope," he said, and smiled. "Yes, sir."

THE KITCHEN DOOR burst open, and Parker Elliot rocketed into the beach house, his gun drawn. Five or six agents followed him, along with several uniformed policemen. They quickly surrounded Rob, who was standing by the telephone, receiver in one hand, the other hand in the air.

Silently, he held out the phone to Elliot.

"Selma wants to talk to you," he said.

Elliot stared at Rob. Blue eyes? The description they had gave him brown eyes. What was going on? Why was he so calm? And where was Jess?

Parker Elliot took the phone, glancing first at the other agents who still had their weapons trained on Carpenter. "Johnson," he said, nodding at the wiry little man to his right. "Search him."

"Yes, sir," Johnson replied. "Okay, Carpenter. On the floor, on your belly, hands on your head!"

"Selma." Elliot spoke into the phone. "Good job. We got the bastard."

"No you didn't, dear."

Elliot's stomach started to hurt. "I don't think I want to hear this."

"I said, get on the floor," Johnson repeated, louder this time.

"Hang on, Selma," Elliot said.

Rob was staring at Johnson as if he were the devil incarnate. "Johnson?" he rasped, his voice barely a whisper. "*Tom* Johnson?"

"Well, yeah. How the heck do you know *me?*" the little man said, confusion on his face.

Rob turned and looked at Elliot in horror. "He's supposed to be watching Jess's house," he breathed. "He's supposed to keep her safe. What the *hell* is he doing *here?*"

"THE FLASHLIGHT'S batteries ran out a month ago," Jess said, digging under the sink, looking for more candles. "Kelsey was playing with it, and I guess it got left on. I kept meaning to pick up new batteries, but every time I went to the store, I couldn't remember if I should get size C or D."

She heard Frank opening the drawers.

"Candles wouldn't be in there," she told him. "Those are the utensil drawers."

"I know," Frank replied.

Something about his voice made her look up.

Something about...

He stood there, smiling at her in the flickering candlelight, holding her longest, sharpest knife. He drew it slowly across his thumb, then glanced down at the line of blood it left behind. "I think it's probably sharp enough," he said in his mild voice.

For one short moment, Jess stared at him, confused. Then, instantly it clicked. She drew in a ragged breath, shock coursing through her veins.

Frank.

All this time, it had been Frank. All those women, raped and murdered...

She bolted for the hall that led to the garage. She had to get out of here. She had to get *Kelsey* out of here....

Frank grabbed her, tackled her. She landed hard on the floor with him on top of her. The knife was still in his hand. He didn't hold it threateningly. He just held it, which was threat enough.

"Now, *that's* not very nice," he said reprovingly. "That's not nice at all."

SELMA WAS SHOUTING, her voice coming out like an enraged chicken over the telephone's tiny speaker. Elliot put the receiver back to his ear as he watched his men wrestle Carpenter to the ground.

"I heard that!" Selma shouted. "If Johnson is there with you, Parker, then Jess is alone in her house with the killer! Rob *isn't* the killer! Frank Madsen is!"

"What?" Elliot felt his teeth clench. As he watched, Rob struggled to get free. "Selma, that's crazy. This guy is nuts. Four of my men can barely hold him down."

"You want to quiet him down? Tell him you'll take him to Jess's house."

"Come on. You have no way of knowing Carpenter *isn't* the killer—"

"I know." Selma's voice was definite. "Parker, you said you trusted my feelings. Well, I've never been so positive about *any*thing. Tell him you'll take him there!"

"Carpenter," Elliot called out. "If you let them put the cuffs on you, I'll take you over to Jess's house."

The man stopped fighting instantly.

"Well, that worked," Elliot said to Selma. "Now what?"

"Now take him to Jess's, dammit!" Selma shouted.

FRANK HAD BROUGHT the length of blue rope into her bedroom with them, and now he sat on her bed, playing with it.

Jess's heart was hammering in her chest. He had ordered her to take off her clothes, but now he seemed to have forgotten about that. She sat on the floor, knees pulled into her chest, hoping... What? That he'd fall asleep? That he'd have a sudden, fatal heart attack? That God would strike him dead with a bolt of lightning?

Lightning lit the dim room with bluish light, and thunder cracked loudly.

You missed, God, she thought.

She hoped with all her heart that Rob would show up, like a knight in shining armor to rescue her. Lord, she could really use him right now. Rob, with his deadly switchblade . . .

But it wasn't going to happen. If she wanted to be saved, she'd have to save herself.

Please, God, she prayed. Whatever happens to me, please keep Kelsey safe. Don't let him find her, don't let him know that she's here. . . .

"I told you to take your clothes off," Frank said sharply.

"Frank." Her voice cracked and she started again. "Frank, we should talk. Maybe I was a little hasty in my decision not to have dinner with you. . . ."

"It's too late to change your mind," he stated, his voice gentle now.

"How can it be too late?" she questioned. Lord, maybe if she could just keep him talking . . .

"You had your chance," he said. "And it *is* too late. Too late indeed."

His wide eyes looked colorless in the candlelight, giving his face an inhuman quality.

"So you're going to kill me." A spark of anger cut through the fear in Jess's stomach. "Just like that."

He shook his head and smiled. "Not just like that. I'm going to take my time."

Fear threatened to overpower her, but she fought hard to keep hold of the anger. *Dammit,* she wasn't going to just sit here and let him kill her. . . .

If he would just make a mistake—just one small mistake. . . .

She needed him to get overconfident, sloppy. . . .

A weapon. She needed a weapon.

She glanced around the room, but there was nothing. She had a stick pin in her jewelry box, but that wouldn't do much against a stainless steel carving knife.

"Take your clothes off," he ordered. "You have to do what I say."

"Why?" Jess argued, her dark eyes flashing. "You're just going to kill me anyway, aren't you?"

"Because," he said. "If you don't do what I say, I'm going to eviscerate you. You know what that word means don't you, Jess? It means that I'd take this knife and cut your belly open and—"

"I *know* what it means."

"Take off your clothes."

He sat up, leaning toward her slightly with the knife, and she began untying her sneakers.

He chuckled. "Good girl."

One mistake, that's all she needed.

Got to find a weapon.

But what?

She didn't have any double-barreled shotguns lying around the house. Or swords. Hell, she didn't even have a baseball bat.

Think, Jess, think.

There was a crowbar, but it didn't do *her* a whole hell of a lot of good where it was out in the garage. And even if she had a chance to run for it, there was no way she'd lead him out there, out to where Kelsey was.

At least he doesn't know that Kelsey is here. She was clinging to that thought like a lifeline. At least Kelsey's safe. Please, Lord, keep Kelsey safe.

There were other knives in the kitchen, but none as large as the one Frank was holding in his hand.

He was watching her closely as she undressed. She wasn't wearing that much, just her T-shirt, the denim skirt, her underwear. She took her time, dragged it out....

How about the living room? What was out in the...

The fireplace poker.

Yes.

But it was out in the living room.

She took off her underwear. She was naked and she was afraid, but she grabbed that fear and stomped it back down to where it came from.

Fear and tears weren't going to keep her alive.

"I'm cold," she said. "Can I put on my robe?"

"No."

He was just sitting there, looking at her.

If he was trying to humiliate and frighten her, it was working.

"Okay, Jess," he said. "Put on your makeup. I want your lips really red. Like blood."

This was it. Her chance.

She trembled, afraid he would see her triumph, afraid he would know.

Her voice shook. "My makeup's in my purse. It's out in the living room."

He smiled. "Well, go and get it."

She nodded, and moved out into the dark hallway.

The living room was even darker. Every muscle in her body screamed for her to head for the door and run. But Kelsey was there, in the car, and her car keys were in her purse....

No, she had to get over to the fireplace, pick up the fire iron without Frank hearing, and then bash him over his head as hard as she possibly could.

Silently she crept into the middle of the living room. She was almost there. Lord, it was so dark.... Just another few feet...

Lightning flashed.

For a moment, it was clear as day in the living room, and Frank smiled at her from in front of the fireplace. He held the fire iron in his hand.

"This what you're looking for?"

Fear surged through her, as darkness collapsed back around them. Jess turned, about to bolt for the door, but his words stopped her.

"Don't move, or I'll kill you where you stand."

She froze, numb with fear, with failure.

She closed her eyes, her breathing coming in sobs.

She felt him lightly touch her foot, and she jerked it away from him. He grabbed her ankle, harder this time, and she felt him slip the rope around her foot.

"I used a slipknot, Jess," he murmured. "Just like the knot Rob showed you how to make earlier tonight."

Oh, Lord, he'd tied the rope around her leg, just like he'd done to those other women.... Those other *dead* women...

The reality that she was going to die at this man's hands hit Jess like a fist to the stomach.

At least he doesn't know that Kelsey's here.

Please, don't let him know that Kelsey's here.

"I don't know," Frank mused. In the darkness, she heard his voice move from the floor to above her head. He was standing up. "Do you think it's tight enough?"

Without warning, Frank yanked the rope. The slipknot tightened, and Jess was jerked off her feet. She hit the floor, hard.

"Yeah, I think it's probably tight enough," Frank said.

The rope had already taken off the top layer of skin around Jess's ankle, but she didn't say a word. She scrambled back, as far away from him as the rope would allow. Her breath was coming in sobs, and it was all she could do to calm herself down. Don't give in to the fear, she commanded herself. Fear won't help you. . . .

But it didn't stop there.

He jerked her back to him, like a fish on a line. When she was in reach, he wrapped the rope around her neck, pulling it tight, so tight that she couldn't breathe.

And he hauled her back into the bedroom.

Jess clawed at the rope, needing a breath, choking, dying. . . .

"Say you're sorry," Frank demanded.

There was a roaring in her ears, but somehow she understood him. She couldn't speak, she could only move her lips. I'm sorry.

He released her.

With a shuddering gasp, Jess drew air, precious air, into her lungs. Her eyes were watering, and her entire body shook.

He had almost killed her. He was going to kill her.

Fear gripped her, blacking out the world for a moment. She lost her balance, pressing her head into the carpet until the room stopped spinning.

At least he doesn't know Kelsey's here.

He tossed her purse down next to her head.

"Well, what are you waiting for?" he said. "Put on your makeup."

He laughed, and the anger came back then, cutting through the fear.

Dammit. Damn *him*.

Frank was taking off his clothes, and she closed her eyes, not wanting to look at him. He tied the other end of the rope to his own ankle, an ankle that was scarred from countless other rope burns.

She wiped her face with her arm, willing the tears to stop. He wanted her to cry, he wanted her to be consumed by the fear.

Over my dead body, Jess thought.

ROB RODE in the back seat of the patrol car, his hands cuffed behind him.

"Can't you make this thing go any faster?" he shouted at Elliot through the metal cage, over the roar of the overextended engine.

"The roads are flooding," Elliot shouted back. "I'm already hydroplaning. We won't do Jess any good if we don't make it there in one piece."

Trying to stay calm, Rob looked out the window, trying to gauge how far they'd come, how much farther they had to go. Ten minutes, he thought. It's going to take us ten more minutes.

At least.

AT LEAST he doesn't know Kelsey's here.

Jess knelt in front of the floor-length mirror that was on her closet door, putting on thick black eye liner. He'd let her take the candle over with her, and it flickered slightly in the breeze from the window that he'd opened.

He liked to smell the fresh night air, he said. It made her feel healthy, yes, sir.

He'd been talking pretty steadily for about five minutes, as he watched her put blush on her cheeks and eye shadow on her eyes. He told her specifically what he was going to do with her, the rope and his knife. His voice was chantlike, monotonous.

It was enough to give her nightmares for the rest of her life. Except it really looked as if her life were going to end very soon. All she had left to put on was her lipstick.

But at least he didn't know Kelsey was here.

After her lipstick was on, he was going to kill her. He had already told her that. Over and over.

And even if she dug around for the lipstick in the bottom of her purse for a while, even if she put it on one lip at a time, very, *very* slowly, there was simply no way it would take longer than five minutes.

Five minutes left to live, and she was still praying for a miracle, still praying for him to make a mistake.

She fumbled for the hard plastic cylinder of lipstick. It was too dark, even with the candlelight, to be able to see down to the bottom of her purse. Her hand closed on something round and smooth—a roll of Life Savers.

"Cleave," Frank was saying. "It's a good word, don't you think? It means to stick closely to, like, 'after you put your lipstick on, I will cleave to you.' It also means to cut or split, like, 'then I will cleave you with this knife.'"

Jess's fingers found another hard, smooth, nearly cylindrical object. It wasn't her lipstick, it wasn't . . .

"It'll be over too soon," Frank continued sadly. "It always is. But, you know, then I'm going to do the exact same thing with your little girl."

Jess looked up sharply, meeting his eyes in the mirror. He was still watching her, and he smiled now at the look of horror on her face.

"Yeah, I'm going to kill the little girl, too, Jess. I know she's sleeping out in your car. You can't fool me."

He knew Kelsey was in the car.

Oh, no, Lord, not Kelsey, too . . .

Jess turned to face him and her purse knocked the candle over and the little light went out, engulfing the room in total darkness.

He pulled hard on the rope, and she was jerked across the dark room toward him. She skidded on the floor, and gasped with shock as she felt the full weight of his body against hers, and the coldness of his knife at her throat.

Not yet, oh, please God, not yet!

ROB PRAYED.

There was nothing else he could do.

Elliot was driving as fast as he could, but the rain just wouldn't let up, and the roads were flooding and—

"Hang on," he heard Elliot shout as the car hit a puddle that must've been eight inches deep. Hang on with what? His teeth? His hands, still cuffed behind his back reached for something, anything to hold on to, but all he came up with was the smooth vinyl of the seat.

The car began to spin out, and Rob dove down, onto the floor of the car, wedging himself between the front and back seats with his knees. His swollen ankle hit something and he shouted with pain.

The car spun around—it seemed like two complete three-sixties to Rob—and smashed into a telephone pole.

JESS COULDN'T SEE Frank's face, but she heard the sound of his lips as he smiled.

"But you haven't got your lipstick on yet," he said, pulling his knife away from her, lifting his body off of hers.

She could hear her own breath coming in gasps, her heart pounding in her ears. Oh, Lord, he knew Kelsey was here....

Don't lose it now, girl, she told herself fiercely. Stay alive. Believe you can, and you will.... You *have* to... Think about what you found in your purse....

"I have to light the candle again," she managed to say, her voice sounding breathy and high. "I think I have some matches in my purse."

"Okay," he said, his voice agreeable, as if she'd suggested coffee after dinner, not light to murder her by.

She found her purse on the floor where she'd dropped it, and she righted the candlestick.

Digging into her purse, she quickly found what she was looking for, and hid it on the floor, under her kneeling legs. The matchbook wasn't hard to identify either, and with shaking hands she struck a match and lit the candle.

She could see Frank in the mirror, lying back on her pillows again, the hand with the knife resting casually against one of her tall bedposts. He was watching her. His eyes still looked inhuman, and a small smile played about the corners of his mouth.

She could see the rope in the mirror, connecting them, ankle to ankle. It was about ten feet long. Ten feet.

If he would only make a mistake...

This just might work. God help her, she wasn't going to die without trying....

ROB PULLED HIMSELF UP, leaning against the wire mesh that separated the front from the back of the patrol car.

Elliot had hit the steering wheel with his face, and his nose was broken and bleeding. He tried to restart the car, but the engine only whined uselessly.

"We're not that far from her house," Rob said, his voice hoarse. "We can cut through backyards. I know a shortcut. Unlock the damn doors!"

Elliot popped the locks and Rob backed against his door, unlatching it. He fell out of the car backward and onto the street. Elliot helped him to his feet.

Rob swore savagely as his weight came down on his bad ankle.

"I don't think you can walk on that," Elliot said.

The rain was still coming down hard and steady. Rob took off at a sprint. "I'm not going to walk," he told Elliot. "I'm going to run."

JESS REACHED INTO her purse one last time and pulled out the lipstick. Really Red, it was called.

She was scared. Lord, she was scared. If this failed, she was dead. This time he *would* kill her, there was no doubt in her mind.

He was talking again, describing the way her blood would spray out from the severed artery in her neck, coating him with a fine, red mist.

She tried not to listen, she couldn't help listening.

"But I'm really gonna love waking up that little girl of yours." Frank laughed, watching for Jess's reaction in the mirror. "I can just imagine what she's going to say when I bring her in here and she sees her mama lying dead on the floor...."

He.

Made.

His.

Mistake.

Jess felt the anger explode inside her, felt the rage expanding, spreading into every single cell in her body. Even her hair tingled.

She leaned close to the mirror, as if she were taking her time putting the lipstick on, and she looked herself in the eye.

Go on, get mad, she told herself. Forget about being afraid. ust get good and mad. Think about Kelsey. Think about what e said he was going to do to Kelsey. That son of a bitch bas-ard is *not* going to touch your child. He will burn in *hell* irst....

Jess could taste the rage, she could feel the adrenaline surg-ng through her body.

Okay, God, she thought, *I'm ready whenever you are. Send e all the strength and all the anger of the thousands, the* mil-ons *of mothers whose children have been brutally murdered y men like this. Give me their strength so this bastard doesn't ave a chance to kill again....*

Jess took a deep breath, filling her lungs with air. She moved er leg slightly, reaching down to pick it up....

Now, God! Send it to me now...!

With an unholy scream, Jess launched herself at Frank. He ut up his knife, bracing himself for her attack, but she swerved t the last minute, scooping up the rope, and looping it tightly round the tall bedpost at the end of the bed.

He lunged for her, but she had tethered him to the bedpost ith only about two feet of slack. He fell with a loud crash onto he hard floor as his feet went out from underneath him. The nife flew from his hand.

She was on him instantly, wrapping the slack from her side f the rope tightly around his neck with her left hand, her right and slashing down at him with her Swiss army knife's sharp-st blade.

He lashed out at her wildly with his fists, raking her with his harp fingernails, punching her.

He flipped over, wrestling her back, the weight of his body ressing down on her.

But still she kept the rope tight, choking him. Still she tabbed at him, blind in her fury.

"You are *not* going to hurt my daughter," she raged. "I'll ill you first, you bastard...."

OB HIT JESS'S front door full force at a dead run, and broke hrough the frame.

His lip was bleeding, and his shoulder felt smashed, but he limbed back to his feet, inside the living room.

"Jess!" he called out, but there was no answer. The house was silent, and very dark.

"Power's out," Elliot said. He had his gun drawn, and he looked around the room carefully.

The flicker of candlelight from the bedroom caught Rob's eye, and he ran toward the door.

"Oh, God," he breathed, looking into the room. "I'm too late."

Jess lay crumpled facedown on the floor in a pool of blood. Frank lay on his back nearby, lifeless eyes staring at the ceiling.

"Get these handcuffs off me," Rob whispered, his face stony in the flickering light.

Swallowing hard, unable to keep the tears from his eyes, Elliot nodded. This was *his* fault. It was *his* responsibility. He was the one who'd ordered Johnson over to Siesta Key. Johnson should have been here, waiting for Jess to come home.

As the cuffs came off him, Rob knelt down next to Jess. He lifted her up, pulling her naked body into his arms, holding her close to him. He closed his eyes, not wanting to see the terrible wound in her throat where her life had seeped away.

God, he'd been too late.

Tears rolled down his cheeks, and he held her tighter. They'd almost made it. Her body was still warm.

He remembered the way she'd held him just hours ago, how fiercely she'd kissed him, her arms tight around his neck.

"Oh, Jess," he whispered. "Please don't be dead. I promise I'll stay with you forever, just don't be dead."

"Rob," she said, her breath hot against his neck. "You came. I knew you'd come...."

Startled, Rob pulled back. Her eyes were open, her throat was...uncut.

"Jess!" he cried. "Oh, my God! You're alive. She's alive! Elliot! She's alive!"

But all that blood...

Quickly he searched her, afraid to find some other fatal, gaping wound. But all he found were scratches on her arms and shoulders, a rope burn around her neck, a horribly abraded ankle.

"I couldn't let him hurt Kelsey," she said, and burst into tears. "Please, Rob, can you help me take a shower?"

SELMA FOUND PARKER ELLIOT standing just inside Jess's open garage door. He was soaking wet, his nose was broken, the front of his shirt was covered with his own blood. And there were tears on his face.

She looked at him quietly for several long moments, then asked, "Where is she?"

"Carpenter's helping her get cleaned up," Elliot said, his voice raspy. "He's going to pack up some of her clothes, some of her kid's things.... Her daughter's been asleep in the back of her car all this time, can you believe that? I'm out here to make sure the kid doesn't wake up and stumble onto that mess in the bedroom."

He laughed, but there was no humor in it. "Damn, Selma," he said. "I made a judgment error, and I put that woman through hell. Not only that, but she ends up doing my job for me. If our roles were reversed, I honestly don't think I could've done what she did."

"She was protecting her daughter. People can do some pretty amazing things for love," Selma said quietly.

Again, Elliot laughed. "You don't have to tell me that. Carpenter would have dived headfirst into the bowels of hell to save Jess." He wiped his eyes and took a deep breath. "God, I'm so envious of them both."

Selma smiled. "Congratulations, dear. I always knew some day you'd admit you're human."

Chapter Twenty

Jess sat on the deck of the beach house, looking out over the ocean.

The late autumn day was chilly, and she was glad for the heavy knit sweater she was wearing.

Kelsey played down on the sand with the neighbors' children, laughing and shrieking as they chased each other here and there across the wide open beach.

The sound of footsteps on the deck stairs made her jump, and she couldn't hide the apprehension in her eyes fast enough when she saw Selma Haverstein's familiar face.

"I startled you," Selma said. "I'm sorry, dear."

Jess shook her head, pushing herself out of the deck chair. She crossed to stand looking over the railing. "That's okay."

"I brought some donuts and coffee . . ."

Jess turned to look at the woman, bemused. After all this time, Selma didn't seem to realize that she never ate donuts and she didn't drink coffee—

"And a cup of tea for you, dear."

"I thought I was beyond these house calls," Jess said evenly, taking the offered paper cup of tea from Selma's hand.

"Everyone needs a house call every now and then," Selma said soothingly as she sat down. "How's the music going?"

Jess tried to make her shoulders relax. Selma could read something into every little twitch, every little movement. And she was usually right. . . .

"I finished my demo tape," Jess replied, taking the top off the cup of tea and balancing it on the wooden railing.

"When can I hear it?"

"I've got copies. You can take one home."

"I'd like that," Selma said. "How about the house? Have they scheduled a closing date?"

Jess nodded. "Next week." She'd put her house on the market, asking way less than it was worth, and she'd found a buyer almost immediately. She didn't care about the money. All she knew was that she couldn't live in that house. Not after what she'd been through there.

Her parents were generously letting her and Kelsey stay in their beach house. They could stay as long as they needed, until they figured out what they were going to do, where they were going to go. . . .

Rob had left her some money. *Some* money? A *lot* of money. Nearly fifty thousand dollars. But she didn't want his money. She wanted *him*.

"I heard Ian's out of rehab," Selma commented.

Jess took a sip of her tea. "He's been sober for thirty days now," she said. "I spoke to him on the phone. He sounded . . . different. Quieter. He apologized for everything, and actually sent me a child support check. He told me he's in therapy now. He's got a lot of issues from his childhood to work out, but I think he might actually be okay."

Selma nodded, taking a bite of a honey-glazed donut. She watched Jess speculatively as she chewed.

"Sleep much lately?"

Jess looked away, not meeting the older woman's eyes as she shook her head very slightly. No.

"Are the nightmares back?"

Jess sighed. The nightmares, the fears, the edginess . . . She couldn't shake it. Especially not at night. She was going to have nightmares about Frank for the rest of her life.

The FBI had searched Frank's downtown apartment, looking for something, *any*thing that would explain why he'd turned to murder. They found that he'd kept journals. Selma told her those journals were quite possibly the most complete account of a serial killer's thoughts and feelings on record. Frank apparently detailed the murders in his daily ramblings—along with conversations he'd had with his long-dead mother. It seemed as if Frank had come from quite a dysfunctional family.

Selma had told Jess that Frank's diary entries were enough to give *any*one nightmares, so Jess hadn't read them. She had enough nightmares of her own already.

The funny thing was, she'd been fine right after it had happened. Or maybe it wasn't so funny, because when she stopped to think about it, she realized that the nightmares had only started when Rob had left.

Rob...

He'd stayed, glued to her side for nearly two weeks after Frank had tried to kill her. After *she'd* killed Frank.

During those weeks he'd told her about everything, about living in New York City with his roommate, Chris—about the night that had ended his life—at least his life as Connor Garrison.

He'd gotten the call around twelve-thirty that night. Chris was in the Bronx, in a bad neighborhood, and his van had broken down. He sounded really scared, and almost begged Rob to drive out and help him. Rob didn't stop to think why Chris didn't call the police. He just hurried out to help his friend.

When he got to the Bronx, Chris was frantic. He started pulling heavy boxes out of the van and throwing them into the back of Rob's beat-up old station wagon. When Rob suggested that they just call a tow truck, Chris kept saying it was too risky, and he couldn't waste all that time.

Chris said he didn't know what was in the boxes. He told Rob it was better if they didn't look. But Rob couldn't leave it at that—he pulled one open.

And found it loaded with cocaine.

Then Chris really lost it. He started crying, saying how he never knew, how afraid he was, how he was already in trouble because the shipment was late....

Rob didn't hesitate. He got the last of the boxes out of the van, threw them into his car, pushed Chris into the front seat and drove to the docks, where they dumped every last bit—ten million dollars' worth—of cocaine into the black waters of the Hudson River.

Then Rob drove to the police station. Chris figured the only chance he had of staying alive would be to ask for police protection. Rob watched as his friend entered the station house, then drove away.

Chris died in a car bomb explosion the next day, while being driven to a "safe" location.

But before Chris died, he'd called Rob, warning him that the syndicate bosses had put out a contract on Rob. Run, Chris had told him, and don't look back.

But Rob couldn't leave town without saying goodbye to his girlfriend, Janey. He went to see her at the restaurant where she worked as a waitress, and she took a break, coming out to talk to him on the sidewalk.

Three minutes after he'd arrived, he held her in his arms as she bled to death, gunned down in a drive-by hit meant to snuff out his own life.

Destroying over ten million dollars of drugs hadn't made him a hero. Two people very close to him had died, and he was a fugitive, with a million dollar contract on his head.

The contract was still out there, not forgiven, never forgotten.

Rob told Jess how he'd run, leaving New York City far behind, how he'd worked hard to lose his Brooklyn accent, how he'd changed his name, his hair, his eyes, the way he dressed. And still he was afraid they would find him.

Worse yet, he was afraid to get close to anyone, for fear they'd get caught in the crossfire, the way Janey had.

And that was why, he'd told her, he had to leave. He wouldn't tell her where he was going or even if he was coming back.

All he told her was to remember that he always kept his promises.

But what had he promised her? Jess thought she could remember a dream she had where Rob promised her he'd stay with her forever. But when had she dreamed it? It had been *months* since she'd had anything but nightmares.

It had been months since Rob left.

Jess had a gut feeling that Selma knew something about where Rob had gone and what he was doing, but the older woman wouldn't say a word.

The sound of tires on her gravel driveway made her look sharply at Selma—who smiled back at her, unfazed by the wary edge in Jess's dark eyes.

"I'm not expecting company," Jess said.

"I am," Selma told her. "I invited a new friend of mine over. I want you to meet him."

Jess felt her face flush with anger. "Tell him to go home. Selma, don't try to set me up this way." She lowered her voice as she heard a car door slam, then footsteps on the gravel. "I don't want to meet anyone. I want Rob to come back."

"Robert Carpenter can't come back, Jess." Selma placed a soothing hand on her arm. "He's gone. But my friend here is—"

Jess pulled away from Selma, turning to run down the stairs, down to the beach, away—

A man stood at the top of the stairs, looking at her. He wore cowboy boots, faded blue jeans, and a soft brown leather jacket over a dark-colored T-shirt. He pulled a cowboy hat off his head, revealing wavy golden hair, a pair of piercing turquoise eyes, and a face she would've recognized anywhere.

Rob.

Her breath caught in her throat.

"Jess, I'd like you to meet Robin Stewart," Selma said, sounding very satisfied. "He's from Memphis. He's down here for a couple weeks of vacation...."

His eyes were guarded, wary, as if he weren't sure she would want him, as if he weren't sure how she'd react.

Witness Protection Program, Jess thought suddenly. If Selma was involved... She was FBI... They must've given him a new name, a new identity, a new *chance*....

Blinking back the tears that sprang into her eyes, she held out her hand. "Pleased to meet you...Robin," she whispered.

Relief spread across his face as he took her fingers in his hand. "Rob for short," he said, and smiled, a big, beautiful smile that nearly made Jess's heart stop because it was so alive.

She smiled back into his eyes, eyes that for the first time since she'd known him held joy and hope. And a promise for the future.

"I realize this is rather sudden," Rob said, his voice sounding as breathless as she felt, "considering how we just met and all, but . . . Will you marry me?"

"Definitely," Jess said, and kissed him.

"Sorry I can't stick around," Selma said, but wasn't surprised when neither of them bothered to say goodbye.

ROB HELD JESS'S HAND tightly as they strolled down the beach. She smiled up at him, her beautiful face alight with happiness. He stopped suddenly, pulling her in close to him, delighting in the feel of her slender body against his.

He kissed her slowly, tenderly, a kiss that mirrored the love she could see in his eyes. He kissed her again, this time invading her senses, making her arms tighten around him, making her heart pound.

"When did you say Kelsey's bedtime was?" he asked hoarsely, closing his eyes and inhaling the sweet scent of her hair, her skin.

"Not soon enough," Jess said, laughter in her voice.

When he opened his eyes, she was smiling at him. She reached up to touch his hair. "This is going to take me some time to get used to," she said. "Along with the cowboy boots and hat . . . partner."

"I got me a little bit of a twang to go 'long with it, too, darlin'," Rob said with an easy smile.

"Why'd you take so long, Rob?" she asked suddenly, looking searchingly into his eyes.

He looked out at the horizon, squinting at the reflection of the sun sparkling on the water. "I didn't get this second chance for free, sweet," he answered quietly. "I had some unfinished business with the Feds. They've been looking for me for years.

"The FBI offered me protection if I agreed to testify against one of the men my roommate used to work for, the man responsible for his and Janey's deaths. It was a coincidence, but his trial had already been scheduled to come up in late September."

Rob pulled her close to him again, loving the way she wrapped her arms around his waist. He kissed the top of her silky hair.

"I was their surprise witness," he said. "I helped them put that bastard away for good. But I couldn't come back. I couldn't even call you. Not until the trial was over. I was in protective custody." He laughed. "I didn't go into the bathroom without three different escorts. And after it was all over, they set me up in Memphis with the Witness Protection Program."

"Memphis," Jess said, looking up at him.

He smiled, and she loved the way his eyes shone with pleasure. "I found a really great house. It's in a nice neighborhood, near the elementary school. It's got a terrific yard, Bug will love it—" He frowned suddenly. "Except...Memphis is kind of far from the ocean."

"I don't care," Jess said.

He pushed her hair back from her face. "Jess, I know how much you love the ocean. You told me that being on the beach on a sunny day was the next best thing to heaven."

"Why should I settle for the next best thing," she said with a smile, pulling his head down and brushing his lips with hers, "when heaven is in Memphis?"

Weddings by DeWilde

Since the turn of the century the elegant and fashionable DeWilde stores have helped brides around the world turn the fantasy of their "Special Day" into reality. But now the store and three generations of family are torn apart by the divorce of Grace and Jeffrey DeWilde. As family members face new challenges and loves—and a long-secret mystery—the lives of Grace and Jeffrey intermingle with store employees, friends and relatives in this fast-paced, glamorous, internationally set series. For weddings and romance, glamour and fun-filled entertainment, enter the world of DeWilde...

Twelve remarkable books, coming to you once a month, beginning in April 1996

Weddings by DeWilde begins with
Shattered Vows
by Jasmine Cresswell

Here's a preview!

"SPEND THE NIGHT with me, Lianne."

No softening lies, no beguiling promises, just the curt offer of a night of sex. She closed her eyes, shutting out temptation. She had never expected to feel this sort of relentless drive for sexual fulfillment, so she had no mechanisms in place for coping with it. "No." The one-word denial was all she could manage to articulate.

His grip on her arms tightened as if he might refuse to accept her answer. Shockingly, she wished for a split second that he would ignore her rejection and simply bundle her into the car and drive her straight to his flat, refusing to take no for an answer. All the pleasures of mindless sex, with none of the responsibility. For a couple of seconds he neither moved nor spoke. Then he released her, turning abruptly to open the door on the passenger side of his Jaguar. "I'll drive you home," he said, his voice hard and flat. "Get in."

The traffic was heavy, and the rain started again as an annoying drizzle that distorted depth perception made driving difficult, but Lianne didn't fool herself that the silence inside the car was caused by the driving conditions. The air around them crackled and sparked with their thwarted desire. Her body was still on fire. Why didn't Gabe say something? she thought, feeling aggrieved.

Perhaps because he was finding it as difficult as she was to think of something appropriate to say. He was thirty years old, long past the stage of needing to bed a woman just so he could record another sexual conquest in his little black book. He'd spent five months dating Julia, which suggested he was a man who valued friendship as an element in his relationships with women. Since he didn't seem to like her very much, he was probably as embarrassed as she was by the stupid, inexplicable intensity of their physical response to each other.

"Maybe we should just set aside a weekend to have wild, uninterrupted sex," she said, thinking aloud. "Maybe that way we'd get whatever it is we feel for each other out of our systems and be able to move on with the rest of our lives."

His mouth quirked into a rueful smile. "Isn't that supposed to be my line?"

"Why? Because you're the man? Are you sexist enough to believe that women don't have sexual urges? I'm just as aware of what's going on between us as you are, Gabe. Am I supposed to pretend I haven't noticed that we practically ignite whenever we touch? And that we have nothing much in common except mutual lust—and a good friend we betrayed?"

Fall in love all over again with

This Time... MARRIAGE

In this collection of original short stories, three brides get a unique chance for a return engagement!

- Being kidnapped from your bridal shower by a one-time love can really put a crimp in your wedding plans! *The Borrowed Bride*— by **Susan Wiggs**, *Romantic Times* Career Achievement Award-winning author.

- After fifteen years a couple reunites for the sake of their child—this time will it end in marriage? *The Forgotten Bride*—by **Janice Kaiser**.

- It's tough to make a good divorce stick—especially when you're thrown together with your ex in a magazine wedding shoot! *The Bygone Bride*— by **Muriel Jensen**.

Don't miss THIS TIME...MARRIAGE, available in April wherever Harlequin books are sold.

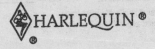

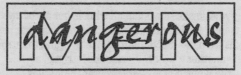